MW01716299

**To anyone—and that's everyone—who's ever said,
"They're playing my song!"**

Chapter One

Halloween 1961

Jimmy Welton was thinking of his father again when the first notes of the song floated into his head. They floated in and they stayed, and he knew as he dressed for work that he'd have another song finished soon. He played the notes in his mind again, mentally matched them to the right guitar chords, and kept humming, not pushing, waiting for the right words to come, too.

Meanwhile, he was due at his after-school job by 5:00. He peered out the grimy apartment window but saw only what he usually saw: A square of cold gray. If he really wanted to see the street below, he had to push up the ancient wooden window and stick his head through it, and even then, he only got a tiny glimpse of daylight. He didn't do it often; he'd become almost resigned to the ugliness of life in the Bronx, in a place they could barely afford.

He laid out a fresh shirt and went into the small bathroom, his mother's cosmetics crowding the tiny sink. He scrubbed his hands and face briefly as he thought of what had been. Before.

Jimmy's life had been just fine until four months ago, when his father, a fireman on Long Island, had been killed in a house fire. After that, they'd found out in a hurry that his life insurance company wouldn't pay out on a technicality, and they'd been forced to sell their house and move to this tall, narrow building on a crowded street with paper-thin walls and a serious roach problem.

Just thinking about his father Phil, a cheerful big man who was always available for a catch or an impromptu football game, even when he was tired from work, made Jimmy feel awful. He'd been told, over and over again, that the grief would get better with time. Well, it wasn't getting better. He missed his dad fiercely, and he was furious at the fire that had taken his life and the clumsiness and mistakes that prevented his fellow firefighters from breaking into the house to save him.

No time to sulk now, though; he had to catch a train and change clothes at the park. Jimmy grabbed a lightweight gray jacket; he'd put it on properly on the train. He checked for subway tokens in his pocket and made sure his wallet, with two measly bucks inside, was secure. Thinking of the song in his head, he also picked up a small notebook and a stubby pencil and stuffed them in his shirt pocket. Maybe he could write down some of it on the subway.

He called a quick goodbye to his twelve-year-old sister Debby as he ran through the stuffy hallway, still crammed with junk from the move that had never found a permanent place. His mother was too weary from her full-time secretarial job to unpack boxes when she got home, and he wasn't interested enough to do it after school.

"Leaving for work!" he bellowed to her as he ran. "Make sure you set the table before Mom gets home."

Debby came to the door of her overcrowded tiny bedroom; in the rush to move, she had refused to get rid of anything she owned, even the baby toys she'd outgrown years before. It was all crammed into the room, with her single cot, a small table she used as a desk, and a small chest of drawers, with her favorite rag doll sitting crookedly on top. To make matters worse, she shared the room with her mother, whose own things were still stuffed haphazardly in shopping bags, because their single small closet was full. "It's Halloween, Jimmy, will you take me trick or treating later?"

"Aren't you too old for that junk?" he said contemptuously. Because he was seventeen and she was twelve, his mom expected him to take her around, since it was a 'new neighborhood' and she wasn't sure people could be trusted here.

"Come on, Jimmy, I have my costume and everything. I'm going as a nurse."

"If I don't get to work fast, I'll *need* a nurse. Trick or treating is dumb, don't you know that? Why don't you grow up?" he said, hurrying out. Jeez. Taking her around like a kid—that was the limit. He probably wouldn't even get home till nine or later; Halloween would be a big night at the park, and they'd want him around till the end, jollying the customers along.

As he reached the hall, though, he felt bad. She was just as trapped as he was, in this awful messy miserable apartment, and she'd looked forward to going out with him.

He stuck his head back inside and called, "Debby!"

"Yes, Jimmy?" she said hopefully. She looked so vulnerable, in her after-school jeans and threadbare t-shirt, that he felt bad all over again, just looking at her. Why couldn't his mom buy her some decent clothes?

"If I'm back early enough," he said, "I'll take you out. Just be ready when I get home. We won't have much time. And if you get lonesome before Mom gets home, Aunt Sairy is upstairs." Their friendly upstairs neighbor was already 'Aunt' to both of them.

"I know." She smiled, though. "Thanks, Jimmy. Thanks a lot."

"Yeah, yeah." He had to run now, but he felt better, knowing she felt better.

He barely got to the station in time to catch the train; it was crowded with commuters, so he didn't get a seat. He didn't dare pull out his notebook, either, but more notes of the song began to drift in as he listened and waited, not trying to force anything.

The other commuters, hanging onto subway straps, glanced at him curiously, and most took a second look. Jimmy was an unusually handsome seventeen-year-old; he'd done some serious growing over the summer, after his dad's death, and now he had almost reached his full height—just shy of six feet tall, with dark silky hair that was much longer than his friends' hair, since his mother didn't earn enough for regular haircut money, either.

Jimmy was supposed to pay for that out of his earnings, but often he spent it on records or new strings for his acoustic guitar, the final birthday gift from his dad just two months before he died; after those purchases, which he found irresistible, he didn't have enough to spare for the regular three-week haircuts he'd always had on Long Island.

As the music continued in his head, Jimmy began to hum, quietly, and his deep blue eyes glowed, under a fringe of lashes all his female relatives envied. He had a thin straight nose and a slim build and had finally begun to shave regularly, which took even more out of his meager earnings for razor blades, but he was proud of his burgeoning beard.

The song was unfinished—no middle eight bars or opening lines, but the melodic line was solid—when the train reached his stop. He jumped onto the platform with a dozen others, then ran up the station steps to the street, where he jogged two more blocks past the sign to the amusement park where he worked.

"Cutting it a little fine, Jimmy?" said one of the ticket takers, grinning as she let him through the turnstiles. "Shouldn't you be bowing to Cinderella right about now?"

"Can it, Marcia!" he growled. He didn't like to be teased about Laurey, the girl who played Cinderella to his Prince Charming.

He slipped into the backstage section and made his way to the dressing rooms. His costume, cleaned and pressed by one of the costume ladies, to whom he smiled thanks, hung on the nail where it always did.

Jimmy quickly stripped down to his underwear and pulled on the pants and heavy tunic, buttoning it with one hand while he tried to write down the chords in his head. He'd forget them if he didn't get them down…

"Finally ready, Jimmy?"

Laurey, in her Cinderella ball gown, glass (plastic) slippers and elbow-length gloves, smiled at him. She liked to tease him, and he didn't like it; he didn't know much about girls, but he knew that he felt different about Laurey and wished she'd take him seriously.

"Yeah, in a minute," he said, struggling with the last buttons. Laurey, pretty blond hair tucked into a bun, stepped in front of him and buttoned the last two buttons, then patted his dark hair down.

Jimmy froze. Something felt really different now, in a *great* way. He had liked Laurey from the minute he met her, and she'd teased him mercilessly the entire time they'd worked together, but when she stood in front of him like this, perfume wafting faintly around him, something just exploded in his head. He wished he had the nerve to take her hand or ask her out. He wished he had the money to do it, too. As it was, the only time he could touch her without worrying about rejection was when they worked together.

She smiled up provocatively, something she did often, he'd noticed; he usually passed it off with a joke. Tonight, though, he said, "Bet your boyfriend would have gotten buttoned up much faster."

He was always trying to find out if she had a boyfriend. A girl that pretty was probably dating the football captain, or something. All he knew was that she lived in the suburbs somewhere, far away from his own neighborhood, and her father was rumored to be rich; she was just doing this job for pin money.

Usually, she joked back, but tonight she said pointedly, "My *boyfriend* would have been here on time."

He looked at her. She seemed really upset. "Did you think I wasn't coming?"

She looked down and fumbled for the words. "I thought—maybe—you'd quit and weren't coming back. And then I'd never know how to find you."

He was stunned. That sounded, for one split second, like he mattered to her. But it couldn't have.

"Come on," he said, in an agony of confusion. "We need to get out there."

"What about this?" Laurey was holding the notebook he wanted to write in. But they were late… and yet, if he didn't write down the chords he'd forget…

"Just a second!" he said, grabbing for the pencil. He threw open the notebook to a clean page and began to write rapidly: A7, C, G, G7…

"What's that?" Laurey asked. "Homework?"

"Naw. It's—nothing."

Jimmy finished writing. He had every bit of it down now; he couldn't forget it. He had never taken formal guitar lessons and couldn't read music, but his dad had taught him some chords, and he took to it like a duck to water. His dad had once said that he could record his stuff on a tape recorder, if they could ever afford one, and then play it back to hear it, whenever he wanted. But until then, Jimmy had decided he'd just write down the chords and the words, as they came to him, and remember them.

"Okay, done," he said, putting away the notebook in his outer jacket pocket and then shutting the jacket into his assigned locker. "Let's go."

Their job was simple—to walk among the customers and interact with them, remaining in character throughout as Cinderella and the Prince. The children squealed in delight when Laurey, moving like an angel, floated into sight, and Jimmy's manly good looks led many older women to ask for pictures with him.

Their big moment came later, when they waltzed together in a cleared space near the carousel.

Jimmy always felt the tinny carousel music they danced to was too slow, but he loved to dance with Laurey. It was the only chance he ever had to hold her, and he relished those few minutes under the stars when they were whirling together in a circle of admirers.

Tonight, though, as they did their dance near the carousel, with the tink-tink-tink of the music behind them, Jimmy noticed Mr. Billings, his boss, standing among the circle of people watching them. He wore his usual topcoat and scarf, wound under his tiny Hitler-like mustache. It was never good news when Mr. Billings came out to supervise.

They finished with Jimmy bowing and Laurey curtseying to him, amid a round of genuine applause. "Kiss her, Prince Charming!" somebody shouted in the crowd.

Laurey heard it, too. She turned to him, her face only inches from his, and he yearned to lean forward and draw her to him in a long, long kiss… one that would last till the park closed.

But Mr. Billings was watching, and he couldn't afford to lose this job… so he leaned in and gave her a tiny, chaste peck on her smooth cheek. She looked disappointed as he drew away.

"Come on, man!" shouted the heckler. "Give her a *real* kiss!"

When Laurey realized he wasn't going to embellish the kiss, she raised her gloved arm and waved sweetly to the crowd. Jimmy did the same, until they dispersed, drawn to other attractions.

A moment later, Mr. Billings was standing in front of them. He drew them into an alley between the arcade building and a souvenir stand. Once they were there, he fumbled out, "Good show, kids. We're doing another one tonight, because it's Halloween, and we have a great crowd."

Jimmy listened with a sinking heart. Since he'd worked there, they'd never just added another show out of the blue. He'd probably even miss the trick or treating he'd promised Debby.

When neither Laurey nor Jimmy said anything, Mr. Billings said, "We'll pay five dollars more—each—for the extra show. And dinner in the park on us. I'll give you a comp slip."

Five dollars extra! Jimmy was stunned. He didn't earn that much in a day, and he sure could use it. He could make some excuse to Debby and call her before the second show, but they really needed the money.

When Laurey saw the glow on Jimmy's face, she said to Mr. Billings, "If Jimmy will stay, so will I."

"It's fine," Jimmy said, trying to conceal his elation. "When's the second show?"

Mr. Billings pulled up his sleeve and consulted the thin watch on his wrist. "Ten o'clock. The park closes at eleven, but you two should be finished before ten-thirty."

He reached into his pocket for a pack of white slips, handing one to each of them. "This is for dinner at any of the vendors' stalls. Be back here ready to go at 9:45. I'll pay you the extra myself before you leave tonight."

Five dollars extra! This made the whole night worthwhile, but Jimmy had to find a pay phone to call Debby and then wait till the teenager in the booth finished a teary fight with her boyfriend. When she came out, Jimmy went in, dropped in a dime and called home. His mother was home and fixing dinner, and she was pleased that he was earning extra for another show. When Debby complained loudly about missing out on trick or treating, her mother admonished her that keeping the job was more important.

Jimmy told his mom not to expect him home till midnight; he hoped to persuade Laurey to go out for a soda after work with the extra money in his pocket. If not, he'd go home and work on the song; he did his best writing in the late-evening hours, when he was alone.

Laurey lingered nearby until he finally said to her, "Aren't you going for dinner?"

"Maybe we could find someplace to eat together."

Funny, it seemed like the longer he worked at the park, the more interested she seemed in him. Ridiculous, of course, since she had guys just about fainting when she smiled at them.

"Okay, then." He led her out to the vendor area, where a variety of hot food was sizzling on grills. "What's your pleasure? Burger? Hot dog? Pizza?"

"Cheeseburger with onions and fries," Laurey said, pointing to the vendor directly in front of them.

"Not onions—how can I breathe in the next dance?"

"Baby," she teased him, but they marched up to the booth together. Just as the vendor turned to ask for their orders, Jimmy felt a tap on his shoulder.

"Hey, Welton!"

Jimmy turned instinctively. It was one of his few new friends from school, Luke Arlington. "Hey, Luke. Just a second." He turned back to the vendor and ordered cheeseburgers, fries and sodas for him and Laurey, handing over the white slips to the counterman.

When he turned back, Luke was still standing there, next to a young man Jimmy had never seen before. He wore a black leather jacket and dark blue jeans, had his medium-brown hair greased back menacingly in a D.A. and gave off an air of devil-may-care ruthlessness.

"Jimmy Welton, meet my good friend, Mark Morgan."

"Hi," Jimmy said, extending his hand to the newcomer.

Mark looked at his hand as though he didn't know what to do with it, then reached out and pumped it with his own. Jimmy noticed his own hand felt bruised when he let it drop.

Mark looked at him, his eyes narrowing. "So what's your job here—you're the handsome prince at the park? So all the girls can swoon over you?" His voice, a normal baritone, escalated suddenly almost to falsetto. He batted his eyelashes girlishly at Jimmy.

Jimmy grimaced. He *hated* being teased about his costume, and now he liked this guy even less.

Luke went on eagerly. "Mark goes to high school downtown, Jimmy. He came out tonight to scout the park."

"What for?" Jimmy asked, not really interested in the answer. The guy struck him as a bad imitation of James Dean. Jimmy had met plenty like him, and they were all bad news.

"For my band to play here," Mark answered, his voice cutting through the windy evening.

Jimmy, who had been ready to walk away, stopped dead. "You have a band?"

"Sure as hell do. I play guitar and sing."

Jimmy had never met *anyone*, boy or girl, who was in a band. Suddenly he wasn't mad about being teased anymore; he was starting to get excited. He tried to seem nonchalant as he asked, "Is it a dance band or country-western, or—"

Mark looked amused. "No, Pretty Boy. It's rock `n roll. Ever hear of it?"

Rock 'n roll! Jimmy would *kill* to hear a live rock 'n roll band.

"Here's your grub," the counterman called, pushing forward plastic trays of burgers, fries and sodas. Jimmy was so caught up in Mark's words that Laurey had to retrieve the tray. She pushed past the engrossed boys toward a small empty table for two, saying pointedly, "Excuse me, please."

Mark looked admiringly after her. "That your girl?" he asked Jimmy.

"Come sit with us," Jimmy said impulsively. "I'd like to hear about your band."

Laurey had already sat down in a flutter of skirts and stripped off her long white gloves so she could eat. She put a couple of napkins carefully at her neckline and refused the ketchup Jimmy offered, saying she didn't want to get it on her dress.

Mark and Luke dragged over chairs and sat close to Jimmy while he negotiated the cheeseburger and fries, gulping the Coke thirstily.

"So what do you play?" he asked finally, trying to articulate just one of the thousand questions that had leaped into his mind.

Mark looked as though he sensed Jimmy's avid curiosity and took his time answering. "All kinds of rock `n roll."

"Bill Haley?" Jimmy questioned. He loved Bill Haley.

"Yeah, we do 'Rock Around the Clock', but we also play Chuck Berry, Elvis, James Brown, Little Richard… lots of artists."

"How many pieces?"

Mark pretended to count on his fingers. "There's me on lead guitar, and Hammy on drums..."

"Hammy?"

"My pal Harmon. Good guy. That's his nickname. Kellen Garrett on electric. He's new this fall."

Jimmy was so excited he could hardly eat. He gave up on the fries and just stuffed the cheeseburger in his mouth, trying to swallow it before it choked him. "So... three guys?"

"Right. I sing lead, Kellen sings harmony. Hammy doesn't sing, just bangs the drums."

Jimmy didn't want to blurt out, *Do you need anyone else?* But he didn't remember ever being more excited in his life.

Mark was clearly pleased to have an attentive audience. While Laurey looked at Jimmy once in a while, he was so thrilled about the band that for once, she wasn't the most important person in the vicinity. He just wanted to know more and more about Mark.

Mark told Jimmy he'd come to the park to meet with Mr. Billings about playing a gig (not *job,* Jimmy noted to himself; they're called *gigs*). If the setup was right, he and the band would come in next week and play for a few days.

"What's the band's name?" Jimmy asked. He realized he should have asked this almost at once.

Mark hesitated. "We've tried a few names, but none of them seem right. Right now, we're the Mark-Tones."

Laurey looked at the huge clock hung on a lamppost. "We need to get back for the next show." She got up and picked up the empty tray. Jimmy would have hurried to take it from her, but he was still focused on the band. She looked disappointed as she carried it past him.

Mark got up, too. He seemed a little lost for words, then said, "You around for a little while?"

"We've got another show to do," Jimmy said apologetically. "For half an hour or so."

"Well—" Mark scratched his head. "I'll see this Billings guy and maybe come see the rest of your show. And we can talk some more. Okay?"

"That's great," Jimmy said gratefully. As Luke, who'd stayed silent throughout the odd dinner, started to turn away with Mark, Jimmy nudged him. "Hey, Luke… thanks."

Luke flashed him a grin. "You owe me, guy."

Jimmy said nothing to Laurey as they returned to the carousel area. Laurey slid the skin-tight gloves up her arms, drew on fresh lipstick and patted down her hair; Jimmy absently plucked at the buttons on his Prince Charming coat, but he was thinking about Mark and the band.

He was thinking so hard, in fact, that he hardly heard the waltz music begin. Laurey waited for him to take her into his arms, but he simply moved around, oblivious to the music. Only after she hissed at him, "Dance, Jimmy!" did he wake out of his somnolent state and reach for her.

They made a couple of weak, clumsy turns—turns Jimmy usually made perfectly—and as the carousel music began to wind down, the applause from the small group of patrons who'd stopped to watch them was more meager than usual. Jimmy just didn't have his mind on the job.

When they'd finished and made their usual bow, Laurey dainty and graceful, Jimmy manly and suave, they were done for the night. The group around them drifted off, no one asking, as they usually did, to pose for pictures with them. But Jimmy saw Mark and Luke standing at the fringe of the group, and he hurried over.

"I was right to call you Pretty Boy," Mark observed. "Bet you got the job 'cause you were *such* a pretty guy."

Jimmy blushed. He knew his good looks were a big factor in getting the Prince Charming job; he had come to the park looking for a job as a waiter or counterman and had been offered the role almost immediately. He'd taken it because it paid more than the usual park job, and his family needed the money. "Did you see Mr. Billings?" he asked.

"Yep." Mark looked pleased with himself. "We're on for five days next week, starting Monday. We start at 4 and play till closing. You gonna come see us?"

Jimmy didn't know what to say. "I'm working," he said finally. "Maybe on a break—"

Mark made it easy. "We'll be on the bandstand," he said, pointing at the well-lit space above and behind him, where throughout the night musicians often played live. "Come over and hear us, yeah?"

"Yeah," Jimmy said. He couldn't wait.

Mark looked him over—a teenage boy in a heavy formal costume, his deep blue eyes shining. "You really like music, huh?"

"Yeah. I really do."

"Your favorites?"

"The guys you play," Jimmy blurted out. "I'm nuts for Elvis, and Bill Haley and Chuck Berry." He hesitated, and then said, "I play guitar a little."

"Really?" Mark looked interested, not amused or indifferent, as Jimmy thought he might.

"Yeah. No lessons, but I can play some chords."

"Maybe you can play something for us after our set next week."

"Maybe," Jimmy said, his heart thumping in his chest.

"Good. I'll be going, then," Mark said.

Jimmy wanted to stop him and talk some more, but suddenly he couldn't think of anything to say. "You live near here?" he finally managed.

Mark tossed his head backward, toward the row of slums right behind the park. Jimmy suddenly felt horribly sorry. He himself lived in a dump, but it wasn't a violent slum. Mark obviously had a much tougher life, but he didn't look like he wanted or needed sympathy, so Jimmy kept his thoughts to himself.

"Okay, then," he said, suddenly at a total loss for words. "See you next week."

"Right." Mark shook his hand, oddly formal for a guy in a black leather jacket, gave a quick smile and disappeared toward the subway station. Luke gave Jimmy a grin and then trailed after Mark.

Jimmy stood looking after them. This might just have been the greatest night of his life.

CHAPTER TWO

Jimmy's extra $5 for the second show helped reconcile Debby to her disappointment at missing out on trick or treating; he took her for an ice-cream soda after school the next day to apologize.

He didn't work the next afternoon, so after the soda, he stayed in the tiny room his mother had allotted to him as man of the house and worked on the song, polishing the chords and the words he'd scratched in his notebook on the subway. He wondered if, when it was finished, he'd ever dare play and sing it for Mark.

Writing the song took him back to the days before his father died. They'd lived in a small house in Baldwin, on the Island, as everyone called it, but it was a happy place, and since Jimmy had come to the Bronx, he'd been anything but happy.

He'd begun writing the song wanting to feel happy again, and let his mind drift back to the good times with his dad, to the baseball games they played, the pool they splashed in at the community center, the sweet-smelling summer nights full of magic and mystery, when they'd lit sparklers in the backyard, where almost anything could happen and it was always more wonderful than anything Jimmy or Debby could ever dream of.

Jimmy let himself remember delicious Thanksgiving dinners at home, Christmas parties for friends and family, singing in the church choir, snowball fights with Debby and his mom while his dad was working. And from those happy times, he found the words to go with the melody.

His cheap school pen raced over the lines of his old notebook (the one he'd never used in French class but found invaluable for writing down chords and lyrics for his songs). He wondered fleetingly whether the song was any good, since it was coming so quickly. Most of the stuff he'd written quickly in the past had been awful. But he was enjoying remembering so much, he didn't stop to worry about it.

Two hours later, he picked up his guitar, tuned a couple of the strings and sang it through once, then twice.

It was finished.

It was right.

He looked at the first verse again:

"Sparklers flare in the dark of night
Magic and my'stery in prisms of white.
Scout trips that last till the dawn's early light—
That's summer; that's freedom; that's home."

In his head he could hear the arrangement, with soft brushes and a light tap on the snare. But he had no access to those things, and even if he did … He sighed. His dad had started teaching him piano chords in June, but he got busy and then it was too late. The piano had been sold to help pay their moving expenses.

There wouldn't be a piano in their home again for a long time, if ever.

"Dinner, Jimmy!" his mother called.

He put away the guitar and got up.

* * *

Jimmy made a point of getting to work early Monday, but at 4:30, there was still no one on the bandstand. Mark *had* said four till closing, right? He was disappointed, but he hoped when it was time for his break, Mark's band would be up there playing.

Jimmy clocked in and found his costume was still being pressed in the wardrobe tent. He went out to get it, past the bandstand, at 4:45.

Mark and two strange boys were there, setting up in quick, practiced movements. "Come on, guys," Mark was exhorting them. "Let's get set up and tuned up quick."

Jimmy stopped, so glad to see Mark that something inside him hurt. "Hi," he said hesitantly.

Mark saw him and grinned. "Hey!"

Jimmy fumbled for something else to say. "I thought you were supposed to start at four."

Mark shrugged, his greased-back hair not moving an inch. "Four, 4:30, whatever."

"But you've got a gig!" Jimmy knew he sounded like one of his teachers, but he couldn't help it; he couldn't imagine arriving late for a job.

"We'll start soon."

"Not if we can't get plugged in, we won't," muttered one of the guys on the bandstand. His voice still sounded in the process of changing, because it went from almost bass to falsetto in the same sentence. Jimmy managed to smother his own grin. This was a *kid*. He'd bet he wasn't more than fifteen—and already in a real rock `n roll band!

"Hey, guys," Mark called to them, sounding much older and more confident. "This is my friend, Jimmy Welton. He's come to hear us play."

Mark had a gift of leadership; the boys stopped setting up and peered at Jimmy, then muttered reluctant hellos. The boy with the squealy high voice nodded indifferently, then went back to plugging in an amplifier. He was a good-looking boy with thick dark hair and dark eyes, wearing a sweatshirt and jeans. The other boy, tall and a little plump, with blondish hair brushed back like Mark's and a sharp-looking jacket over striped pants, set up a primitive-looking drum kit, checking each piece as it went on.

"That's Hammy," Mark told Jimmy. "Great drummer. And Kellen Garrett on bass. He's new this month." He grinned. "Finally old enough to go out nights, for our gigs."

"Kellen?" Jimmy said tentatively. "Is that--?"

"Irish, yeah," the boy said to him, checking the dials on the amp. "You don't like the Irish?"

"Uh—no. I'm part Irish too."

Kellen merely nodded and picked up his guitar to tune it.

Jimmy waved up to Hammy, who waved back. He and Kellen looked relaxed, like they knew what they were doing and had done it often. They worked together on the final setup, while Jimmy watched, envying the easy camaraderie.

Mark took his guitar from a beautiful, new-looking case on the ground. "Nice case," Jimmy said, trying to sound cool. "How long you and Hammy been together?"

Mark shrugged, which seemed characteristic of his personality. "Just a few months in the band. Hammy's been my friend forever, though." And while he seemed cooler than cool, in Jimmy's eyes, he took his time tuning his instrument, listening carefully and turning the keys until they were just so on the neck of the guitar.

Jimmy caught sight of the big clock nearby; he was due to waltz with Laurey in ten minutes, and he still hadn't picked up his costume. "Gotta go," he said hastily. "I'm working."

Mark shrugged again. "Come on back when you're done."

Jimmy wished he didn't have to go, but at this rate, he'd have to change in the costume tent, if he didn't want to be late. He sprinted to the tent, picked up his jacket and pants and ducked inside to change. He arranged to leave his own clothes there till the end of the night. Then he rushed back.

As he passed the bandstand, he noted that the band had managed to plug in the electric cords and was beginning their set. Mark was singing an unfamiliar but catchy song with a good backbeat, which surprised Jimmy, as he listened to the radio all the time and thought he knew most of the rock `n roll songs on the record charts.

But there was no time to stop. He did his waltz with Laurey and posed for pictures for longer than usual, grudging every minute that the patrons delayed him, then rushed back to change into his own clothes before clocking out. He was in such a hurry that he barely spoke to Laurey, who stared after him in bewilderment.

The band was still on the bandstand, and Mark was talking to the few people who wandered nearby. "Thanks for listening, folks," he said. "Now we're gonna play Bill Haley's 'Rock Around the Clock'. If you know it, just clap your hands or stamp your feet to help us out, okay?"

The band broke into the high-energy song, with Mark counting off, "One, two, 3:00, 4:00 rock!" in a clear tenor voice that cut like glass through the night, amplified by the tinny microphone. Mark handled the microphone as though he'd used one all his life and played the chords of the song with tremendous verve, while behind him, Hammy banged lustily on the drums and Kellen strummed a massive guitar that looked like something he'd bought to grow into, as Jimmy's mother had often said before he'd hit his own growth spurt a few months before.

Jimmy listened closely. Mark had a great voice, though he was apparently the only one singing: Kellen just focused on playing behind him, and Hammy had no mike at all; Jimmy remembered that Mark had said he didn't sing. Still, a good drummer was a rare commodity to a band, and this guy was good: He was hammering away at the high-hat and cymbals and keeping a good solid beat.

"Rock Around the Clock" ran less than three minutes, and when Mark and the band finished with a flourish and a final crash of Hammy's drums, only a few people bothered to clap. Jimmy thought that was sad; the band was trying hard, even if they weren't playing the kind of music these people wanted to hear. He was surprised, though; rock `n roll was everywhere these days, and it was becoming more and more popular. To compensate, Jimmy clapped hard and whistled.

Mark acknowledged the sound with a rueful grin. "Thanks, everybody. We'll take a short break and be right back and play for you some more. Enjoy the rides, now!"

He took off his guitar, leaned it against the amp behind him and motioned to Kellen and Hammy, who left their instruments to come off the bandstand and crowd around Jimmy.

"How'd we sound?" Mark asked, affecting a casual tone, but Jimmy could tell he really wanted to know. Realizing that made Jimmy feel warm inside.

"You're a great band," Jimmy told him. "Good beat, good guitar. Great song selection."

Mark snorted. "You've heard *one*!"

"What about that song you played at the start?"

"Oh, that—I wrote that."

There was literally nothing Mark could have said that excited Jimmy more. "You write songs?"

"Yeah." Mark looked at him hard. "What, you too?"

"Yes!" Jimmy blurted out. "In fact, I just finished a new one."

"Wanna play it for us after we finish tonight?" Mark asked.

Play his song for Mark! He'd never played anything he'd written for *anyone* except his dad, because no one else understood what music did to Jimmy the way his father did. He missed those sessions with Phil, missed his comments and honest pleasure in Jimmy's melodies and words. And of course he hadn't played the latest song for anyone. Now he had the chance to perform again. Still, he tried to keep cool as he answered.

"I'd—like that."

"Then you'll stick around till midnight?"

Jimmy thought about the subway. He wasn't even sure they ran after midnight. He'd have to call his mom...

Mark said, "I'll see you get home okay. But it would be great to hear the new song, right, guys?"

Kellen and Hammy nodded silently. They didn't seem to have much to say around Mark, who was clearly the leading light in the band.

Jimmy made his phone call in the office tent and stayed for the rest of Mark's band's set. They played for a half hour, took off ten minutes, went back for another half hour, and finally packed up as the loudspeaker announced the park closing.

"Come on, fellas," Mark said. "We're done here."

He was quick to put away his guitar and waited for Hammy and Kellen to pack up their stuff. Hammy had the biggest load, carrying the big drum set, and Kellen and Mark helped him. It took them quite a while to get out of the park and back to the subway platform.

Mark saw Jimmy looking at him apprehensively. "They run till 4 am," he said, "but after midnight they're further apart. You could wait 20 minutes for a train after midnight."

"I'm still getting used to it," Jimmy muttered, feeling stupid.

"You new here?"

"Yeah. Used to live in Baldwin."

"Where's that?"

"Long Island."

A train stopped then, and they piled in. A few minutes later, they got out and took the stairs to a street with a sad-looking bar on the right side. "In there," Mark said. "We leave Hammy's kit in back."

Jimmy thought that made sense, because no one wanted to lug that heavy kit back and forth every night. The bar looked a little seedy, but he decided not to sweat it and followed the boys inside.

The bar looked seedy inside, too, but they must have been well known here, because the barman motioned to Hammy to put his kit away and poured drinks for them without a word.

"Thanks, Mick," Mark said appreciatively, sipping what looked to Jimmy like a Coke, though he suspected it was more than that. He said to Jimmy, "You want something?"

"A Coke would be great," Jimmy answered, mentally trying to decide if he had enough coins in his pocket to pay for it and tip Mick too.

Then Mark pushed his guitar case toward Jimmy. "Here, play us your song."

Jimmy took out the guitar and checked the tuning; it was still pretty good, though he re-tuned the E string. Then he strummed the guitar lightly; it had a good acoustic sound and felt good in his arms. "Okay. Here's the one I just finished."

Mark, Hammy and Kellen watched and waited, sipping their drinks. He took a deep breath, hoped he'd remember all the chords and the words, propped his foot up against the bar rail and broke into the number.

"Sparklers flare in the dark of night
Magic and my'stery in prisms of white.
Scout trips that last till the dawn's early light—
That's summer; that's freedom; that's home.

"Thanksgiving turkey and stuffing in fall
Hit records spin at the last Christmas ball
Snowball fights at the schoolyard wall
Hold tight; these days won't stay.

"Home is the one place that never lets go
Mem'ries take hold, till they're all that you know.
Bathing your heart in a warm gentle glow.
Wrapped in the gauze of love.

"Baseball games and lemonade
Lining the streets for the kids' parade.
Families where happy is the way that you're made
Why can't it all stay the same?

"If only the world could be sweeter and kind
Put my heart in a cushion, I'm sure I won't mind
Wrapped in soft fibers I'd always rewind.
Wrapped in the gauze of love.

"Seasons to grow and seasons to change
Still, life goes on even when it gets strange
When a new world demands what you can't re-arrange.
And the home you remember is gone.

"Yet thinking back happens, it's hard not to glow
When that memory pops up, it's something to show
Doesn't matter where else I go
When I'm here I'll always know
I'm wrapped in the gauze of love."

When he finished, there was a moment of absolute silence.

Jimmy looked at them nervously. He hadn't really sung much since he stopped going to church choir regularly, and he might not have been completely on-key, but still—

"That's *great,*" Mark said finally, and his eyes lit up in appreciation. "That's a really *great* song." He thought for a moment. "It's like—what everybody dreams of for their life, all those details you put in. It's all about the little things. You absolutely killed it."

Hammy nodded, raised his glass toward Jimmy and said, "Gave me goosebumps, man."

Kellen, who was scowling over a loaded Coke himself (with his voice breaking all over, Jimmy was surprised they served him at all), said, "Really good. You should record that."

"Really? You think so?" Jimmy said, pleased that it went over so well. But he hoped to hear more about the song itself, what they liked, what they didn't.

Mark nodded emphatically and patted the stool next to him. Jimmy put the guitar back in its case and climbed on the stool. "You have a great voice, too. You sing in bands before?"

"No," Jimmy said. "Just my church choir."

"How touching," Kellen cracked. "He sings in the church choir. For God."

If they hadn't been so enthusiastic about the song, Jimmy might have felt hurt; as it was, he grinned. "Well, God seems to like it."

Mark peppered him with questions: what kind of musical training did he have? How long had he been playing? What else had he written?

Jimmy admitted his dad had taught him all he knew, but his dad hadn't taken any lessons and couldn't read music; he was really just a natural musician. Jimmy had been playing since he was about eight, when he first showed interest, and he'd gotten a guitar finally on his last birthday.

How did he write down his songs, if he didn't read music?

Jimmy explained that he wrote down the chords and the lyrics and played it over and over till he knew the melody by heart. He didn't have a tape recorder, and if he didn't remember a song the day after he wrote it, he just figured it wasn't much good.

The only other song he felt comfortable talking about was something he had written very recently, a dance song with comic overtones. He called it "Bawk Bawk", and said it was silly, but was meant to be a parody of The Twist.

"Play that one!" Kellen said, slugging down the rest of his Coke.

"Yeah," Mark said. "Let's hear it."

"Uh-uh," Jimmy said, feeling embarrassed that he'd even mentioned it. "It's a joke. No way."

"It might be good," Hammy offered. "You never know."

It struck Jimmy that Hammy hadn't said anything except nice things to him since they were introduced. He also seemed a few years older than Mark, but either way, he was a good guy.

Mark settled the matter by jumping off the barstool, reaching into the guitar case for his instrument and putting it firmly in Jimmy's hands. He then pushed his glass toward him and said, "Have a real drink. Looks like you need it."

Jimmy hesitated for a moment, then took a good slug and felt it burn down into his stomach. Only then would he trust himself to strum the first chords of "Bawk Bawk". He'd written it in a sardonic mood one day, when he heard Debby playing "The Twist" on her record player and wanted to make fun of it. It had never occurred to him he'd end up playing it for a bunch of guys in a seedy bar after midnight.

Jimmy took a deep breath and launched into the song, speaking as well as singing it. After he'd written it, he'd realized he could even dance it a little, too, and he made gestures as well: Imitating a chicken, clicking his heels together, clapping his hands. His father had told him he was a natural showman, so he gave it his all.

When he began to ham it up in the dance part, the boys began to laugh, and they laughed right through to the end. Jimmy finished with the high whistle he'd learned the previous summer, and a final click of his heels before bowing to them.

Mark, Kellen and Hammy applauded enthusiastically, and Mick, who'd come back to see if they wanted another round, said to him, "Terrific, fella. Funniest thing I've seen since 'The Ed Sullivan Show'. You a comic?"

"Are you kidding? He's a musician!" Mark roared. "A *great* musician! And 'Bawk Bawk's a number-one hit if ever I heard one!"

He jumped onto the floor and imitated Jimmy, clicking his heels together, arms flailing like a chicken, and making the 'bawk bawk' sound. In a minute, Hammy and Kellen were following him.

"Play it again, Jimmy!" Mark shouted. "So we can dance it this time!"

Jimmy felt sheepish, but the others were bouncing around with such energy that he had to try. The clock over the cash register read past 1:00 now, but he was having so much fun he didn't want to go home, though he knew he had school in the morning.

By now, Kellen and Hammy had caught something of the melody and lyrics, so they echoed Jimmy's 'bawk bawk' along with the dance moves. They laughed, sang and danced right through the song, and at the end, even Mark got down on the floor for the chicken moves and joined Jimmy in the final high whistle.

It was the most fun Jimmy could remember having since his dad died, and he wished it didn't have to end, but finally, reluctantly, he said, "I really have to go now."

Mark hesitated, then said, "You want to come out with us again tomorrow?"

His light-colored eyes looked concerned, as though he hadn't made the invitation enticing enough.

But Jimmy was enthralled.

"Sure," he said without hesitation.

"Great." Mark looked relieved.

It took more than a half hour for Jimmy to catch a train home. He finally snuck into the apartment at 2:15. His mother, who seemed to have a sixth sense when he was out, came to the door of Debby's room and hissed, "Where have you been?"

Jimmy's heart sank. The last thing he could bear was to be grounded and miss his chance to see Mark and the boys again. "I went out with some guys after work," he said carefully. "We talked about work. It was pretty much... uh... required."

"Will it happen again?"

He took a deep breath and took the plunge. "They've—uh—asked me to meet tomorrow night too."

His mother took a deep breath of her own. "Jimmy, I need you home at a decent hour. And you have to get to school on time in the mornings."

His mother had never cared about his interest in music, or his father's interest, either. To her, it was a negligible hobby she was almost sorry he had passed on to his son. She had never even suggested piano lessons when he was younger. But he couldn't bear not seeing Mark and the others again. This was something he had to do.

"Mom," he said carefully, "I really need this extra time at work. To learn new stuff."

"And maybe get promoted?"

He had no idea how he could get promoted from waltzing with Laurey, but it was worth at least a little white lie. "Maybe," he said. "I don't know."

"Are they paying you overtime, at least?"

"Uh—not—not yet." He didn't know where this was going.

"Well, if they do, you can keep more money to spend on yourself."

He'd been expecting a storm. She handed him, instead, a soft caress. He thought about how hard it had been for her, these last few months, and how she'd cried every night into her pillow when she'd thought they were both asleep, in the first few weeks after his father died. He was suddenly grateful to her, and he loved her very much.

"Thanks, Mom," he said. "Good night, now."

He kissed her, something he didn't do often, and went into his tiny bedroom. She stood looking after him, wondering what new thing had caught his attention so completely and whether it would turn out to be good for him or not.

She hoped it was something his father would approve of.

Then she went back into Debby's room and softly closed the door.

CHAPTER THREE

The next night after work, Jimmy helped the others carry Hammy's drum kit, and they got to the bar just after midnight. It had been a long night, doing his show with Laurey and watching Mark and the others play, but he loved their act and was excited for what would happen afterward.

This time they sat in a booth. Mark ordered his usual rum and Coke, and Jimmy asked for a plain Coke. He'd put extra coins in his pocket for the occasion, along with an extra subway token.

When the drinks sat on the table in front of them, Mark took a slug and looked at Jimmy. "So, you want to join us?"

"Uh—what?" Jimmy didn't want to sound stupid, but he was a little stunned.

"Join us—the band. You want to be part of our band? We could use another guitar."

Jimmy looked hard at him. Mark was grinning broadly.

Hammy and Kellen were grinning, too. Obviously, Mark had discussed it with them.

"We'd like to have you," Mark said. "You play with us, split the take from our gigs. We might even sing some of your songs." He stopped and looked at Jimmy, who was looking uncertain. "What do you want—an engagement ring?"

Jimmy pulled himself together. *Yes, he wanted to join the band!*

"I want to," he said carefully. "I just don't know if I—can." It cost him a lot to say that.

Mark frowned. "Why not?"

"I don't—have much free time," Jimmy said, fighting the urge to scream, "Yes! Yes!" He went on, painfully, "I need my job after school. Things are—pretty tight at home, since my dad died."

"Oh," Mark said, after hesitating a moment. "Sorry." He dug into his pocket, pulled out a pack of cheap cigarettes, proffered it to Jimmy. "Smoke?"

"No, thanks," Jimmy said. "I don't smoke." It was also the first time he'd seen Mark with cigarettes.

Mark pulled out one, reached for a matchbook lying in a bowl on the table, struck a light, and inhaled deeply, like a devoted smoker. "Sure?"

"It's—not good for your voice, is it?"

"The hell with that. They taste fantastic! I've been smoking since I was ten. I'll never give them up."

"They're—expensive, aren't they?"

"Look, Jimmy, let's talk about what we want to talk about. You've got talent. You sing great, and those songs you played for us are fantastic. I'd love to work them into the act and play them at every gig. But I also want you with us. You can keep your job and play Prince Charming. We'll get other gigs, that won't interfere. Everything split evenly, four ways. I was our lead singer, but you can sing lead on some songs. And play bass. We need a bass bad."

Jimmy looked at him hesitantly. He wanted to do this so much! And if he could earn a little extra, he was sure his mother would like it. He just didn't know how she'd take the news that he was in a rock `n roll band.

"Well," he said at last, "if I can keep my job—"

Mark whooped and banged on the bar. "Mick! Rum and Coke for our new bandmate!"

"I'm underage," Jimmy tried to whisper to him.

"Who cares?" Mark roared. He jumped off his stool and lifted Jimmy high in the air and spun him around exuberantly.

"Hey!" Jimmy protested, feeling a little giddy himself, "put me down!" Guys didn't pick up guys; guys only picked up *girls* if they really, really liked them, and if the girls were light enough.

"Yeah, yeah!" Mark spun him some more and then set him down. Kellen, smiling, clapped him on the shoulder. Hammy clasped his hand.

"So," Jimmy said, getting back on the barstool and saluting his new bandmates with his drink, "when's our first rehearsal?"

* * *

Jimmy and the band convened at Mark's house on Saturday afternoon. Jimmy knew of the grinding poverty Mark must live in, though he obviously had enough for cigarettes and liquor. But though Jimmy knew they were being paid for the gig at the park, he expected Mark's house would be a tiny walkup where they could barely move around, let alone play loudly.

Jimmy got to the subway stop with his guitar in hand twenty minutes before he was due at Mark's house. Mark had given him the address and told him how to walk from the subway, but he was confused; all the buildings around him were beautiful, large one-family homes. They were beautifully maintained and obviously expensive, and Jimmy was *so* confused, he walked past Mark's block three times before finding the correct number.

By the time he rang the bell at the top of a flight of steep stairs, he was breathless from more than the climb. He'd been sure Mark was dirt poor; hadn't he tossed his head toward the slums when Jimmy first asked where he lived?

Well, he told himself, trying to be fair, *he* could *just as easily have meant this very wealthy neighborhood, situated well behind the slum areas.* For sure, Mark hadn't wanted him to *know* he was rich when they first met.

Then Mark opened the door. "Hey, you're early," he said, pleased. "Come on in. We can talk till the others get here."

Jimmy stepped into a fabulous foyer, with marble posts edging the curtains in the plush living room to his left, spotless black and white tiled floors, and more beautiful paintings hung on the walls than he'd ever seen, outside a museum. He just looked at Mark, who wore a T-shirt and jeans and had his brownish hair combed back in the D.A. he'd affected at the park.

"Jimmy? What's up?"

Jimmy felt like he should offer to take off his shoes, but Mark was wearing boots with Cuban heels and walking unconcerned on the rich tiled floors. But this was not okay; he'd been sure Mark was one thing, and Mark was obviously something completely different.

"Hey yourself," he said. "Looks like you forgot to mention something."

"Like what?"

He gestured. "Like this! You're not some greaser; you're rich."

Mark looked embarrassed. "Well—uh—it's not the easiest thing to talk about. C'mon, we can play in here." He opened a door halfway down the hall, and Jimmy saw a fully-furnished music room, with music stands, chairs, rows of record albums on shelves and a little upright piano against the far wall.

Instead of putting down his guitar case, Jimmy faced him. "You let me think you were poor!" he accused Mark. "You let me think you had nothing! And then I come here, and—I don't know who you are!"

"Sure you do," Mark answered calmly. "I'm the guy you met at the park. I've just got some—extra baggage." He gave a sheepish smile and moved over to the piano. "You play this at all? I can play a little."

Jimmy gave up. Mark didn't want to talk about being rich, he just wanted to make music. Jimmy wouldn't goad him into a confession at their first rehearsal. "I tried it," he said. "With my dad. Didn't get far."

Mark nodded, then straddled the piano bench. It was clear as he played a hot "Chopsticks" that he didn't read music, either. But that was okay; they'd figure things out together.

"What songs do you do in your sets?" Jimmy asked. "Besides what I've heard?"

Mark named them—current popular rock songs, some older, more obscure stuff, some folk music for a change, one or two R&B selections. "We pick songs from B sides a lot, so other bands don't play all our stuff if we're on the same bill. If they don't know the songs, they can't play them. But if we could start writing and playing more of our own, that'd be a lot better."

Jimmy undid his guitar case, took out his instrument and began to tune the strings. "Good idea," he agreed. "It's fresh, anyway, and we can do great harmonies."

"I knew you'd like that!" Mark approved. "Let's start with the two you played for us, that great one and 'Bawk Bawk'."

"You're kidding!" Jimmy said. "You *want* to learn 'Bawk Bawk'?"

"Chicken arms and all!" Mark laughed. "Dance numbers go over well, and I want to play something kids can dance to."

Before Jimmy could protest any further, the bell rang again. Hammy and Kellen showed up, lugging their equipment, and once they were set up, Mark persuaded Jimmy to start 'Bawk Bawk'. Jimmy played and sang it a couple of times, till Hammy picked up the rhythm and banged his drums, and Kellen began to strum some chords along with him.

Mark focused on the gestures, the 'bawk bawk' chicken arms flapping up and down, the little trot he did with his feet, the up and down motion of his head.

"Hey, how about this?" he said a few minutes later, pumping his arms and swinging his hips wildly.

Jimmy looked at him and burst out laughing. The others did too, and Mark, who was 'bawk bawking' with great abandon, flopped down on the rich maroon carpet and laughed, his face turned into the nap, until tears rolled down his cheeks.

When he finally stopped, he said, "But I do have an idea. Why don't we add something to the final 'Bawk Bawk'?"

"Like what?"

"Like your head." Mark thrust his head forward and back wildly, like a chicken, and once Jimmy could control his laughter, he agreed.

They practiced the song for a couple of hours, while Kellen came up with a couple of original guitar riffs and Jimmy, singing lead, and Mark, singing harmony, were in perfect alignment on the vocal. They took turns practicing the dance moves, which sent Kellen and Hammy into paroxysms of laughter.

"That's fantastic," Hammy approved when he finally calmed down. "What a sound!"

"We'll knock the kids out with this one," Mark said, playing a few compatible chords on the piano. "They'll beg for it, every night."

"When's our next gig?" Jimmy asked. No one had mentioned it, and after all, that was a major reason he'd agreed to join the group.

Hammy looked at Mark. Kellen looked at Mark.

Mark looked down at the carpet he'd been lying on, laughing. "Well… something's bound to turn up."

"Oh, no," Jimmy groaned. "I thought you guys had regular gigs."

"Don't worry," Hammy assured him. "Mark always finds places for us to play. He's great at it. The park thing was new, but didn't Mr. Billings say he'd have us back?"

"In June," Mark said. "Not much help right now."

"The holiday gigs are coming up," Hammy said. "We should get our share."

"We need a manager," Kellen said.

"We've talked about it," Mark argued. "They're not easy to get, and they always want a percentage of your take."

"If they get you the gig and take care of your business, don't they deserve a percentage?" Jimmy asked. It only seemed fair to him.

Mark shrugged. "The ones I've met seem pretty shady. Don't trust any of them."

"Has anybody asked to manage you?"

Mark flushed. "Not yet."

"How many have you met?"

Kellen shrugged. "Half dozen or so. We've played at local amateur night gigs where they had managers and agents. *Said* they were looking for new talent. I think they're all nuts. Always talking about how they can get you a record deal. Sheesh. If it was that easy, everybody'd have a record."

Mark took charge. "I'll get us a gig in the next week. I can pull some strings. Now let's get to this other song. Jimmy?"

Jimmy went into his guitar case to get out the sheets on which he'd written the lyrics and chords of the song. He showed it to the others and promised he'd make copies they could all practice with when they weren't together.

Mark signaled him to give the count-in and he did, and they burst into the song, huddled around him so they could see his handwritten notes, singing where they could, just trying to get the melody line right. When it was over, Mark said with satisfaction, "You sing lead on that one. It's yours, and you sound great on it."

"Can you sing harmony?" Jimmy asked Mark.

"Sure, I'll give it a shot."

"Okay, let's try it." Jimmy nodded them back in, did the count-in again, and they burst into it.

As Mark added his voice to Jimmy's, something changed.

Mark leaned his head close to Jimmy's, and sang along sweetly with him, his voice a third below Jimmy's on the melody line. The sound of these two young voices mingling, breathing together in immediate, perfect sync, their energy combining beautifully, took Jimmy's song of love and longing and transformed it into something completely different. It made the song something that stood on its own.

It made the song dynamic in a way that Jimmy singing it alone had never done.

They continued into the second verse, then the chorus, with Hammy drumming lightly behind them and Kellen adding improvised licks on his electric guitar.

The sound was electrifying.

Mark dropped out as Jimmy sang the last lines, then came in for the last eight bars.

They finished together, holding the final note for eight beats, instinctively knowing how best to end it. They looked at each other, knowing that something very special had just happened.

Mark had a half-smile and a gleam in his eye. Jimmy wore a wide grin.

When they stopped, Hammy cocked his head at the two singers. "I got goosebumps, man."

Kellen nodded slowly. "Me too." For once, there were no squeaky tones in his changing voice.

Mark and Jimmy looked at each other. They had sounded like—Jimmy didn't know what. He'd never heard a sound like that before, not even harmonizing with the others in his choir. What they did together was… magical.

"Man, that was *great*!" Hammy banged one of his hi-hats. "That was fucking *great*!"

Jimmy was more startled by Hammy's casual use of profanity than the clash of the hi-hat. He tried not to let it show. Musicians drank, smoked and cursed. He'd have to get used to it.

Mark said nothing for a minute. Jimmy was trying to understand what had just happened.

They had sung a song together, and it was pure, strong and soaring.

If they could do this on other songs, then what *couldn't* they do? On impulse, Jimmy said, "You have other songs you've written?"

Mark looked at him. "A few, yeah. Not good enough for the band yet, but I'm working on more."

"Let's try them," Jimmy said.

Mark went to a bureau set in the wall and began pulling out drawers. Pages of music fluttered through the air and fell on the floor, but he didn't bother to pick them up, just kept thrusting his hands into thick piles and letting them fall where they would.

He came back with two sheets of paper: They looked much like Jimmy's own scribblings, with guitar chords and lyrics written haphazardly, side by side, in Mark's sloppy handwriting.

Jimmy leaned over one sheet intently. "What's this? It looks good."

Mark picked up his instrument. "It's not bad. Listen."

Unself-consciously, he played and sang the song.

Jimmy was electrified. This guy! This guy who loved rock 'n roll, who had his own band, who could sing and harmonize like nobody's business, this guy was rapidly becoming really important in his life.

Jimmy had never had a best friend, but he was beginning to realize that the longer he hung around Mark, the likelier it was that Mark would become his best friend.

He loved what he knew about him, so far. He didn't even really mind that he was rich.

"Okay, let's try it," Mark said, nodding to Kellen and Hammy.

Jimmy stepped close to him and strummed the chords as he and Mark sang the words, with Mark automatically taking lead and Jimmy singing a perfect automatic harmony behind him.

Hammy's drumming became more frenetic as their voices rose together, with Kellen playing an energetic lead guitar.

Mark finished with an exuberant chord, and they all chortled.

"This is—fucking *perfect*, man," Hammy declared, with a final cymbal crash. "*Serious* goosebumps."

"We need more rehearsal," Jimmy said, just as Mark said, "We need a gig!"

They all laughed, just as the door to the music room opened, letting in a puff of cool air, and a woman peeked in.

Mark stiffened. Jimmy, knowing nothing about the newcomer, instinctively straightened up.

The woman who walked in looked between forty and forty-five and was quite beautiful, with that indefinable, timeless chic of New York women: Expensive perfume and a long trailing coat even Jimmy knew had to be mink. Her high-heeled pumps looked brand new and untouched, whereas Jimmy's mother's shoes were beginning to look very worn, after weeks of heavy wear in her office. The woman's lovely red hair was bound in a perfect French knot that she'd obviously spent time and money at a hair salon to get, and her makeup looked, of course, as though she weren't wearing any.

She trailed into the room, as Mark's face tightened, and said, "Mark, you didn't tell me you'd invited friends over."

Mark sounded resentful as he answered, "We're just rehearsing." He reached a hand toward Jimmy. "Mom, this is Jimmy Welton. He just joined the band. You know Hammy and Kellen."

"Of course, boys. How are you?" She didn't wait for an answer, or glance at any of them. "Mark, are you about ready to wrap up? Your father has an important dinner tonight, and of course he wants you to come."

"Nobody has dinner at 4:30," Mark muttered, glancing at the antique wall clock.

But Hammy and Kellen took the hint, starting to pack up their instruments. The woman had put a total damper on their rehearsal, merely by her presence. As soon as she came in, Jimmy began to wonder if they'd even get another gig. She made him feel they were just kids fiddling with instruments in music class. The magic was gone from the afternoon.

All the same, he'd been taught how to meet people. "How do you do, ma'am?" he said softly, holding out his hand for her to shake. He gave her a smile and held it, the crystal-blue eyes liquid in his young face, his smile revealing even white teeth.

The woman responded as many women had responded since he began to grow again last summer. She took his hand, smiled back uncertainly and said, "Happy to meet you, Jimmy."

"Thank you, Mrs. Morgan. I'm happy Mark invited me to join the band."

Mark's mother looked at Mark for a moment, then back at Jimmy, and reached over to pat his hand lightly. Jimmy had the feeling she might not even know her son had a band, but how could she not? She was his mother, wasn't she?

"All right," Mark blared suddenly, almost making Jimmy jump, "if you're going, then go. I'll let you know about the next… er, meeting." He was careful not to say 'rehearsal', and Jimmy suddenly wondered if Mark had even told his mother the band was now being paid to play. It seemed odd that she received the information so casually.

He looked quickly at Mark, to see if he minded, but Mark had put away his guitar and taken a stray piece of string from the top of the little piano; he absently rolled the string into a ball in his hand. He seemed to have forgotten Jimmy altogether.

The other boys packed up and left quickly, with Kellen helping Hammy drag his drum kit. When the front door closed behind them, Mrs. Morgan turned to Mark, though Jimmy was still packing up.

"I hope you're not still seeing a lot of them," she said. "They're not the kind of boys who—well, that you should be spending a lot of time with."

Mark looked at her resentfully. "What's wrong with them?"

"They're not… well, they're not people we know. I don't know their families."

Mark pressed his lips together in sudden anger and then spat out his response. "You want to know about their families? They're dirt poor, and Hammy's dad has been in prison three times, and Kellen's mom drinks and has been married twice, and I doubt you'd actually want to meet *any* of them," Mark said, his seething resentment turning his eyes the darkest brown Jimmy had seen since they'd met. "But it's not the prison or the drinking that's a problem, is it? It's the fact that they're *poor*." Mark almost hissed the words. "*That's* the part that makes you throw a fit."

Mrs. Morgan finally noticed Jimmy and indicated him with a dip of her lovely head. "Mark, this isn't really the time—"

Then Mark suddenly burst out, as though he'd been suppressing strong emotions for a while. "So who *can* I be friends with? Between your silly charity meetings and Dad's wining and dining the New York elite so he can someday be an Assemblyman—"

Jimmy didn't know how to get out of this mess, but he wanted out as soon as possible. Like a flash, he put his guitar in its case and strapped it firmly. "Thanks, Mark," he said, a little breathlessly. "See you soon." And he headed quickly for the front door.

"Don't go yet!" Mark's answer was a literal cry from the heart, and Jimmy, who already was on his way out the door, turned back to look at him. In Mark's face, where before there had been laughter and intensity, was a look of total misery. Jimmy had never seen anyone's emotions change that quickly.

Jimmy, who had wanted nothing more than to escape the confrontation, came back at once. Mark pulled himself together. "Let's go back inside," he said hoarsely. "Let's talk about your song."

"Don't be too long," Mrs. Morgan said, as Jimmy, legs trembling a little, took a few steps into the music room Mark indicated, and Mark shut the door firmly behind him.

"She almost never comes in here," he said reassuringly, his rage seemingly dissipated. "She knows this is *my* space."

Jimmy sat down suddenly on one of the comfortable sofas lining the wall, the deep emotions making him tremble. His legs were folding under him. His own mother had *never* talked to him like this. "Intense, isn't it?" Mark said, with a crooked grin. "It gets like that sometimes. Don't let it bother you. Too bad it had to happen today."

He sounded as cheerful as though he himself hadn't been spewing rage just a few moments before.

Jimmy looked up at him shakily, stunned at the split-second change of mood. Who *was* he, anyway?

Mark knew what he was thinking. Without a transition, he said, "That song of yours. There's a line I wasn't quite sure about… "

"Which one?" Jimmy asked. His mind turned with relief to his lyric, as Mark had obviously intended.

He got out the lyric sheet and Mark squinted over it. "Damn, another headache. Hold it a sec, okay? Back in a jif."

He bounded out and came back in a few minutes, looking better. "Sorry. Have to take my pills, and then I feel better. I probably need glasses, because after a while everything just swims around, and I can't see that well." He knelt down by Jimmy and pointed at a line near the bottom. He hummed it. "That the tune?"

"Yeah. What's wrong with your head?"

Mark made a face. "Sometimes when I'm tired, my head hurts, that's all. The doctor gave me pills, and as long as I take them, I'm fine." He looked at Jimmy. "That song—it's so sad. But it makes you feel better, at the same time."

Jimmy said, "I wrote it thinking about my dad and how he was killed fighting that house fire—"

Mark looked at him somberly. "Jimmy, really?" He put a hand on Jimmy's shoulder. "I'm sorry. That's rough."

Jimmy stared at him as his mind worked busily. This guy! This guy who understood him in a way *no one* understood him. Right then and there, he knew he and Mark could write songs together, songs that would *work*.

What *couldn't* they do together?

He hoped all this didn't show on his face as he asked, "What should it be?"

Mark considered. "I'll work on it and tell you at the next rehearsal."

"When's that?"

"I'll call you. Soon."

Jimmy started packing his guitar again. "Don't want you late for dinner."

"Oh, sure," Mark mocked him. "I just *love* sitting with all those middle-aged women trying to be polite and not ask them to move their fat asses out of my way."

"Mark!"

"Well, they *do* have fat asses, and they *are* in my way."

"You don't have to *say* it!"

"Nope—I could be a kiss-ass and only say nice things, just like you. Then *I* could be a prince too."

Jimmy threw a halfhearted punch at his face, and Mark chased him out of the house. "Prince Charming, Prince Charming, come wake me up with a big wet kiss!"

"You're sick!" Jimmy hollered back at him from the sidewalk. He was relieved that Mark seemed back to his usual self.

"Next time, come earlier!" Mark called after him.

"You stop being rich, and I will!"

Chapter Four

Mark called the next day and asked if they could meet at the bar; they served sandwiches from lunchtime on. Jimmy agreed to come after school Monday. He knew that Mark wanted to see him as much as he wanted to see Mark.

They met at the bar and Jimmy, feeling prosperous with five dollars in his pocket, bought himself a Coke and a burger. Mark ordered the same, and they sat silent after Mick, who always seemed to be there, went to put in the order.

"We got a gig," Mark said abruptly, breaking the silence. "Saturday night at Marvin's on 59th, on the West Side. You know it?"

"No. I don't know any bars around here—except this one."

"This is a good one," Mark agreed. "Marvin's is good, too. They have a nice band setup, and we're booked from 7 to midnight. Fifteen bucks for the night."

"Fifteen each?" Jimmy got excited.

"Fifteen for four of us. Split four ways, that's—"

"Three seventy-five each," Jimmy said flatly.

"I'm not good at math."

"Well, I am. I wish you'd let me know before you booked it."

"It's not exactly a fortune, is it?"

Jimmy looked at Mark's broad grin. "Not enough to buy your house," he agreed, "but I'll take it."

"Great. I've already told Kellen and Hammy."

"So I'm the last to know?"

"Yes, sweet prince. It's not my fault you weren't home the first time I called. Now, about what we wear—"

Jimmy sobered. "I can't afford much, but—"

"The code is all black. Jeans, black shirts, leather jackets."

"Don't own a leather jacket," Jimmy mumbled, feeling poor and out of place.

"I'll lend you one. No sweat. We're about the same size."

"You got more than one?"

"It's great to be rich," Mark laughed. "You can try it on at rehearsal Saturday afternoon. We'll leave for Marvin's from my house."

Jimmy just sat looking at him, smiling. He was doing just what he wanted to do, and it felt *great*.

Mark looked at him and again that strange telepathy was working between them; he seemed to know just what Jimmy was thinking. He said, "Do you really want to be a musician in a band? I mean, full-time? For good?"

Jimmy thought about it. "When I talked to my dad about a career, we thought about my being a music teacher. We never thought I could perform or write songs. But now I want to." He paused. "What about you?"

Mark laughed. "I wanted to be a big finance guy, the kind my dad works for. I guess I thought if I was a rich big shot, he'd pay attention to me."

Jimmy looked sharply at him. Mark had stopped laughing, and the look on his face was unbearably sad.

Jimmy couldn't stand it. "Then I guess we'd better *all* become rich and famous, and then your dad'll be working for *all* of us!"

Mark thought about that, then he grinned and slapped Jimmy's arm. "You're so right! Let's work on *that*!"

* * *

The Saturday rehearsal started at noon. Jimmy was surprised that Hammy, always so prompt, arrived late, a little out of breath, his clothes covered with hair. When Jimmy asked him about it as Hammy hurriedly set up his kit, Hammy said simply, "Weekend job at a vet's office."

"So do the animals—"

"The animals like me," Hammy laughed, and brushed at the hairs ineffectually. Mark had to get his father's hair remover brush to help him get rid of the individual cat and dog hairs before they even started.

They rehearsed for hours, with several repeats of "Bawk Bawk", which they planned to put in that night. Before they stopped rehearsing at five, they'd locked in their playlist and knew how Mark would introduce each song. They also knew all the intros and lead-ins, and who did the counts. They sounded good, and Jimmy, who'd never played guitar in front of a live audience, was both nervous and excited. He couldn't wait to get on the bandstand.

They changed into their stage clothes at Mark's house; Marvin's had no dressing room. Jimmy noticed Mark wore a lightweight black shirt; his own was heavier. Mark saw him looking at it. "You tend to sweat under the lights. Lighter is better," he suggested.

"I'll get a lighter one with my next paycheck." Jimmy wondered whether he'd ever make any real money playing with the Mark-Tones. On the other hand, he'd just started with them, and you couldn't expect to be a millionaire playing rock 'n roll! Only people like Elvis were millionaires. But he knew they would have fun.

They arrived at Marvin's before 7:00 and helped Hammy move his equipment onto the small platform that passed as a stage. Marvin had some extra lights and a single microphone, which Mark immediately commandeered. "The singer needs the mike, boys," he drawled. "Else they can't hear me."

"So *that's* why you sing lead," Kellen grumbled. "So you have an excuse to hog the mike."

"You're so right," Mark said, blowing him a kiss.

At 7:05, they were ready to play, though the room was only half-full. Jimmy peeked through the kitchen door at the audience: Twelve tables with one or two couples, all pleasantly half-crocked. The men ranged in age from mid-twenties to forties, while the women ran from twenties to late thirties. There were no teenagers, and he was disappointed; maybe they wouldn't respond as well to the band. They looked like people who'd dance to Mantovani or Percy Faith but had never heard of Chuck Berry.

On the other hand, Jimmy comforted himself, Marvin had booked them, and he had to know what his customers liked.

Mark nodded to Marvin, who brought the bar lights down and bellowed, "Hey, everybody, here's tonight's entertainment. Say hello to my friends, the Mark-Tones!" There was a smattering of light applause to greet them.

Mark stood at the mike, brownish hair brushed back, black jacket collar turned up. "'Evening, folks. We're so glad to be here. Think we'll start off with something you all likely know. Just clap your hands to help us along, okay?"

He began the lead-in to "Rock Around the Clock", and Hammy jumped on the drums. Jimmy and Kellen leaped in on guitar, and they were off.

Within a minute, they knew something was happening. The customers began to clap their hands and hum along, and Mark, cruising on the vocals, pumped up the energy. They strung the song out for a lot longer than it was originally meant to be—five or six minutes compared to the two minutes the song usually lasted—and nobody complained. They just clapped like mad.

Mark introduced other songs, and the audience seemed to like it. They continued to clap and the group, feeling appreciated, smiled more and more broadly.

"Okay," Mark said after an energetic version of "Jailhouse Rock". "Here's our newest member, Jimmy Welton, who plays guitar and sings with us. Hope you'll give him a warm welcome, folks; it's his first time."

The audience, hearing the double entendre, whooped and cheered as Jimmy waved sickly from the bandstand.

Mark went on, "Jimmy's got a great new song we hope you'll get up and dance to. It's so new, we're playing it here for the first time. *I* don't even know it!"

The audience chuckled—they clearly liked Mark—but Jimmy was suddenly nervous as Mark swung the microphone toward him. They'd liked the first songs, and Jimmy had kept up fine with Kellen on guitar, but he and Mark hadn't sung harmony yet, and the new song that Mark had generously allotted lead to him wasn't coming up till later. He *had* to put "Bawk Bawk" over.

He took a deep breath and stepped up to the mike, trying to sound reassuring and confident. "Hi, folks. This is new, and, well, we hope you like it. It's a dance song, and we'll do all the moves up here, and you can just follow us. The song is called 'Bawk Bawk'."

He did the four-count lead-in and Kellen came in behind him, with Mark backing him up. Hammy bashed out a steady rhythm, and Jimmy launched into the vocal, trying to pump up the energy with exuberant gestures. He strutted, he clucked, he waved, he pumped his elbows together like a chicken.

The audience just about died laughing.

No one clapped. No one stomped their feet. No one got up and danced.

But they did laugh their heads off, all the time Jimmy was singing. They laughed so much they could hardly hear the vocal, though he kept going doggedly till the end. He remembered to do the high whistle and the click of his heels, and when he bobbed his head like a chicken for the final notes, the audience all but fell out of their seats. Jimmy began to feel like a fool.

Hammy played the last beats on the drums, and Kellen finished strumming his guitar with a flourish.

As the last notes died away, Jimmy gave an embarrassed nod to the audience. They finally stopped laughing.

They began to clap.

They began to cheer.

In a moment, the room was echoing with stomping feet and yelling patrons.

Mark deliberately stepped back and glanced at Kellen to do the same, so Jimmy could have the spotlight. Jimmy bowed and nodded, then nodded again.

They didn't stop. Someone in the front hollered, "Again!" and behind him, others took up the cry.

Jimmy didn't know what to do. He looked frantically at Mark, who stepped forward, toward the microphone. "Thanks, folks," he said, smiling. "Guess you liked that one, huh?"

A wall of sound answered him.

Mark waited until it died down. It took a full minute. Then he went on, "We'll play it again later—" He had to stop, because the cheering had become literally deafening. When it subsided enough for him to speak, he said, "We'll play a lot more for you too, but right now, we're gonna take a short break—" A gaggle of boos broke out. "—and we'll be back very soon. So order another drink, light up a smoke and thanks!"

He stepped back from the mike and put down his guitar, which was the signal for everyone else to unload their instruments as well. Hammy put down his drumsticks and followed the others into the back of the kitchen, where Marvin had graciously given them a tiny table with an ashtray and some chairs to relax between sets. There was also a light curtain they could pull for privacy, which cast their rest area into semi-darkness.

Mark stretched out on a chair and lit a cigarette. "Did you *hear* that? *Did* you?"

"We're not deaf," Kellen said mildly. "We all heard it."

Hammy grinned. "Gave me goosebumps, man."

Mark pounded on the table and gave a mock glare to Jimmy. "They loved you!"

Jimmy sat uncomfortably. He still couldn't believe the wave of sound that had swept over them onstage, and he wanted to savor it. "Yeah, pretty good, huh?"

"So when do we play it again?" Hammy wanted to know. "Right after the break?"

Mark shook his head. "No, let's stay with our set list. Let 'em wait a while. We haven't done some of our best stuff yet, plus we still have the new song, 'Wrapped in Gauze', and they'll love that."

"Should we close with that one?"

Mark pondered. "Maybe next to closing." He grinned. "Let's close with 'Bawk Bawk'. This way, they'll stick around, and maybe next time, they'll get up and dance." He inhaled deeply on the cigarette.

The boys gulped down Cokes and took a couple more minutes to savor the sweetness of their sudden success.

When they went back out, the people sitting at tables gave them a warm round of applause. The boys waved and grinned and picked up their instruments again.

Jimmy stood back while Mark sang lead on "Jailhouse Rock", and the audience whooped over their version. He played along on "Johnny B. Goode" but didn't sing, and they liked that one, too. The audience had decided they liked the band, so they were happy with just about everything they played, and they hummed along or tapped their feet on the heavier rock numbers.

It went the same way all night, until they came to the last half hour of the gig. Jimmy felt keyed up but very alive, and he and Mark had already harmonized on two songs the audience applauded wildly.

Now it was time to sing "Wrapped in Gauze," and he stepped forward confidently, Mark stepping up to harmonize with him. He gave the count-in, and they attacked the song, voices blending beautifully as Hammy banged the hi-hats and Kellen strummed furiously on his electric guitar.

"Sparklers flare in the dark of night,
Magic and my'stry in prisms of white.
… Doesn't matter where else I go
When I'm here I'll always know
I'm wrapped in the gauze of love."

This was the best reaction all night. The audience, now considerably thinned out since the early evening, rose to their feet and roared. They listened to the song, and it seemed to catch at their throats. A few people picked up the words and began to sing along, while others rose just to rock slowly in place.

When Mark and Jimmy sang the final poignant notes, there was a tiny silence before the remaining audience cheered lustily.

"Thank you, folks," Jimmy said, speaking into the microphone again, and a little surprised that he felt so comfortable. "We're glad you enjoyed tonight. We have just one more song to do for you, and hey, you asked for it. Here it is, one more time—'Bawk Bawk'."

The audience, which had been swaying and clapping, now cheered again, as Jimmy strummed the opening and swung into the song, clicking his heels, bobbing his head and flapping his arms.

They'd been waiting for it, because the whole place, in a minute, was 'bawk bawking' all over the dance floor, with the men doing the chicken 'bawk' and the women bobbing their heads and clicking their heels.

It was their most exciting rendition yet, and the band finished on an upbeat, exuberant at their success.

As they made their way offstage, men and women stopped them and told them how much they'd enjoyed it. A few offered them cash tips. The boys, embarrassed, smiled, thanked them and finally escaped.

When they'd packed up, Mark found Marvin to collect their fee. Marvin seemed almost as happy as Jimmy was with their success. "Nice going, guys," he said. "My people had a lot of fun tonight."

"So did we," Jimmy said, when it seemed no one else would speak up. He knew Mark would speak for the group, but Hammy and Kellen had been there longer; you'd think they were dummies, for all they said. "We appreciate it."

"Well, then," Marvin hesitated, "maybe you could come in again. Maybe something regular? That last song was pretty great. So was the other one you did." Jimmy knew he meant "Wrapped in Gauze," and his heart glowed in his chest. What a night!

Mark took charge of the negotiations. "We'd love a regular gig here, if we can work out the money. How often would you want us?"

"Well, I haven't thought much about it. But maybe—Friday, Saturday, Sunday nights? Every week, starting next weekend?"

Mark hesitated. "Every weekend?"

"Well, we can talk about that. And we can talk about the money too. I'd just like to know if you're interested. Are you?"

Jimmy nodded at once. He would have to cut back on his job at the park, but he could probably make more money doing this. Imagine getting *paid* to play and sing rock `n roll!

He noticed the others were noncommittal. Maybe he'd have to start learning how to play hard to get, like girls were supposed to do. But in his case, they were too interested in chasing him. The only one who *didn't* chase him, he thought, was Laurey.

"We'll think about it," Mark said. "Why don't you think about an offer and call me this week?"

His smooth delivery was a little surprising to Jimmy. He didn't know Mark could do that.

"Here's your take, boys," Marvin said genially, handing Mark some bills and coins. "Don't let him keep it all, now. You just get ready to play for me regular, and keep that 'Bawk Bawk' song in every time. I'll make sure you have good audiences like tonight."

He walked away, and without discussing it, the band went right back to their old bar hangout for what Mark called 'real drinks'. Once there, the boys crowded around Mark, as he counted out each man's split. Jimmy was excited to get his, even if it *was* only $3.75. It was the first money he'd ever earned in his life as a musician. His dad would have been so proud. When that thought occurred to him, he didn't realize his eyes were glistening.

When Mark pushed a rum and Coke at him, Jimmy didn't hesitate; he took a big swig and handed it back. When Mark then lit a cigarette and offered it to Jimmy, he firmly pushed down his revulsion and his impulse to refuse, took it and inhaled deeply, then choked as the smoke got into his lungs.

"Now you're a real musician," Kellen said with satisfaction. "Smoking and drinking like the rest of us."

Jimmy tried another draw on the cigarette before handing it back to Mark, but he couldn't help it: he choked and coughed so hard he almost retched up the rum he'd just swallowed.

"You'll get used to it," Mark said comfortingly. "Nothing like a butt to keep you mellow."

Jimmy doubted he'd ever get used to it, but he stayed quiet as the others celebrated. He couldn't speak without coughing.

"Best one yet," Hammy said with satisfaction. "Mark, how much you think we should ask for a regular weekend gig?"

Mark inhaled deeply and took a slug of rum and Coke before he answered. "I think we ask for $100 and take $80," he said. "That's $20 each, every weekend." He swallowed another slug before adding, "There's always a negotiation. If I back down from $100, Marvin'll think he won something. You always want them to think they've won."

"Sounds like the son of a lawyer," said Kellen.

"Lucky he is," Hammy chimed in. "He'll get a good deal for us."

"That sound about right?" Mark asked.

"I'm okay with it," Kellen said.

"Me too," Jimmy said. It was the first time he could talk without coughing.

Mark slapped Jimmy on the back. "Atta boy. You'll get the knack of smoking. Soon you won't be able to live without 'em, like me."

"Bad for the voice," Jimmy croaked, and he sounded so awful the others burst out laughing. When they stopped laughing and he stopped coughing, he had a question. "Are we still gonna be the Mark-Tones?"

"Unless you have a better idea," Mark said.

"How about—the GooseBumps?"

"What?" Hammy asked.

"You keep saying it, Hammy—the songs give you goosebumps. And I did meet Mark on Halloween—the night you're *supposed* to get goosebumps."

"Goosebumps," Mark mused. "Goosebumps. Hey, Jimmy, where's your notebook?"

Jimmy unstrapped his guitar case and handed it to him.

Mark flipped to a blank page in the school notebook, picked up a pencil lying on the bar and wrote "Goosebumps." He sat looking at it.

"Different spelling?" Kellen suggested.

Mark wrote 'Guzbumps'. Then 'Goocebumps'. He sat looking at it some more.

Jimmy took the notebook from his hand and wrote 'Gusbumps'.

Mark took it back from him and again wrote "Goosebumps." He thought about it. "I like it, spelled regular like this," he said. "You guys?"

Jimmy looked again and had an idea. "No. Spell it with a capital B in the middle; makes it look distinctive." He wrote out "GooseBumps" in large, clear letters on the page.

Hammy and Kellen peered over his shoulder. "Okay by me," Hammy said. "Better than Mark-Tones."

Kellen said, "Yeah, I can see us now, picking up a gold record with that name."

Mark said, "First you better see us *making* a record. Then we can get to the gold part."

They all laughed at that, and when Jimmy laughed, it was the first time he could make a sound without coughing or choking.

Chapter Five

Mark got them $80 per weekend at Marvin's, paid in cash after the Sunday-night show, and suddenly Jimmy had a source of income larger than his pay from the park. He kept his job anyway, more to see Laurey than anything else, because he still hadn't gotten up the nerve to ask her out, but now that he knew he'd make a clear $20 per weekend, it made a lot of things possible.

First, he was able to give his mother more money for the household, and though they bickered about it, in the end he made her accept $10 every week. The remaining $10 from the gig and the park money, about $5 a week, gave him the kind of spending money he'd never had before, and he resolved to save as much as he could. He tried to put away at least $8 every week, and most of the time, he succeeded. The stack of bills and coins he kept in an old cigar box in his room grew and grew, week by week.

They officially adopted The GooseBumps as their band name, and Marvin put it on the signs he posted outside the club, advertising their weekend appearances. Mark asked everyone to buy new black shirts and tight black pants, plus boots with the new Cuban heels—it was one of the weeks Jimmy didn't save anything, but he wasn't sorry. Dressed like that, they all looked sharp, and they even seemed to sound better. They were more confident, and that's how they came across onstage.

"Bawk Bawk" remained the most popular song in their repertoire, with the boys performing it at least twice every night, and some nights three, when things got really raucous. People started hearing about the 'chicken dance' and coming in to try it, and sometimes they had forty people on the tiny tiled floor at Marvin's, bawk-bawking enthusiastically, flapping their arms and clicking their heels.

"Wrapped in Gauze" was popular, too, and since typically they played it at the end of their set, people came to expect it and know it. Many times, they sang along with the band, clapped their hands and pounded their tables. Marvin talked about installing soundproof tiles in the front room, though he never did.

Jimmy's mother and sister finally came to see the band play one night, after Jimmy talked enthusiastically about their reception for some time. Apart from the weekend gigs, nothing had changed at home, with his mother still trudging off every day to her secretarial job and hoping the measly insurance money she'd finally wangled for the claim from their father's death would come in every mail.

Jimmy made sure they had a center table in front, and Marvin provided free drinks, though his mom only ordered Cokes for her and Debby. She hadn't heard him play since his father taught him the first chords, so she had no idea how hard he had practiced or how far he had come. She also didn't know Jimmy had started writing songs, though he tried to prepare her ahead of time for "Bawk Bawk". She met Mark, Kellen and Hammy before they went on and had something nice to say to each of them.

With Jimmy's mother watching, the group felt obliged to deliver a rocking performance. As usual, they started with "Rock Around the Clock" and did many Carl Perkins and Elvis and Chuck Berry songs afterward, all of which got a good reception.

Then Jimmy stepped forward and the audience, knowing what was coming, yelled, "Bawk Bawk!"

They were on their feet and ready to dance.

His mom and Debby looked bewildered, but when Jimmy introduced it and the band launched into it, they were stunned by the wall of sound that vibrated around them. The audience loved it.

When the band took a break, Jimmy breathlessly brought them outside and asked, "So, what do you think?"

"That song, Jimmy," Debby blurted out, "did you write that?"

"'Bawk Bawk'? Yeah, I wrote it. Do you like it?"

"Like it? I could dance all night to it!" Debby started flapping her arms and clicking her heels. "Will you play it again, Jimmy? *Please?*"

"We always play it at least twice," Jimmy said. "But if you can't stay—"

"Debby does have school tomorrow," his mother murmured. "It was very nice, Jimmy, really."

Jimmy felt completely deflated. At that moment, he missed his father so much, he could have broken down and cried, right there on the crummy sidewalk in front of Marvin's. When he could control his voice, he said, "Why don't you come back in and hear the other number I wrote? I'll get Mark to do it right away, so you can just slip out afterward."

"Come on, Mom, can we stay?" Debby pleaded. "Just for a few more minutes? To hear Jimmy's other song?"

He grinned at her; Debby had always been a fan, and he appreciated her. She grinned back; she was having fun.

His mom reluctantly acquiesced, and Jimmy got Mark to change the set order so they could play "Wrapped in Gauze" right away.

As he played, though the audience was wildly receptive, he watched his mom and Debby closely. His mom listened to the lyrics intently, a hint of a tear in her eye. Debby's smile was too bright, and at the end she put her hand over her eyes.

The next day, she said to him, "It's about Dad, isn't it? That song? About Dad and us?"

"Well, sort of. It's about our life before. I was trying to remember the good stuff."

"It hurt my heart, Jimmy. It really did."

It was the nicest thing he'd ever heard from his sister. He gave her an impulsive hug.

One evening, as the band came in to set up at the start of a weekend, Marvin said he wanted to speak to them before they started. They went to his office in the back, and without small talk, he said, "How'd you guys like to make a record?"

They stared at him and each other. Making a record was an unheard-of dream. It was what they all talked about and dreamt of. They had no idea it could really happen.

Marvin said to them, "I've been asking around. There are places here in the city where you can pay for a 45, a single—two songs, front and back—and have them cut as many copies as you want. I thought we could maybe do that and then sell the copies here. The crowd would love it. And you'd have a sample, if you ever wanted to take it to a record company and try to get a real contract."

Mark was the first to be able to speak. He said, "Wow, Marvin, that'd be great, but—"

"I know, I know," Marvin said. "Your dad has to look over the contract, so he knows you guys won't get cheated, right? We'll draw up something simple, and if he's satisfied, we all sign on the dotted line, right? I'm thinking we sell the records for a buck each and you guys get 10 cents of each record, since I'm paying for the recording in the first place."

"At least 20 cents," Mark said. "We'll go from there."

Marvin laughed. "You little gutter rat! Twenty cents! You'd think I *wasn't* paying for it in the first place! I have to make my money back, Mark, surely you can see that."

"Sure," Mark said, "but after that the risk is as much ours as yours. Maybe no one'll want to buy it, and then we'll all be stuck. But if they do, you're selling it at the club and that's the only place they can get it, so we should get a higher royalty to compensate for the lack of distribution."

Jimmy wasn't sure he even understood what Mark had just said, because when Mark started talking business, he talked bewilderingly fast. But he seemed to be fighting for more money for them, which he was sure, knowing Mark, they'd all split four ways, as usual. The thought of actually *making a record* just made his head spin!

By the time he tuned in to the conversation again, Mark and Marvin seemed to have ironed out their differences, because they were now talking about which songs to record. "'Bawk Bawk', of course," Marvin said, "and then how about that song you always end with?"

"`Wrapped in Gauze'"?" Mark said. "Yeah, we can do that." He gave Jimmy a broad grin. "But we'll need a higher royalty on those, since Jimmy wrote them both."

"Why, you stinker—"

"Those are the ones people come in to hear," Mark explained. "And we don't need to *pay* royalties to any other writers, since Jimmy wrote them. Might as well have the best ones on the record."

After the show that night, the boys repaired to the bar, ordered drinks from Mick, lit cigarettes (all but Jimmy) and celebrated their good fortune. "A record!" Kellen sighed blissfully. "Never thought it'd happen!"

"Imagine recording 'Bawk Bawk'," Mark chuckled. "That song we all laughed at the first time we heard it."

"*Everyone* laughs when they first hear it," Hammy said. "The second time they get up and dance, and after that, they're so happy they don't care *what* we're singing."

Marvin, true to his word, booked time in a Brooklyn studio for them the following week, and Mark managed to get them twenty cents' royalty per record sold, four cents per man and an additional four cents to Jimmy as the songwriter. Mark believed in splitting things evenly; he said each man contributed to their success.

Jimmy went with the others to record "Bawk Bawk" and "Wrapped in Gauze". It took them only an hour at the studio, after the engineer set up the microphones and explained how to sing into them for maximum effect. Hammy did a powerful drumming job, and Kellen's guitar licks were better than usual.

They were told to come the next day to pick up the acetate and the copies they wanted pressed.

Mark told the studio session people to make 200 copies.

The initial 200 records sold at the club in the first week, and Jimmy pocketed $16 in royalties, extra money he loved earning for work he'd already done. They had a 'hot platter', and from then on Marvin had hundreds of extra copies pressed every week to sell.

That same week, Jimmy went to his job at the park and ran into Laurey just as she'd finished dressing as Cinderella. "Does my sash look okay?" she asked, twirling in front of him.

Obediently, he looked it over. "It looks fine."

She stopped and seemed to search for words. Finally, she said, "I hear you're in a—in a band now."

He didn't know how she knew. He said, "Uh—yeah—I am." Then, because she seemed to expect it, and because he really wanted it too, he added, "Maybe you'd come to see us play sometime? We have a record now."

"A record! Gosh!" For a minute she couldn't say anything, then she said, "Why didn't you ever tell me, Jimmy? That you were playing in a band? That's exciting!"

"I didn't think you'd care." He was just being honest, but he was unprepared for her reaction.

For a minute, she just looked at him, and then he saw tears pooling in her eyes.

A moment later, she was pounding on his chest with her fists. "You always say that—that you think I won't care. But I do! I do!"

"Hey, stop it!" He grabbed her fists to stop her; the pounding really hurt. But then she looked up at him and he suddenly felt that same elation he'd felt before, that flooding sweetness in his body. He looked down at her, brushed the tears off her face and kissed her.

They kissed for a long time, until Laurey stepped away suddenly and said, "You haven't even changed yet; we need to get out there."

"Oh. You're right," Jimmy said, at a complete loss. Kissing her was so hypnotic that he hardly knew what to do once it was over. He had to get his costume on, but he couldn't think what else to do, until she pushed him and said, "Hurry!"

Jimmy got into his costume in record time, and they did their act and their dance. Afterward, when he'd finished changing, he waited for her, and when she came out, in a blue wool knee-length dress and a light coat, he said to her, "Will you come see the band?"

She tried to seem casual about it. "Yeah, I'd like that."

"We play Fridays through Sundays at Marvin's in Manhattan," he told her, and took a piece of paper out of his notebook to write down the address for her. While he was writing, he asked her, trying to be casual, "How about giving me your number, so I can call to remind you?"

She took the pen from him and wrote it down on a blank sheet in his notebook. He stared at the number, trying to memorize it, thinking it might ignite on the page before he could. He'd gotten her number, after dreaming about it for so long. And it had been so easy; all he'd had to do was ask!

He wondered if it were true that she really had feelings for him apart from friendship. If so, he'd hit the jackpot. Those kisses earlier, which he could still feel on his lips, were the most exciting moments he could remember ever having—better even than a standing ovation at Marvin's.

"What night will you come?" he asked, hoping the show that night would be extra-good.

"Probably Saturday. I go out with my friends that night, so I may come with them."

He hoped there would be no guys among those friends and said boldly, "If you let me know, I'll get you and your friends a table by the bandstand."

She gave him back the piece of paper he'd written on, so he could add the phone number of the little apartment in the Bronx. "Good night," she said reluctantly.

"Good night." But he wanted to turn cartwheels and do handsprings all the way home.

He had finally kissed Laurey, and she was coming to see him play!

* * *

He was still high when he went to rehearsal Friday afternoon. Mark stared at him when he arrived.

"What's with your hair?"

"What's wrong with it?" Jimmy knew better than to sound defensive; sooner or later, Mark would *tell* him what was wrong with it, so he might as well just hear him out.

"It looks—good." Mark walked around him, looking at the silky strands of hair combed down around Jimmy's ears. "What did you do to it?"

Jimmy said, puzzled, "I just washed it. I wanted a haircut, but the barbershop always closes before I can get there, most days, so it got a little long."

"I like it." Mark looked at him again. "Maybe we can do something with this."

When Kellen and Hammy arrived, Mark asked what they thought of Jimmy's hair. They both liked it, too. Mark got combs for everyone, and they practiced combing their hair down around their ears, the way Jimmy had. They had to wet the combs to make it work, and Mark had to unravel his precious duck tail, but eventually they all had their hair combed down around their ears. Kellen's looked silly, Hammy's like the moths had eaten it—he was on his way to balding early—but Mark and Jimmy were closest in style, and after tilting his head in the mirror several times, Mark announced, "We need to wear our hair like this from now on. It's a great look."

Kellen and Hammy made no objection. They had learned when Mark decided something about the band, they would eventually go along with it. Jimmy was glad he didn't need to worry about the barbershop anymore.

"That's settled," Mark said with satisfaction. "We all get haircuts—or whatever—by tomorrow night, and then we turn up with the new style. It'll be our new look."

Jimmy checked the mirror carefully the next day, before heading to Mark's for a final rehearsal. He was wearing his newest black shirt and his best tight black pants, and he'd gone over his hair minutely, every strand was even and neat, though longer than he'd ever worn it. His mother hadn't complained, and even Debby told him he looked 'dreamy'. He hoped Laurey would be impressed… if she came to see them.

He asked Marvin to hold a table 'ringside' for her and her friends (he hoped there weren't more than four of them) and played with great enthusiasm when they started, hoping to keep a high charge of energy. The band sounded unusually good that night, and all their songs went well; the audience, as big a crowd as they'd ever had, responded with appreciation.

Then she walked in, with three girlfriends, and Marvin seated them down front. They had just started "Splish Splash" and were rocking out, but he caught the quizzical look in her eyes as she looked at him on the bandstand. He picked up the beat a little and sang louder; Mark gave him a speculative look.

Finally, the song was over, and they were bowing and thanking the audience. Laurey clapped, along with her friends, but Jimmy didn't think she looked really impressed. He hoped she'd stay at least till the break, so he could talk to her.

Mark signaled the band for a break a few minutes later, so Jimmy stepped forward to introduce 'Bawk Bawk', always a highlight for the audience. He played it enthusiastically and did the moves with extra verve, but he couldn't help but notice she wasn't dancing along, though her friends were; Laurey looked like she was about to collapse in laughter. *Well, everyone else did the first time they heard it.*

They finished with the usual flourish, the clicking heels and the bobbing head, to wild applause from the regulars, and Jimmy thanked them and said the band was taking a break. They left the bandstand, and he went over to Laurey's table.

"So you came," he said, trying to sound casual.

Laurey smiled; she looked extra pretty in a black dress with a full skirt and high heels. "What was that last song? It was a riot."

"Oh! That's one of mine." When she looked puzzled, he elaborated. "I wrote it. It's become kind of a—thing—around here."

"Love 'Bawk Bawk', Jimmy!" called one of the girls who came in often. She was a pretty blonde in a tight skirt and lots of eye makeup. "You gonna play it again tonight?"

"Yep," he called back. "At closing, like always. You gonna stick around to hear it?"

"I just might." She gave him a flirtatious look and he waved to her. Then he looked down at Laurey, whose face looked like she'd just swallowed something sour.

"I guess all the girls like guitar players," she said when she saw him looking at her.

"It's fun."

"I'll bet." She introduced him to her friends, and he joked with them extravagantly, though he barely paid attention to their names; he wanted to talk to Laurey so badly, and now that she was here, in front of him, he couldn't think of anything to say. He couldn't dance with her at the club, only at the park, and he couldn't find the right way to keep the conversation going.

"What do you think of our music?" he finally asked, knowing it was the wrong way to go about it. You shouldn't *ask* for compliments.

"Is it all *your* music?" she asked innocently. "I mean, I've heard 'Splish Splash' before."

"That one's by Bobby Darin." He fidgeted, wanting to take her in his arms, but he knew he couldn't.

"Do you have to go back?" she asked, looking at him.

"Uh—no, not yet. We can talk some more."

"So you *write* songs, too?" She looked up at him as though he climbed mountains as well, with pure admiration in her eyes.

"Only a few, so far. You like songwriters?"

"I do now," she said, and he almost shivered, he was so thrilled.

"Introduce us, Jimmy?" came Mark's voice behind him.

He almost groaned. Just what he needed. But he made quick introductions of his three bandmates, and Mark, in particular, made a fuss over Laurey. "You're the girl who plays Cinderella, right? Boy, do you look great in that costume." He gave her a wink.

"Thanks," she said, but she was looking at Jimmy.

"Stick around for the next set?" he asked, as the others started to climb onto the bandstand.

"Uh, I guess so," she said, and her friends murmured a quick assent.

He gave her what he hoped looked like a special smile. "Okay, then. We'll play some good ones for you."

She and her friends stayed till closing, and he spent every break at her table. She enjoyed "Heartbreak Hotel" and "Jailhouse Rock", but her favorite by far was "Wrapped in Gauze", which they played just before closing the night with "Bawk Bawk" again.

They packed up to go quickly, and he invited her to come with them to the bar, but she thought she'd stayed out long enough. "Come back again?" he asked her. They were standing on the sidewalk outside Marvin's, as the lights went off inside, one by one.

She hesitated. "I'd like to. That song, Jimmy, the other one you wrote—"

"Yes?"

"That's a beautiful song, Jimmy. I'd like the band at my wedding to play that song." She leaned in and gave him a quick kiss on the mouth. "Good night."

He floated all the way home.

* * *

The following month, the screaming started.

The GooseBumps were becoming a tighter unit, with good timing and good rhythm; Mark and Jimmy, working together, had strengthened their sung harmonies into something truly beautiful. In fact, when they harmonized on a song, customers stopped talking and drinking and just listened. It was the ultimate tribute.

Over the weeks, their audience began to change, as well. Once their new haircuts were well established at Marvin's, new customers began to come in—teenage girls, from seventeen up, who clapped loudly and cheered, pounding on the tables, for "Bawk Bawk" and "Wrapped in Gauze". Patrons in their forties gave way to customers in their thirties, who got up unself-consciously to dance and enjoy themselves, often right up to their last set. They bought copies of the record, as well, and Mark's distribution of their 'royalties', as he liked to put it, went from a few dollars a week to a respectable sum. Soon Jimmy was earning more in record royalties than he did in his park job.

Laurey and her friends became regulars, and they invited others of the same age. Jimmy quit working at the park, to give more time to the GooseBumps, which was providing much more income. But knowing he'd see Laurey every weekend and having her phone number so he could take her out for a soda or a movie on other nights, made all the difference. They were officially dating now, with good night kisses and all (which never failed to thrill him), and he didn't miss playing Prince Charming, though Mark continued to call him that. Jimmy figured he was just jealous.

Rehearsals Friday, Saturday and Sunday afternoons became standard, while Mark and Jimmy often got together at other times, just for fun. They talked music all the time and worked on new songs they had begun to write together, but Jimmy never said a word about Mark's mother, and Mark never brought up the subject. It was as though the outburst at his house on Jimmy's first visit had never happened.

The rehearsal time bonded them together as a group, and Jimmy got to know more about his bandmates, bit by bit. Hammy's father *had* been in prison, but he was out now and looking for a job, which wasn't easy for an ex-con. He'd been convicted twice of petty theft and imprisoned for a few months, here and there. Most recently he'd been a house painter, before he stole from a family whose house he was painting, and he was slowly trying to work his way back to respectability, while Hammy's mother worked full-time as a telephone operator to support Hammy's three little sisters.

Kellen's mother *did* have a drinking problem, so he didn't invite the band over often. Jimmy, looking around the cramped, messy little apartment Kellen lived in with his mom, shuddered inwardly. Even his own awful apartment was better than that. Both Kellen and Hammy still lived at home, because they couldn't support themselves independently, and they were proud that the money they brought in from Marvin's helped their families.

Hammy was 20, Kellen 19, but they had only part-time jobs apart from the band. Hammy's job at the vet's office too often meant he arrived with animal hair on his shirt and required a vigorous brush-down before going onstage (Jimmy figured Hammy was as kind to the animals as he was to other people). Kellen made change for children at a kiddie arcade near his home and admitted he enjoyed wearing the change belt more than the rest of the job; he hoped to be successful with the GooseBumps so he could eventually give it up. Mark, the youngest and most business-savvy, thanks to his well-connected attorney father, was just 18 and happy to be done with high school; despite his parents' urging, he refused to consider college, as long as he could earn even a little money playing rock `n roll.

The night of the first uncontrollable audience, they'd played a raucous set, including three separate renditions of "Bawk Bawk", which was going over better and better, week by week. There were new girls at the club now, girls over 21 who came by themselves and ordered liquor (Marvin was strict about not serving under-age people), and they were a bit high when Jimmy announced the song and broke into it.

When it was over, the cheering turned into screaming. The band bowed once, and then again. But the girls kept screaming.

Mark stepped forward to quiet them down. "Thanks very much," he started, but the screams from the audience were drowning him out, even with the microphone. He tried again but could not make himself heard.

He looked at the band. "Let's go," he tried to shout, but they were unable to hear him. Jimmy, though, saw he was looking worried and made frantic motions to the others, who held tightly to their instruments as they trooped offstage.

That seemed to be the signal for the girls to rush forward. Mark, Jimmy, Kellen and Hammy barely escaped in time, as they came running forward, screaming all the way, their arms outstretched as if to engulf them.

Marvin, looking really worried now, pulled them through the curtain and parked them in the kitchen. "Don't move!" he warned them. "I'll get them out and lock the door."

He emptied the place efficiently in just a few minutes, with the help of his silent but heavily muscled bouncer by the front door. Even then, it wasn't easy, but Marvin, determined to protect his band, got rid of the girls, including Laurey and her friends, who had as usual been at ringside.

"They're gone," he said, coming back to the kitchen. "You guys okay?"

"No harm done," Mark said, though he still looked unnerved.

"There's such a thing as too popular," Marvin tried to joke, but he too seemed shaken. "Just stick around a while, okay? Don't go home yet. Just in case."

The boys sat quietly in the kitchen, where a sympathetic barman brought them drinks.

Then the bouncer, who'd been watching the windows, came back. "They're still out there, sir," he said to Marvin, who started toward the front with him.

True to his word, there were knots of girls—probably three dozen in all—still milling around the front door. When they saw Marvin, they began to shout, "We want Mark! We want Jimmy!"

"I'll go talk to them," Mark said bravely.

Marvin held him back. "You're gonna reason with a mob? They'll trample you to death. Stay here."

Marvin went to the phone and nodded to the bouncer, who picked up the baseball bat he'd stashed in the coat-check room. "Police, right now," he said into the receiver. A moment later: "We have a riot building here. I need police protection right now… As many as you can spare."

He gave the name and address of the bar and hung up.

The boys sat tensely. Three long minutes went by.

Suddenly, there was a crash of glass, as the girls, who had shoved against the windowpane, pounded it to the splitting point. As the glass flew all over the front tables and flooring, the girls began to pour in, still screaming.

"Get out!" Marvin yelled at the boys. "Through the back door! Now!"

Jimmy, Mark and the others picked up their instruments and ran for their lives. The back door was always kept locked, but one of the bartenders opened it and held it as they scrambled out. Fortunately for them, the alleyway behind was empty; the girls hadn't thought to station anyone there.

Panic-stricken, the boys ran a block. No one tried to stop them. They turned back to the street where Marvin's was situated, now a full block away from the screaming mob. But as soon as they turned onto the street, headed the other way, the girls saw them.

"There they are! Jimmy, I love you! Kellen, I love you!"

"Grab them!"

As the boys began frantically to sprint in the opposite direction, police cars pulled up. Mark whistled harshly and brought a cruiser to a stop. Instantly, he yanked open the door and scrambled inside, pulling Jimmy and the others with him. "Thank God," he said breathlessly.

The two officers in front turned around. "We have a report of a riot," one said.

Mark pointed toward Marvin's, but he was too late: the girls had reached the police cruiser, and seeing the band inside, tried to yank open the doors.

"Floor it, Jack!" said the officer riding shotgun.

The driver did, and the girls clinging to the doors fell away, though not before they had managed to pull open the door and half-drag Hammy out of the seat. The other boys grabbed his left arm and left leg and held on grimly. When the cruiser had gone several blocks, he finally managed to pull the door shut with his right hand. He was trembling badly.

"Jesus," he said.

Mark patted him. "Okay, Hammy? Almost lost you back there."

"Not funny, Mark," Kellen said. He was squashed between Mark and Hammy, still clutching the drummer with both hands. "Those girls could've killed him."

"They ripped off my sleeve," Hammy said, looking at his arm, where the fabric had indeed been torn off.

"Be thankful. Could've been your head," Mark told him.

"What the hell happened back there?" the policeman asked, pulling onto a quiet side street.

Mark and Jimmy took turns explaining they had no idea how the girls had gotten so out of control that they'd tried to rush the stage and then smashed in the windows of Marvin's club.

"You must be a pretty good band," one of the officers said, while the other said, "Shut up, okay? These kids are scared out of their minds."

He considered for a minute. "We'll go back there to help out, but first we'll get you four home. I'm not putting you out on the street for those girls to swallow up… so, where to?"

Mark gave his address, and the police cruiser dropped him off. The street was quiet, but they waited till he was inside and the front door closed before they pulled away.

Hammy was next. He lived in a poor neighborhood further north. He thanked the police profusely before getting out and running inside.

Kellen's apartment was on a street with a lot of old brownstones. He untangled his guitar from Jimmy's and said good night. "Hope we don't have to do this again," he said as he left.

Jimmy was the last dropped off, at his apartment house in the Bronx. "Thanks so much," he said gratefully to the policemen. He hoped his mother wouldn't realize a police car had brought him home; he'd never hear the end of it.

"We'll go back there," the police officer said to him. "Hope it's over by now."

"I hope so, too," Jimmy said fervently. He hoped it would never happen again. It was one thing for them to like you, another for them to rush you in the club, where people were supposed to be civilized.

He had no idea it was just beginning.

CHAPTER SIX

The next morning, newspaper reporters started calling.

When Jimmy got home from school, reporters were waiting in front of his building. They wanted to know what had happened; the reports of a riot had come over the AP wire.

Jimmy was stunned. "How'd you find me?" he asked.

"Marvin told us where you lived," one reporter said. "What happened there? Was it really a riot?"

"I—I'm not sure," Jimmy said. On one hand, he was thrilled that any reporter wanted to talk to him. On the other hand, he had no idea they'd hunt him down. This was almost as scary as being pursued by the girls last night.

"It's okay, kid," said one veteran in a trench coat and stained old hat. "We just want to write something about this. Can you help us out?"

Jimmy thought of inviting them in, but he knew his mother would never recover if she came home to find a gaggle of reporters in her living room. Besides, he wasn't eager to advertise their poverty. "Can you wait here a minute?" he asked. "I'll be right back."

Reluctantly the reporters let him go inside, where he rushed upstairs frantically and called Mark. "These guys were sitting on my doorstep when I got back from school!" he exclaimed. "What should I do?"

Mark was similarly inundated. "They've been here with me for an hour. Why don't you just send 'em to me and I'll talk to them all?"

Jimmy could hear an undertone of enjoyment in Mark's voice. The son of a gun was having fun with this! Suddenly, a little voice inside him said, *If Mark can talk to them, so can I.* I *was there, too.*

"Never mind," he said. "I guess I can give them a story just as well. Did you talk to Marvin today?"

"He's closing temporarily," Mark said. "Has to repair those smashed windows. He'll call us when he's ready to open again."

"We're not fired, are we?" Jimmy asked anxiously.

Mark laughed. "Fired because we're too popular? Not hardly. That riot was good for business. Besides, his insurance will cover it. He figures a week or so for repairs, and we're back onstage, but he'll have better security, this time."

"Okay," Jimmy said. "See you later, maybe."

"Yeah. Come over Friday, even though we're not doing a show. We can rehearse—oh, no, we can't, not without Hammy's kit—but we can mess around. Anyway, all publicity is good publicity!"

Jimmy went back outside. The reporters were still there, and they started on him as soon as he appeared.

Jimmy explained that their band, the GooseBumps, had played a regular weekend gig at Marvin's for about six weeks, that he had no idea who had started the riot and that it had never happened before. He admitted to being scared when the girls had started pouring into the club through the windows.

When the reporters got through with basic details, they asked about the band, and Jimmy told them he'd joined the band at Halloween, that he played bass guitar and had written two songs in their nightly set. He gave the names of the other band members.

One reporter grinned, writing busily. "Now that's—um—Mark Morgan who started the band, and you're Jimmy Welton, right? Age?"

"Seventeen."

"Still in high school?"

"Yes, sir. Graduating in June."

"Good. Most of these jokers in bands drop out long before they get a diploma… You plan to keep playing with the GooseBumps after you graduate?"

Jimmy thought about that. His father had hoped he'd go to college and become a teacher; they'd talked about his teaching music. On the other hand, he had no idea that Jimmy would land in a band, or that it would pay him anything. But he knew his answer. "I'll play with the GooseBumps as long as they want me."

"Good answer," said the veteran. He closed his notebook. "Okay, I'll talk to Marvin and get something in the paper today." He glanced at Jimmy. "And you, Dreamy Eyes, maybe we can get a picture? I can send a photographer."

Jimmy had a better idea. "How about a picture of all four of us? That would be great PR."

"If a riot can be called PR… Okay, chum, I guess we can do that."

The boys gathered at Mark's house to take the photo, and it ran on page two of the New York papers the next day, next to the story of the riot. Jimmy called Laurey, and she ran right out and bought all the papers. She said she was starting a scrapbook.

The photo was extremely flattering to Jimmy. He'd been told since he began to grow taller last year that he was very good-looking, and occasionally his dad had teased him about having 'movie-star looks'. Mark never missed a chance to call him Prince Charming. But the photo of him leaning against a wall in Mark's music room, smiling slightly, was a revelation. Kellen and Hammy were openly envious, and Mark thought they should make a poster and sell it at the club. "They'd buy more copies of that than the record," he said. Jimmy didn't know if he was joking or jealous.

Laurey cut the photo out of the paper and carried it in her wallet.

His mother began to make comments about "When your band makes it big", which she'd never even hinted at before. He began to realize that she wouldn't try to stop his music career.

Marvin called them down to the club a few days later. He was still making repairs, grumbling about 'those crazy girls', but he wanted to talk to them before the club re-opened.

"CLOSED FOR REPAIRS" signs still plastered the locked doors, and Mark had to knock for the silent bouncer to let him in. "Feels like a speakeasy," he said, walking in with the others. "All we need is the secret password."

The glass on the floor had been meticulously swept up, though pieces of broken chairs and tables still lay in clumps on the scratched floor. "It'll all be cleaned up," Marvin said, waving at the mess. "New stuff coming next week. Nothing to worry about."

At one of the few unbroken tables by the bandstand, where Hammy's drum kit was still set up and fortunately undamaged, sat a man, sipping a drink and smoking a cigarette.

He looked around forty, wearing a pristine gray suit and blue silk tie. His dark hair was beautifully cut and combed back from his thin face, and his dark eyes looked alert and friendly. He wore a beautiful slender gold watch on his left wrist.

Marvin, standing behind Jimmy, said quietly in his ear, "That's a Patek Philippe watch, if you've never seen one. It's worth a fortune."

In a heartier tone, meant to be heard, he said, "Come on over and meet my friend Dary Dover. He asked to meet you guys, seeing as how you caused the riot."

At once the man put down his cigarette and glass and stood up, in one fluid graceful motion. He was taller than Jimmy had thought—over six feet—with the easy grace of a panther. He extended his hand to each boy as Marvin introduced them. "So good to meet you all! Please, sit down."

The boys sat in chairs already arranged around the table. He smiled warmly at each of them, revealing glistening white teeth.

"So, you're the GooseBumps! And the girls here at Marvin's like you so much that you caused a riot."

"Among our many other talents," Mark said. He was watching Dover closely.

Dary laughed appreciatively. "And you do have many." He tapped the table. "Marvin and I are old friends, and he kindly gave me a copy of your record. I listened to it six times without stopping last night. I loved it."

The boys looked at each other.

Dary pretended not to see it and went on. "I've become a big fan, just from hearing the record. Marvin says you also do a dance onstage?"

Jimmy explained how "Bawk Bawk" had been written as a joke but become a dance favorite at the club.

"Ah, yes, Jimmy—the dreamboat." Jimmy blushed. "Don't be embarrassed, son. Good looks are always marketable. That photo in the paper could sell a lot of records."

He let that last sentence hang in the air, and then added deliberately, "Suppose you tell me about your other music. I know the songs on the record; what's the rest of your playlist?"

Mark, after glancing at the others, told him they played mostly covers of songs that had already been recorded by other singers.

"Well," Dary observed, "you won't get far doing that. Too many other acts are doing it, too. You have to do something to stand out."

Mark looked offended, so Jimmy spoke up. "We get great response with 'Bawk Bawk' and 'Wrapped in Gauze'. And we're thinking about writing more songs, so we *can* stand out more." They had never talked about it, but he figured it didn't hurt to sound like they were planning for the future. "I meant," he added, "Mark and I were talking about writing more songs together."

Dary nodded. "Those songs written down and copyrighted?"

Until that moment, Jimmy had never thought of copyrighting his music. "Uh—no. I can't read music. I just—hear it in my head and write down the lyrics and the chords, so I can remember it."

Dary looked thoughtful. "I'll get people to transcribe the songs and then copyright them—" He saw an instinctive scowl on Mark's face and turned to him. "In *Jimmy's* name, okay? It'll belong to *him*. No one's getting ripped off here."

Mark didn't like the implication. "'Ripped off'? What's that? Manager talk for *stealing from us*? And what exactly do *you* do, Mr. Dary Dover? Why are we even here? Marvin wanted us to meet you, but what for?"

Dary didn't seem fazed at the question. "'Ripped off' does mean stealing from someone, yes. And that's not my plan. I've done a lot of different things. I've been in advertising, and I've been in the movie business. I've been very successful, and I've had some big failures, and I've enjoyed the whole ride. And now, after hearing your record, I want to manage you guys. I think I could do great things for you."

The words had been spoken. Kellen and Hammy said nothing, but their eyes were on fire, fastened on Dary. Mark looked at him with a dazed expression. Jimmy felt as though Dary had just handed him the keys to Fort Knox.

Mark was the first to speak. "What kind of 'great things'?"

Dary went on, as though this were a normal conversation and not potentially life changing. "Well, I can get you better known, for sure. At this point, you need PR." He grinned, suddenly looking boyish. "Any band that can start a riot in a club *has* to be worth newspaper space!" He looked at all of them again, his expression sobering. "I can get you better gigs—sorry, Marvin, but it's true—and I think I can help you get a real record deal, on a good label, and become a national presence. In fact, if my hunch is correct, I think you can be the biggest act in show business."

The boys looked at each other. They had literally never imagined anything like this.

Dary continued to speak calmly, as though he hadn't just blown into the club and upended their lives. "First, though, I have to see you perform live, to be sure about your stage presence. Marvin's won't be open again for a week. Are you playing anywhere else?"

Kellen shook his head as if he couldn't believe it. "We just caused a riot, and you don't think we have stage presence?"

Mark took charge. "We've had a regular gig with Marvin every weekend for months. This—thing that happened was unexpected."

Dary nodded, as though everything was clear. "Right. I think I can get you into a friend's club uptown for a night or two. Would you be open to doing that?"

"For free?" Mark asked.

Jimmy wanted to scream. *Here they had a chance to get a manager, and Mark was worried about price?*

Dary looked appreciatively at Mark. "You're right to want to get paid. That's good business. I can probably get you fifty bucks for the evening." And as their eyes grew big, he added, "Fifty bucks for the whole band. No commission, though; we haven't signed anything yet. Let's say this one is on me. So, if my friend says yes, will you do it?"

Mark glanced at the others and saw assent in their eyes. "Yeah, okay. How soon will we know?"

Dary stretched out his long legs under the table. "I'll call him today and get you in this week, I hope. All right?"

"Yeah." Mark leaned forward. "What else can you do for us, Dary?"

Jimmy noticed he used Dary's first name, and that Dary didn't flinch when he heard it. He just smiled. "I have more in mind, but that's all you need to know for now. Just play the gig and let me judge your stage presence for myself. And give me your number, so I can call you when it's set up."

"Who have you managed before?" Mark asked.

Dary spread his long slender hands wide. "You're the first." He looked blandly at Mark, as though daring him to argue.

Mark studied him for a moment, then swallowed hard. "Well, Mr. Dary Dover, you've got nerve; I'll give you that. And what kind of name is *Dary Dover*, anyway?"

Dary looked amused. "It's my legal name. My grandfather used it when he started a new life, farming in Idaho, instead of robbing banks and rustling cattle. He used it so they wouldn't hang him. My parents gave it to me so *I* wouldn't ever be tempted to rob banks." Dary said this with an absolutely straight face. Jimmy looked hard at him but saw no hint of humor, and judging by Mark's wide eyes, he wasn't laughing, either.

"That's a beautiful watch," Mark said finally, indicating Dary's wrist. "Patek Philippe, I think?"

Dary nodded, never taking his eyes off Mark's face. "How do you know?"

"My father has one," Mark answered. "You get it here in New York?"

"No." For the first time, Dary's voice was hard. "I won it."

"You mean like in a sales contest, or something?"

"No. In a poker game."

It was Mark's turn to look hard at him. "You must be good."

Dary's hard look vanished, and he smiled again. "You wouldn't want to play me." Then Dary's tone went lighter, and he laughed. "See, Mark, if you ask me a question, you'll always get an answer—one way or the other."

True to his word, Dary got them a gig three nights later for $50 at The Tempo Club on West 86th Street. Jimmy was elated that he'd earn twice his usual nightly fee for one night's work instead of three and excited about what this could lead to.

Mark got them together for a rehearsal beforehand. Marvin sent Hammy's drum kit and copies of their record by cab to Mark's house, and everyone felt sharp when they left for the club. Mark had not put out the word to Marvin's patrons that they were playing at The Tempo, fearing it might spark another riot. But he was told they always had a good young crowd at the Tempo, and they were ready to rock.

Dary was already there when they came in to set up, smiling warmly, and told them he would sit through their whole set.

They were booked from 8:00 to midnight, and their set that night was exuberant and exciting. The audience was new to them, as The Tempo Club didn't attract the same patrons as Marvin's place. As usual, "Bawk Bawk" brought laughter when Jimmy first introduced it, but soon people were dancing and enjoying themselves and shouting for an encore. "Wrapped in Gauze", at the end, featuring Mark and Jimmy's flawless harmonies, brought a moment of utter silence before the stamping and clapping began.

It was a very good night for the GooseBumps.

Dary stayed after the club closed to talk to them. As they packed up, he told them what he'd seen in them: That their musicianship, their bond as friends and bandmates, their sense of humor, all of it, could help make them the biggest act in show business. Hearing this a second time stunned all four boys into silence. He liked their longer haircuts, which he said made them stand out among other bands, but thought they should also start wearing nice suits onstage. He would send them to his tailor and pay all the charges. The suits would be modern and fashionable, he assured them. They had to *look* big-time to *become* big-time.

He also promised he'd get them a record deal for a full album, with a national tour to follow and possibly some television appearances, along with as much radio play as possible. Mark told him he and Jimmy were writing new songs all the time. They'd be ready to record whenever he asked.

First, though, they needed a management contract. Dary pulled a sheaf of papers from his pocket.

Mark sat down at once to read them. Dary told him tolerantly to take them home to his dad and get his opinion. He knew Mark's dad's legal reputation, and he felt they couldn't get better advice. Get his input and come back with their questions.

He presented his new business card with a flourish. It read "DARY DOVER, Artists' Manager" in heavy black script.

"I thought you never managed anyone before," Jimmy said, reading the card. He was feeling a lot more comfortable with this uptown guy who reacted so comfortably to their questions and concerns. "And where's your watch?" The beautiful Patek Philippe wasn't on Dary's wrist tonight.

Dary looked surprised, gazing down at his bare arm. "Guess I forgot it after my shower. I'll remember it next time... What else did you say, Jimmy?"

"I said I thought you never managed anyone before."

Dary smiled over Mark's head at him. "Yeah, well... I thought it was time to commit myself."

"Or we'll have you committed," Mark said, and ended their first business meeting with firm handshakes and a round of warm laughter.

* * *

The GooseBumps signed an open-ended management contract with Dary Dover the following week, after Mark's attorney father went over every clause minutely and bargained Dary down from his requested twenty percent commission to the standard fifteen percent. He insisted that Jimmy's mother sign for Jimmy, who at 17 was too young to sign a legally binding contract, and that the other boys, all under 21, have a parent or guardian sign for them.

When they had all signed on the dotted line, Dary went to work, with a handful of GooseBumps records and a determination none of them had ever seen. He haunted recording label offices, and if he couldn't get in to see the president, he dated the receptionist until she opened the door for him. He went to newspapers, magazines and television stations, suggesting they do follow-up stories on the band that had caused a riot in Manhattan. He went to other clubs for bookings, promising unending profits if the GooseBumps played there. After all, you never knew when the customers might start a riot trying to get to the band, which was good for business, even if it was bad for the crockery. The club owners listened ominously, booked the band cautiously and doubled their accident insurance.

Meanwhile, with Marvin's opening again, Marvin told the band he would have a Carey Car waiting in the alley behind the club every night they played. He wanted to take the cost of the cars out of their pay, but Dary said he'd pay for it himself, which was generous, since he received no commissions for the boys' gigs at Marvin's or the records they sold there. When Mark asked him about it, he said simply that he didn't want them trampled to death before they could make him a fortune.

He also had them fitted for stage clothes and as promised, fronted the cost. The very chic tailor they saw, who told them proudly he also made both Dary's street clothes *and* his evening wear, took their measurements carefully and showed them a deep gray fabric Dary had picked out for them.

A week later they had beautiful new suits with round collars and black silk ties. The tailor gave them immaculate white shirts as well and advised them not to drink coffee while wearing them.

The night they re-opened at Marvin's, they were a sensation. When they were introduced, the girls crowding the tables, including Laurey and her friends, not only clapped and cheered, but actually *screamed*. They quieted down when Mark introduced each number, but when the songs were over, they screamed again.

They jammed the dance floor for "Bawk Bawk", dancing with each other if a convenient boy wasn't available, and when the band finished singing "Wrapped in Gauze", several girls had tears in their eyes.

Mark thanked the audience, signed off and said with relief to the others, "I saw a lot of them leaving. We won't have any trouble tonight."

Since they were all sharing one Carey Car, Jimmy invited Laurey to come with them; they would drop her off as well.

As soon as they opened the door into the alley, they knew Mark was wrong.

At least half the audience, some of whom had been in the club, others who had not, were waiting for them, shrieking in delight. The car, which was supposed to be waiting for them in the alley, was nowhere in sight.

Mark backed into the club again, slamming and locking the door. "Now what?"

"Call Dary," Jimmy said. "He was supposed to have this set up."

"*Marvin* was supposed to have this set up," Mark corrected him. When they tracked Marvin down, he was cowering in the cold storage unit. Mark, disgusted, called Dary from the office phone.

"Wait there," Dary instructed them. "I'll have that damn car there in five minutes, or Carey Cars will lose a *very* good customer."

Six minutes later, a car pulled to the front of Marvin's, and the boys and Laurey ran out and got in, and not a moment too soon—the girls had moved toward the front of the club again, ready to corner their prey, and Jimmy, the last one, only managed to dart into the car a split second before it pulled away from the curb with a screech. The girls ran after it at top speed for a couple of blocks, then reluctantly gave up.

"How long do you think they'll do this?" Hammy asked Mark.

"As long as Jimmy has those precious baby-blues—" Jimmy hit Mark, and he subsided.

Inside Marvin's they were protected. Girls came up for autographs, and the boys were happy to oblige. Dary sent them for a photo session and the result was a pack of 8x10 pictures they could sign, which the girls were thrilled to have.

Jimmy tried not to count, but he seemed to be the one they approached most often. He signed napkins, handkerchiefs,

GooseBumps photos, the paper envelopes their records came in. Mark signed less often but seemed to inspire more loyalty; at least three girls swore they were madly in love with him, and they began to wear buttons that read "I love Mark" when they played at Marvin's. Hammy and Kellen had their fans too, and most made it clear they were open to anything the band had in mind, which rather shocked the boys, at least at first.

Dary explained that fans were always to be treated as politely as possible, even if the boys were not in the mood to be welcoming. "If you're tired, you're nice to them," he said. "If you're hungry, you're nice to them. If you're going to fall over from exhaustion, you're still nice to them. They're the source of all your success."

They kept asking about a recording contract, but it was slow in coming. Then Dary asked if they would tour the tri-state area, playing small clubs, amusement parks ("Back to Jimmy's old stomping grounds," Mark snorted) and even some private country clubs, to prove they could perform live in different venues with different audiences.

They were willing, though they hated to forego their weekends at Marvin's. He assured them of a steady gig when they got back, so Dary booked them to play one-night stands on a six-week tri-state tour, to tighten up their playing and illuminate their stage presence.

Jimmy faced the hardest decision. He'd get his high-school diploma in June if he could just stick it out for a few more months, but this was a once-in-a-lifetime opportunity, and he couldn't turn it down. He'd miss six entire six weeks at school, and with it most of the preparation for his final exams in the spring.

He and his mother had a knock-down, drag-out fight about what he was throwing away, and how much his father had wanted him to go on to college (which without the insurance money or a scholarship, would be impossible anyway). After a long day and night of bleating at each other, Jimmy agreed to sit down with his school counselor to see if they could work it out.

The counselor was reluctant to give him any hope, but when Jimmy pointed out that if he were sick and in bed, the school would work with him to help him pass, and he was only asking for the same opportunity, he saw reason. "I'll ask your teachers for your assignments, and you can take them with you, then take extra tutoring when you get back," he said. "But I warn you, we can only do this once. And I'm only doing it because my daughter really likes your band. You'll be expected to attend school after that, till graduation."

"I understand, sir," Jimmy said. "All I'm asking for is the chance." He ended up with a thick sheaf of papers listing his reading and assignments for the next six weeks. He made sure to pack his notebooks and school supplies, along with his guitar and sheet music.

Dary traveled with them to many shows, but it was a slog from the beginning. The boys found that many of their 'deluxe' accommodations were less than deluxe. They were booked into clubs where they were expected to sleep on the floor in the back. They were booked into clubs where the accommodations were two chairs pulled together, a ripped quilt and a filthy old pillow on a table. There were clubs with no washroom facilities, which meant, in late winter, being lucky enough to find a sink with water warm enough to splash on their faces so they could shave.

When it got cold enough, they piled on top of one another to keep warm, since the club owners seldom included any kind of bedding. They kept a battered old coffee pot, a gift from Kellen's mother, plugged in day and night, and drank gallons of cheap coffee and hot chocolate. Dary brought them boxes of Ritz crackers and told them not to complain; there would be lots of these on their way to the top, and if they couldn't stand a little discomfort, they shouldn't be in show business. They noticed, though, that Dary always managed to get the most deluxe sleeping quarters for himself, which he passed off as his prerogative as the manager. This usually meant he had the only room with a real bed and a door that locked. The boys squeezed together into whatever was left over. When their complaints got overwhelming, Dary would treat them to a good meal in a local diner, where they ate ravenously.

The awfulness of their surroundings after Dary left them began to get to them, and instead of complaining about it, they joked about it, onstage. Mark and Jimmy led the way, and Jimmy, a wicked mimic, managed to imitate every one of the terrible club owners, which almost got them cancelled.

They did their laundry in the club's deep sinks, dried it furtively on their own shirts and bundled up against the icy winds, which somehow never affected their singing voices. Jimmy and Mark spent endless hours writing new songs together and playing them for Kellen and Hammy. When they got back to the city, they'd play them for Dary, but meanwhile, good or bad, they went into the act.

Jimmy faithfully did his schoolwork and wrote long letters to Laurey; he even called her once a week long-distance, just to hear her voice. They were falling more and more in love and missed each other more and more. Jimmy swore that when he got back home, he and Laurey would spend more time together.

Meanwhile, he had finally become a smoker, as Mark kept offering him cigarettes day and night, until he got hooked. By the time the tour was over, Jimmy was spending some of his pocket money on cigarettes, every other day. He couldn't keep up with Mark in the rum and Coke department, but soon he was puffing with the best of them, and enjoying it, as Mark had promised he would.

The audiences, meanwhile, began to love them as the audiences at Marvin's had loved them. Though they seldom played more than once at any venue, the crowds came to drink, stayed to dance and ended up cheering for them and asking for autographs. There were no riots, but all the boys had one or two girls willing to give their all for music, and all, except Jimmy, took full advantage. They teased Jimmy that he was a prude ("She'll never know; come on, man, life's an adventure!"), but Jimmy just said, "*I'll* know. And that's enough."

They returned to New York in mid-March, cold, hungry, and thin, and with clothes that looked much the worse for their haphazard laundering, but the band had become a tight, focused unit onstage. Dary was ecstatic with their development and planned another round of attacks at the major labels, as soon as they started back at Marvin's.

He didn't have to wait long. The day after they got home, they got an offer from AMX Records.

* * *

Dary had hit AMX months before, but they were in the midst of a staff turnover and couldn't spare the time to consider new artists.

With the turnover now behind them, and new management in place, they were starting up the hunt again for the Next Big Thing, and Dary's extravagant pitch had stuck in their minds. They dug out the record he'd brought and played it.

That was all it took. They called Dary in.

He negotiated with them for a week before he mentioned it to the band. They were back in New York playing at Marvin's, signing photos, and ducking into the Carey car in the alley after every performance. Sometimes one adventurous girl would get close enough to nip at their sleeve or collar, but they learned to run pretty fast.

When the girl was pretty enough, Kellen or Hammy learned to pretend to fall down, and thus they caught the girl trying to catch them. It was enough for these girls if one of the GooseBumps was interested; none of them wanted to push their luck by trying for Mark or Jimmy, even though the girls often told them furtively, "You're my favorite."

Dary told them about the record deal the Saturday after they returned from the tour. AMX Records was offering them a chance to re-record "Bawk Bawk" and put it out as a single. If it charted, they'd spring for an album, which could include "Wrapped in Gauze", which Dary did not feel was as strong as their dance number, though their audiences loved it. It was a chance for the band, at last. The royalty they offered was next to nothing, but after a long argument with Mark and his father, who both wanted more, the band signed a contract with AMX Records.

They cut the new single in the studio a couple of weeks later and it hit the charts almost as soon as it came out, a month after that. By now, they were deep into spring, and Dary announced they would perform at more prestigious clubs than Marvin's. The tour they'd braved in the winter had made that possible.

"Bawk Bawk" went to #51 on the Billboard chart during its first week out, and Dary visited thirty record stores in the city and bought dozens of copies at each place. He brought them to the club, so they could sell them from the floor, and every night they did the song in their set, more copies sold.

In week 2, it charted at #27. Dary visited record stores, called in to teen radio stations and requested the song, and asked every DJ he knew or could cajole to play it.

By week 3, its chart position had rocketed to #11. By now, other people were calling in to radio shows to request it, and DJ's were playing it several times a day. Dary now visited radio stations to ask for guest interviews with the band.

In week 4, the music papers had "Bawk Bawk" at #4, with the record selling like fury. Dary introduced the boys to a music publisher. When Dary explained that publishing meant that no matter who recorded their songs, they would always make money in royalties, whenever they were played, they eagerly agreed: This would be another income stream to benefit from. All the songs would be credited Morgan-Welton, whether they both worked on them or not. By now, Mark and Jimmy were a single unit: Best friends as well as songwriting partners.

The band got together in late May to discuss the songs they'd record on their first LP, and in early June they were in the studio. "Wrapped in Gauze" was an obvious choice, and Mark had written a couple of others he hoped were good enough to record. Their producer said they were, and he was also enthusiastic about the newer songs Jimmy and Mark had written together.

They spent two intense days laying down the tracks, with Jimmy happily missing all the senior-class activities he'd looked forward to for years.

By now Dary had them performing all over New York. When the album came out, he told them he'd get them radio and TV appearances, which made them all wildly excited. The crowds of girls were getting larger and more enthusiastic, and by now it was hit or miss whether the boys would get into and out of the clubs unharmed; Carey Cars now picked them up before and after their shows, and when they arrived at the stage door, they had to take a deep breath and sprint for the club entrance, with someone else holding the door open and slamming and locking it behind them.

Once or twice they almost didn't make it; Hammy tripped on the steps of one club and almost fell down backward, endangering the others, and they barely escaped with their heads and clothes intact. Another time, they were chased from the stage by excited girls, and the Carey car wasn't waiting in the alley as usual, but the girls were. That night they all ran for their lives, just barely outrunning the girls. From then on, Dary had off-duty police officers driving what he laughingly called their getaway cars. But coming out to face a mob intent on tearing them apart—that never happened again. Dary was genuinely shaken and promised it wouldn't, and it didn't.

Dary also hired a PR guy to help them, saying they needed lots of publicity now, with the wild interest they were generating at the clubs. His office sent out a daily stream of GooseBumps-related news, though no matter what they did, the supply never quite met the demand.

Dary whitewashed parts of the boys' story to fit what he thought the fans would want: Kellen's alcoholic mother became a devoted housewife whose life was committed to her family; Hammy's father's prison stints were explained away as 'overseas business deals' that took him away for months or sometimes years at a time, when Hammy heroically stepped in to watch over the family in his absence. The fans, predictably, ate up the sanitized life stories; it only made them that much more insatiable for the boys themselves.

Dary also beefed up the number of people around the band. Mark's buddy Anthony, who'd once worked for a newspaper, was hired, with a couple of other friends, to act as 'roadies' and handle their equipment at club dates. Long gone were the days of the boys themselves wrestling Hammy's drum kit up the steps of the subway; Tony, Rory and Matt took care of their instruments and frequently took care of the boys as well. As time went by, the GooseBumps began to rely on them more and more. Because everyone in their inner circle was a friend, and so much was happening so fast, the GooseBumps family became tight and close.

The GooseBumps would keep most of this 'family' for the rest of their lives.

Chapter Seven

When Dary told them he'd arranged for them to appear live on the *Hollywood's Talent Palace* television show, they were thrilled. It was the biggest talent showcase in America, and Dary had gotten them both an opening and a closing spot on the show, where they could sing two songs each. They were flying to Los Angeles for the show at the end of July.

"Bawk Bawk" ended its run on the charts at #2, but with their album now flooding record stores, "Wrapped in Gauze" was also coming up fast. They could turn on the radio any hour of the day and hear it. Mark began to carry a transistor radio everywhere.

The GooseBumps had arrived.

Jimmy's high-school graduation turned out a lot differently than he'd pictured it. Though his mother and sister had new dresses and shoes for the day, he did not expect—or want—the crowd of teenagers who flooded the grounds of his high school hoping to see him. (Naturally, Dary had published the name of his high school and the fact that he'd be attending the graduation ceremony.)

The principal and several teachers ran interference. Like everyone else, he wore a mortarboard and black graduation gown, but unlike his classmates, who walked in proudly, heads held high, Jimmy kept his head down. There had been too many photos of him in the newspapers, too much notice of his crystal-blue eyes. So he did his best to hide them as he marched around the school gymnasium with the other graduates. Mark, Hammy and Kellen snuck in wearing Halloween costumes and masks and sat in bleachers high up in the back. Laurey joined them in a demure blue shirtwaist dress.

When the students were called to the stage to receive their diplomas, the principal deliberately used a different name for Jimmy. After he handed the diploma to the person ahead of him, Helen Walker, he called, "James Williams."

Jimmy walked to stage center, his bandmates and Laurey clapping madly. Mark even managed a wolf whistle, and Jimmy couldn't help grinning as he reached out to shake the principal's hand.

Then a girl's squealy voice erupted in the darkness: "*That's Jimmy Welton!* Jimmy, we love you!"

Jimmy dropped the principal's hand, grabbed his diploma and literally ran from the stage, not waiting for the school photographer to snap the obligatory graduation shot. The girls were right behind him.

Jimmy ran out of the gym, clutching his diploma, his mortarboard askew on his head, his hands damp with tension. He stopped long enough to snatch off the mortarboard, found an empty hallway and ran down it. He was followed ten seconds later by a group of screaming girls and pushed open the fire door at the end of the hall with no idea where he was going.

He ran onto the lawn that led to the baseball field, when suddenly a car pulled up beside him. "Get in!" Mark shouted at him. The back door was already open.

Jimmy jumped in and the car roared away. For a long moment, he couldn't breathe; he could barely pull in enough air to clear his lungs.

When he felt a little better, he sat up. Hammy, Kellen and Laurey were in back, Mark in the passenger seat in front. Dary was driving what looked like a Cadillac or a Thunderbird.

"Do we pick up your mother and sister?" he asked briefly.

"I think they'll just go home," Jimmy answered. "I don't think anyone knew they were here."

"You didn't think anyone would try to destroy your graduation, either."

"We need more security," Mark told Dary crisply.

"I'll get more," Dary sighed.

* * *

By the end of June, everything they did was news, with the *Hollywood's Talent Palace* show being the biggest news of all. Dary flew them and their families to L.A. and put them in a suite at the Beverly Hills Hotel. They would play two shows afterward at the Hollywood Bowl, and Mark insisted they spend long afternoons rehearsing, choosing a playlist, getting fitted for new stage clothes, writing new songs with Jimmy.

Mark had a new song, "The Bridge Across Tomorrow", a soulful ballad he sang lead on, with Jimmy singing the harmony their audiences now expected. The arrangement had Hammy alternating between drums and tambourine, and Kellen playing a special guitar lick in the middle. Dary liked it and told Mark they'd record it as a single when the *Hollywood's Talent Palace* show was over.

"What if we bomb on the show?" Mark asked practically. Dary laughed in his face.

Their days now included at least one group interview every day and several individual ones. Dary had put out the highlights of their individual biographies for the press to use in their stories. He emphasized the death of Jimmy's heroic fireman father, Mark's 'fortunate' upbringing as an only child in a wealthy and well-connected family (including many quotes and photos from his preening mother), Hammy's loving siblings and Kellen's streak of independence that saw him working his first job (window washing) at age twelve. Jimmy's fans wept for his loss and daydreamed about spending time with him. All the boys were single (Dary kept Laurey in the background) and therefore considered available. That little bit of fantasy kept them accessible to the fans.

Dary was talking to companies who wanted to license their images to sell various products they assured him they could have out 'next week' if he wanted.

Everything now was geared to the TV show in L.A. and the live shows afterward. If they did well, it could take their star even higher, even faster. The band found it hard to believe they could move faster or higher, but it seemed to be happening more, every day.

Dary kept them playing in clubs, and now he was getting top dollar; he got them a one-week gig for $2,000 at a Manhattan club where the bouncers had to turn hundreds away every night. It was the most they'd ever earned at one time. But what Dary wanted was happening: The band had settled into a tight cohesive unit that worked together beautifully.

By the time they reached L.A., things became surreal. The Los Angeles International Airport was clogged with thousands of girls who had come out to greet them, screaming lustily as they set foot on the ground, cheering like mad, and holding up placards like "Never go home, GooseBumps!" It was an undeniable thrill.

By now they had to resort to ingenious diversions to get away, and while the roadies waited for their bags at the airport, Dary and the GooseBumps got away in a hearse that pulled up on the tarmac. The boys piled in and were whisked away, and a moment after the girls snapped their photos and screamed for them, suddenly they were no longer there. It was like watching a magic trick, their most fabulous disappearance to date.

The bungalow at the Beverly Hills Hotel had all the other bungalows around it booked and security around the clock, to keep the GooseBumps safe. Kellen looked at the welcoming baskets of wine and fruit and let out a whistle. "Do you realize we've been inside meat wagons, police cars, an ambulance and now a *hearse*? Is that what stardom's supposed to be?"

The phone rang off the hook. People were coming in; room service delivering meals, men with racks of clothes to show them;

a local jeweler with a locked briefcase; beautiful young women in evening gowns, though it was only four in the afternoon.

Mark pointed the girls out to Jimmy. "Hookers," he said. "Take your pick." He rubbed his hands together in anticipation.

Jimmy thought of Laurey, who was staying in one of the nearby bungalows with his sister and mother. "No, thanks," he said to Mark. "Not for me."

Mark shrugged. "In a month you'll think different," he said. "Meanwhile, more for me." His eyes shone lasciviously.

The next two days were the most exciting of Jimmy's life. He and the band rehearsed at the Palace after sneaking out through the hotel grounds at 5 am, to get away before the legions of fans took up their vigil. They couldn't leave their dressing room once they finished rehearsing and sent Tony out for food.

The show went out live at 6:00 that night, and the boys were ready well before that. They were scheduled to sing "Bawk Bawk" and "Wrapped in Gauze", along with "Bridge Across Tomorrow" and a newer song, and Jimmy and Mark spent some of their free time in the dressing room writing another new one for their upcoming album.

The Palace seated a thousand people. Thirty-five thousand had applied for tickets, and more than half of those who'd gotten seats were screaming young females.

The stage manager came to get them set up behind the curtain, telling them they'd be introduced by the show's guest host, a fading crooner.

They couldn't hear his introduction; the screaming was just too loud. But a voice from the wings hissed, "You're on!" just before the curtain rolled back, and they looked up into the lights as they'd been instructed and smiled as they hit the first chords of "Bawk Bawk".

The girls went insane.

In later years, when Jimmy was asked when he knew they'd become stars, that was the moment he thought of. Always.

As he began to flap his arms, the girls flapped their arms and stomped their feet. From one heartbeat to the next, Jimmy could feel the theater rocking beneath his feet. He could feel the vibrations through the soles of his boots.

He went crazy on the moves, dancing around, stomping his feet, bobbing his head. By now some of the girls had started to dance in the aisles, with frantic ushers trying to stop them.

As he got toward the end, Mark stepped up next to him to do the final high-pitched whistle, and the girls literally jumped in the air, screaming so loudly the last notes of the song were lost altogether.

Police officers patrolled the theater, in case the girls tried to rush the stage, but as soon as the song was over, the GooseBumps hardly waited for the crescendo of applause to die down before they started "Bridge Across Tomorrow".

When that ended, the boys bowed to the gaggle of screams, clutched their guitars and literally ran off the stage as the commercial began. While stagehands set up for the next act, Dary pulled the boys into their dressing room and locked the door.

As the music careened on and the host came back on to introduce the next act, the boys watched the TV monitor silently. "Well, girls, I guess you enjoyed the GooseBumps, didn't you?" asked the host, and the scream that went up all but deafened him.

"Going well, isn't it?" Dary asked, and there was a twinkle in his eye. When no one answered, he said, "You need to change for the next half. Get moving."

Mechanically, still stunned by their reception, the boys took off their light-colored suits and replaced them with new, darker jackets and shirts.

"Well, boys, after tonight we're stars," Mark proclaimed. "It's everything we've ever wanted."

"Speak for yourself," Hammy retorted.

Jimmy said nothing. He wasn't sure it was what *he* wanted. All he'd wanted to do was play with the band and sing his song. And now that the whole world had literally gone insane for them, what were they supposed to do for an encore?

"I'm hungry," Kellen said.

"That's all you got?" Mark asked. "I tell you we're stars now, and you're *hungry*?"

"He's shallow," Hammy shrugged. "What can you say?"

"No kidding, guys," Kellen said. "I would kill for some scrambled eggs and bacon."

Dary picked up the phone on the makeup table.

"How much time before we go back on?" Hammy asked.

Mark looked at the clock on the wall. "About thirty minutes… you crazy, Kellen? You can have *anything you want* now, man, anything! Why do you want scrambled eggs and bacon?"

"Okay… a steak?" Kellen asked. "Can I have that?"

Dary spoke softly into the phone for a minute. "Coming right up."

Mark lit a cigarette, fiddling for a matchbook. "First thing tomorrow, I'm buying a solid gold lighter. *Two* solid gold lighters. One for each pocket."

"First thing tomorrow, I'm buying a car," Hammy announced. "So my old man doesn't need to steal them anymore."

Jimmy thought about what he'd buy, and his face suddenly lit up. "Dary? How much money *do* we have?"

"Now?" Dary thought about it for a minute. "Well—you can probably draw a couple of thousand now, if you want it, Jimmy. Something you want?"

"We all do!" Mark shouted, drowning out Jimmy's response. "We've been waiting all our *lives* for this, Dary, don't you get it?"

Dary answered him dryly. "No, Mark, I don't. You've *had* money all your life. I can't imagine why this is such a big deal for you."

"Because it's *mine*!" Mark shouted. "Because *I* earned it, not my dad!" He looked around at the others, who were all staring at him. "Well, a quarter of it, anyway," he mumbled.

"A quarter minus my commission," Dary said in that same dry tone.

There was a knock on the door and a shouted voice behind it. "Your food, sir."

Dary opened the door just enough to accept the tray with a steak and mashed potatoes. Next to the plate was a bowl of green peas.

"Put a napkin on and eat fast," he instructed Kellen.

But before Kellen, who was truly ravenous, could get halfway through the steak, another knock on the door summoned them to the wings for their next appearance.

"I'm still starving!" Kellen complained.

"Wipe your mouth. I'll have them heat it up after," Dary said, all but pushing them out of the dressing room.

Their second set sounded as though the first had been merely a warmup. The girls, having waited through several less-than-stellar acts, were ready to scream when the GooseBumps appeared again, and though Jimmy and Mark did a great harmony on "Wrapped in Gauze", most of the audience never heard it.

The boys played with real zest and energy, but the audience wanted little more than to look at them, scream for them and sigh for them. Those who hadn't already fainted were in tears.

They finished that second set and bowed. The girls, knowing this was their last appearance, screamed even louder. The boys gave a final, grateful duck of their heads and ran off the stage.

The big show was over. Historians of twentieth-century culture agreed later, in dozens of books and articles, that *this* was the night the entire world fell in love with the GooseBumps.

CHAPTER EIGHT

The national tour began after they recorded their album. It would be released just as they began touring major cities that summer.

They started with shows in Los Angeles, which had already been sold out for weeks. They continued with shows in San Francisco, Portland and Seattle before moving on to Phoenix and Denver.

Ten thousand fan letters now arrived daily, along with requests for photographs and appearances and offers to license GooseBumps merchandise. It was a time of total madness.

Dary started a national fan club and hired an accountant, who all but drowned in the money rolling in every week. Besides the tour money, they had royalties from their album and the singles being released from it, with the records, in some cases, being played all day long on certain radio stations. Their singles were being certified gold every other day. None of them could go out without being mobbed, and to keep the police, roadies and private security from being overworked, they spent most of their time inside.

Jimmy, who had enjoyed running track in high school, thought at times he'd go mad from the enforced inactivity. After the tour ended, when it got too bad, he jumped in a chauffeured car Dary kept on retainer and went to Mark's house, where they continued to write and record new songs on elaborate and expensive new tape recorders. They bought a lot of expensive equipment now, toys they couldn't show off or use outside their homes. They chafed at the restrictions of fame, but Dary assured them it would get better.

With the money pouring in, when he began drawing a weekly paycheck from Dary's office, Jimmy insisted his mother quit her job and stay home, as she had before his father died, and though it put him further from the action in New York, he also persuaded Dary to buy back their old house in Baldwin, which his mother missed terribly. After the negotiation ended (Jimmy was determined to keep throwing money at the sellers until they just gave up), Dary shook his head. "You just gave them a twelve-thousand-dollar profit for living in a new house for one year."

"I don't care," Jimmy said. "Mom wants to go home."

Before school started again in September, she and Debby were settled back in their old house, the ugly old apartment in the Bronx now a distant memory. Jimmy moved back with them, though he was hardly ever there; the demands of the GooseBumps meant he was gone almost all day, every day. By the time the tour finished in the Midwest states, their album had gone gold, hit the #1 spot on the Billboard charts, and stayed there for a phenomenal twenty weeks.

* * *

Once it did, they became prisoners. Dary booked them for another tour, on the East Coast this time, which would last eight weeks and end in a triumphant show in New York; Dary was asking for Madison Square Garden.

Trapped in their suites all day, stuck together for hundreds of hours, the boys watched TV, answered fan letters, worked on new songs and read dozens of articles about their fame, their success and how happy they must be now. They performed every night and traveled late at night to avoid the fans, but it wasn't always easy.

Ingenious fans, unable to buy concert tickets, tried to pass through the gates with counterfeit tickets and had to be carried off by police, often screaming and crying. A few actually mailed themselves to the GooseBumps, but the postal service usually uncovered them, in boxes punched full of air holes, and sent them home in hysterics, threatening to jail them for postal fraud. Just in case, Dary's secretary was instructed to go through every parcel sent to the boys. More often, they received letters with lipstick kisses on the envelopes and offers to marry them and/or have their babies, with or without a wedding ring.

The number of girls who would go to bed with them just because they were the GooseBumps was astonishing. Even Kellen and Hammy, who considered themselves fairly shock-proof, were stunned at the number and type of offers made, and how often it happened. They took full advantage, thinking nothing of it, until Dary warned them about the possibilities for both sexual diseases and possible blackmail, resulting from a girl getting pregnant. This slowed them down somewhat, though nothing could actually stop them.

Mark, Kellen and Hammy enjoyed multiple bouts of sexual pleasure each day with as many girls as they could, while Jimmy abstained (for a while) because he and Laurey had come to an 'understanding', though Dary continually warned *him* that it was death for a pop star to be seen as 'taken', and that while he had no objection to Laurey's being around at times, she was never to be photographed alone with him or seen in any way that could be construed by photographers or reporters as a 'date'. Jimmy agreed, and Laurey decided she would stay away from the tour and simply see him when he came home. And when she agreed to stay away, he went wild, too.

The boys shared suites in every city they played, and every suite, by contract, had bedrooms off the central hallway, with a living room, fully-stocked kitchen and multiple bathrooms. The bedrooms were in use all day, every day, with the boys taking turns having girls in there. When Dary asked them whether they couldn't slow down a little, Mark asked him indignantly what they were supposed to do in their off hours.

"We can't use the hotel pool. We can't go downtown. Hell, we can't even *leave the suite*! Even when we sleep late and then do two photo shoots, three interviews and a show every night, there's still nothing to do afterward! What do you expect?"

Dary sighed. He didn't really expect much different. But even he was a little shocked at the extent to which the boys were drinking, smoking, and sleeping around. He sent in tailors to custom fit them for new wardrobes and salesmen who brought them toys and electronics to play with, but they were still often wildly bored.

After a great show in San Francisco, Jimmy woke suddenly in the early morning hours and noticed that Kellen, who slept in the bed next to him, was gone. The covers were rumpled and thrown back. Jimmy thought of going back to sleep but realized he wasn't sleepy. He wondered where Kellen was and decided to get up and find him.

When he came sleepily into the hallway, he saw that the kitchen light was on.

When he walked in, he saw Kellen, in pajamas, huddled over a large bowl at the counter. "Hey, Kellen, what's up?" he asked. (Though he always called Harmon 'Hammy,' he'd never gotten close enough to Kellen to use a nickname with him.)

Kellen turned around and saw him. "I'm cooking."

"You're what?"

"Cooking. I got hungry, and I've been wanting to try out some of this stuff."

Jimmy walked over to look. Kellen was breaking eggs into a large mixing bowl and shaking in salt and pepper. "What are you making?"

Kellen's eyes glowed. "A souffle!"

"A souffle?" Jimmy had never heard of it. It was nothing his mother had ever cooked for the family, he was sure.

Kellen stirred the egg mixture as he talked. "It's got eggs and cheese and all kinds of good things. It's really hard to make, too. You've got to eat it the minute it comes out of the oven, or it'll go bad. And you've got to be careful cooking it, or it will fall. The slightest sound or puff of cold air at the wrong moment could ruin it."

"That sounds interesting." Jimmy was more awake now. "Can I watch you cook?"

"Only if you promise to stay quiet and taste it when it's done."

"Deal."

Kellen stirred busily for a while, then turned to check on something else bubbling on the stove. "What's that?" Jimmy asked.

"Flour and butter," Kellen muttered. He carefully poured in a measurement of milk. After that, he crumbled bits of cheese into the mixture and used a blender to whip egg whites to a peak.

The sound of the blender brought Hammy, yawning, out of the bedroom he shared with Mark.

"Jam session?" he asked through half-closed eyes.

"Midnight snack," Jimmy answered. "Kellen is cooking."

"Cooking?" Hammy said, dumbfounded.

"So what?" Kellen challenged him. "Some of the best chefs in the world are men."

"Uh—yeah, no problem," Hammy said. He inspected the kitchen, asked what Kellen was cooking, and received the same explanation. He, too, decided to stay.

When Mark finally came out of his room, he had a naked girl with him, and the souffle was in the oven. Kellen carefully set the timer. "How long have you been doing this?" he asked.

The girl giggled. "Oooh, Kellen can cook… the girls will love that!"

Kellen, busily running water into the dirty bowls, gave Mark one swift look, and two minutes later, the girl, hastily dressed, was walking out the door. "Call me!" she shot back at Mark.

"Yeah, yeah, yeah," he said, now looking with interest at the kitchen. "So, what's all this, Kelley?"

"I get tired eating the same stuff," Kellen said defensively. "Don't you? And I never got to help my mom in the kitchen at home."

Jimmy and Mark exchanged looks; considering his mother's alcohol problem, it was probably a blessing.

"So," Kellen went on, "when we started traveling, I started sneaking into hotel kitchens late at night. There were usually people there—"

"You mean getting breakfast ready?" Mark interrupted.

Kellen glared at him. "It's called 'prepping', dummy. Cooks do it every day. They prep every meal, every day, and I got them to show me some stuff. I tried out the recipes after everyone went to bed. I even bought some cookbooks." He gestured at an open book on the counter, to which he'd been referring periodically.

"Now I know what to get you for Christmas," Jimmy muttered.

"Set the table, guys," Kellen said. "I want everything ready when this comes out." He set out a cooling rack, potholders and flatware, and the boys, used to doing chores at home, took down plates and napkins from the cupboards and arranged them around the table.

Mark looked at Kellen while he finished setting the table. "Y'know, this could be a great song… about something you don't expect from someone you know."

Jimmy picked up on his wavelength immediately. "Souffle… my friend whom I never knew before, taught me about himself one day," he sang softly.

"Be right back!" Mark said and ran for his guitar.

The two boys sat in the living room, facing each other, Jimmy's notebook and pen ready. They strummed and talked, each taking a line, the songwriting going quickly.

"Time to eat, guys!" Kellen called, but Mark and Jimmy, intent on composing, didn't hear him.

"Hurry up, guys! Put the guitars down! We have to eat as soon as this comes out!" he called again. He began to open the oven door.

"Coming!" Mark said, and excited about the burgeoning song, strummed his fingers across the strings of the guitar, then clapped his hand over it sharply.

Kellen, in the process of lifting the souffle triumphantly out of the oven, watched speechlessly as it collapsed into the pan.

Jimmy and Mark couldn't help it. They fell on the floor, laughing hysterically.

Kellen gave them a look they never forgot.

He made them eat every bite of the ruined souffle and never forgave them.

* * *

They recorded "Souffle" before they left the West Coast, in a rush session Dary set up after hearing the tape they sent him. It sold a million copies in its first week of release, and hit #1 on the Billboard chart, where it stayed for the next ten weeks.

By this time, "Wrapped in Gauze" had been #1 for eight weeks, and only "Souffle" knocked it off the top spot.

Mark and Jimmy became fixtures in the kitchen when Kellen cooked, and they watched and often helped him, which sometimes led to more musical inspirations. Kellen wasn't choosy; he could whip up a rib roast or a baked Alaska, and when he learned to make steak Diane, he liked it so much he made it every other night for four weeks in a row. The boys became heartily sick of it. But they got two more songs out of it, which they would record for the next album Dary was planning. They would go into the studio two weeks after the tour ended, and the tentative album title was *The Spice Rack.*

Kellen continued to experiment, getting into pastries and desserts (Mark especially enjoyed his strawberry shortcake), and for Hammy's birthday in August, when they were in Atlanta, he made an enormous three-tiered cake topped with plastic figures set around a beach scene, with a naked girl on top of the Hammy figure.

Hammy loved it.

Only Jimmy noticed that while Kellen still played guitar energetically on the road, his focus was becoming less on the music and more on his cooking. He was reluctant to interrupt his days in the kitchen to rehearse new songs and downright sullen about going into the studio to cut more records. He'd already arranged to spend his vacation from the band on a serious cooking course in Paris and only after nonstop hectoring from Mark did he agree to come back for a new tour in the fall.

Dary tried to persuade him that while cooking was a nice hobby, his real job was with the band. Kellen retorted that since Dary couldn't earn a commission from his cooking, it made sense that he'd try to keep him in a place where he *could* get a commission selling his music. Further, he didn't consider Dary the manager of his life, only the manager of the band.

Much as Jimmy didn't want to face the fact, he was beginning to realize that the GooseBumps were starting to fracture. Kellen's newfound passion for cooking was the first crack; the second was Hammy.

This came, in part, because Dary was so unhappy about the dissipation he saw in the boys, who spent most weeks of that year on the road. Knowing how bored they got, and how easily they could fall into the wrong habits, Dary tried to keep the boys entertained while they were trapped in their hotel rooms on the road. He sent in salesmen, who brought them new fashions, shoes, jewelry, records, tape recorders and stereo systems; he arranged to close amusement parks in the cities they played so they could visit by themselves, riding their favorite rides over and over. In a conciliatory gesture to Kellen, he even sent a Cordon Bleu-trained chef, who gave him cooking lessons for the entire week they played in Chicago. But nothing excited Hammy like the financial advisor he sent, who in an afternoon's intense conversation managed to get Hammy excited about owning real estate.

Within a month, Hammy was buying books on real estate investing and persuading Dary to set aside a portion of every check he earned, to invest in up-and-coming properties. His first acquisitions included apartments in the Bronx, a house in Florida (Dary arranged for a property manager to take care of it for him), and an office building in Staten Island. As he grew more interested in his holdings, he made hurried flights to New York and back while still on tour, just to talk to the building contractors and learn the nuts and bolts of building, from the ground up.

As Kellen became more and more absorbed in the world of cooking, Hammy became passionate about developing a real-estate empire. There were moments when Mark and Jimmy looked at each other in despair, wondering why the band suddenly seemed less important to everyone else than it did to them.

All the boys now contributed significantly to their household's income: Kellen and Hammy bought homes for their parents, as Jimmy had, and with the money Mark was making, he persuaded his father to give up his legal practice and begin planning his run for the New York State Assembly. His father only agreed to do it after he supervised the setup of legal corporations for each boy, to make their tax burden easier, and introduced them to an investment counselor, who promised them all kinds of returns on the investments they made in his suggested portfolio of oil wells, stocks and bonds, and gold. In return, Mark promised to appear at campaign rallies for his father to help him win the youth vote. (In spite of Mark's help, his father failed to win the seat, after campaigning enthusiastically for three straight months.)

TIME Magazine did a cover story on the band, calling it 'The Year of the GooseBumps', and CBS planned a one-hour Christmas special, with clips of their shows and their songs. No one was sure how long the trend would last, though Mark told anyone who asked that the GooseBumps were here to stay.

He had no idea how long that might be.

He had no idea—nor did anyone else—that it would be forever.

Chapter Nine

Autumn 1964

"Gimme a hit," Jimmy said as he fell into a chair in the living room of their latest suite in Chicago.

Mark lit a joint and inhaled deeply, then passed it to Jimmy, who did the same.

"Ow, boy, this is getting old," Hammy complained, his long legs folding under him on the couch. He took a hit when Jimmy passed the joint to him and passed it in turn to Kellen.

The boys sat toking, getting more and more mellow, while their staff brought in their luggage, depositing it in each of the four bedrooms (by now, the GooseBumps each rated their own rooms at every hotel, though they still preferred being close to each other). They also lugged in the instruments, including Hammy's drum kit and a Mellotron, a piano-like instrument with a keyboard Mark and Jimmy used to compose on. These they set up in the living room, knowing the boys would both rehearse and compose there.

When they were finished, the roadies waited to see if they wanted anything else.

"You feel like cooking tonight, Kellen?" Jimmy asked.

"Nah… let's order in. I'll do something fancy tomorrow."

Kellen always intended to do 'something fancy' tomorrow. At this point, though, tomorrow never came. Between the punishing show schedule, the travel and the drugs, he was too worn out most of the time to do anything. Jimmy peered at him. Kellen had slid onto the love seat and lay prone, not moving.

"You look old," Jimmy said to him. "Have you looked at yourself lately? This can't be good for you." It worried Jimmy; Kellen was just two years his senior.

"Says you," Kellen said drowsily. "You don't look too hot either, these days."

"Maybe you're just sick of looking at him," Mark put in. "I know I am."

In the act of taking another toke, Jimmy stopped and put it down in a convenient ashtray. "We'll see about that," he announced, marching into the suite bathroom.

He turned on every light in the room and peered searchingly into the full-length mirror on the door.

Kellen was right.

The crystal-blue eyes were a little blurry right now, but the fan of long lashes around them remained the same, and when he shook his head during a song, the silky brown hair he kept in the familiar GooseBumps haircut still evoked screams of love from the fans. His skin was clear and glowing, his mouth as romantic as ever. His waist was nearly as slim as when they'd set out on their first tour.

But in those eyes were the remnants of a thousand cigarettes, too much alcohol, too little sleep, too little exercise and the faintest dissatisfaction with the life he was leading. If he looked for it, he could see it. He was growing up, it was true, but the *way* he was growing up wasn't what his family had envisioned for him. The money, the fame, the drugs, the constant pressure to produce more and more, were all taking their toll.

Jimmy wasn't yet twenty-one years old, and he was heartily sick of being a GooseBump, with contracts already signed for years of more tours, more records and more TV and radio appearances. Dary was talking about their making a movie soon. Jimmy dreaded the thought. He didn't see how they could be more famous than they already were: last month a mountaineer had planted one of their albums on top of Mount Everest and sent them a photograph to prove it. Their work was enshrined in the Library of Congress and the British Museum. He and Mark had provided their original manuscripts of "Souffle" and "Bridge Across Tomorrow" to the Smithsonian Institute for a special exhibit on American music.

Their concerts still sold out in hours, their records disappeared from stores in massive quantities, and there was no sign it was stopping. At first, Dary had assumed with everyone else that the GooseBumps were a fad that American teenagers would soon move on from, and he'd expected that one day he'd have to tell them *he* was moving on, too.

All they'd done since then was soar upward. If anything, they were *more* popular now, with a larger catalogue of songs, and a dozen gold records. Many went platinum in a matter of weeks. No one in the music industry had ever seen anything like the level of sales the GooseBumps brought in.

The GooseBumps themselves couldn't explain it. They were no better looking or more skilled musicians than other groups. But they had something. They were confident, after all the onstage experience, and their songs went over so well that other artists rushed to cover them. They were wonderfully funny in interviews and unfailingly polite to their fans. Most of all, they were still the closest of friends. What they did on their own time, Jimmy considered his due.

He hadn't seen Laurey in almost a year. There had been an ugly scene when he returned, exhausted, from the last tour in Asia, with her nagging him to take her along on the next one. She said she didn't know how long she could wait for him, since he was off playing around with all those girls (he was grateful she didn't know how right she was). Even in his state of foggy fatigue, he knew he didn't want her around to tie him down and rain on his parade. He'd responded sharply, she'd burst into tears, and they hadn't seen each other again.

He sometimes felt guilty about her. She'd been the first girl he'd ever had a serious crush on. But his friendship with Mark, bound as it was by their music and the enforced imprisonment of their fame, was really precious to him. What they were doing together was once in a lifetime; he couldn't let Mark down. Mark had been let down enough by his parents, who'd had him as a lark, and once he was here, had gone on with their lives, hiring nannies and nurses to raise him, without his ever finding a single person who really loved him.

That indifference had turned Mark into a cynic, tough but tender on the inside, kind when it occurred to him but more often greedy for things he had no real interest in. He had sex with more girls than any of them, drank and smoked more than anyone else, started drugging sooner and with more passionate interest than anyone. On some level, Jimmy knew their fame and what came with it meant less to Mark than to anyone else. With all their success, he hadn't found what he really wanted.

"What's going on, Prince Charming?" Mark had come into the bathroom and was regarding him with interest. "Forget about Kellen. He's never gotten over those baby blues of yours. You're still as *gorgeous* as ever."

Jimmy spoke the first thoughts in his mind. "We're getting corrupted, Mark. We're starting to dissipate."

"Dissipate? What the hell does that mean?" Mark shouted with laughter. "It's not like we're the picture of Dorian Gray, or something."

"Maybe it's okay for *you* to get old before you're thirty, but I'm done with it," Jimmy retorted.

"What the hell—?" Mark regarded him quizzically. "Musicians are *dead* by the time they're thirty. By twenty-five we'll be in a nursing home." He looked at the opulent suite behind him. "And what a way to go, hey!"

Jimmy looked at himself again, and suddenly, he couldn't stand it. He couldn't stop the fans from trying to pour into their hotel rooms or go out for a quiet walk by himself, but there was one thing he *could* do.

Jimmy ran past Mark out of the bathroom. The roadies were still there. They tended to burn out fast and quit almost as fast as Dary hired them. The newest was a young guy called Jeff, an eager beaver with inexhaustible energy and a receding hairline, just a few years older than the GooseBumps.

Jimmy called him into his bedroom and opened his suitcase. He took out two huge cartons of cigarettes and gave them to Jeff. "Don't give these back to me," he instructed. "I'm quitting."

"Cold turkey?" Jeff said. "Isn't that dangerous?"

"The hell with it. It's bad for my voice and awful for my lungs. I'm not a smoker anymore. Take 'em." Jimmy nodded to his stash. "That also goes for booze and pot. No more. Don't give me any, no matter what I tell you."

Jeff took the cartons. "You sure?"

"I'm sure. You give me a butt, even if I'm screaming at you, even if I'm begging you, and you're fired. You got it?"

"Yes, sir." Jeff stopped for a minute and thought. "Maybe I should get you some lemon drops. They're supposed to help when you're quitting smoking." He grinned. "I'm not sure *anything* helps when you're quitting booze and pot."

Jimmy nodded. "Good idea. They'll help my throat." He watched as Jeff started out of the bedroom, then said, "Hey, don't go yet."

Jeff stopped.

"I want to go for a run tomorrow," Jimmy said.

Jeff stared at him.

Jimmy went on, as though what he was saying was perfectly normal. "Around ten o'clock. Didn't I see a high school across the street?"

Jeff swallowed. "Well—yeah—but even if we could use their track—"

What was the point of being a star if you couldn't demand things once in a while? Jimmy decided now was a very good time to start. "Good. Get the track for ten o'clock. And see if the others want to run, too."

Jeff left as though he were escaping a lunatic asylum. God knows what it would take, in terms of protection, for Jimmy to run alone on a track in the morning. But whatever it was, it was going to happen.

His bandmates laughed at him and predicted he'd be back on nicotine in twenty-four hours. He didn't laugh.

The next morning, having somehow sweated out the night without a cigarette or alcohol, Jimmy woke up to the call of the hotel operator, who informed him in dulcet tones that it was 9:30, and a beautiful day outside.

Jimmy jumped out of bed and into the shower. He dressed in his loosest pants, with an old crummy t-shirt and sneakers so old and worn, he'd only packed them to wear in case of a flood. Then he called Jeff's room. "Ready to run?"

"Uh—yep—we're all set," Jeff stuttered.

"Good. Come to the suite in three minutes."

Jimmy burst open the doors of his bandmate's rooms. Kellen was passed out, half on and half off the bed. Jimmy tried to wake him up, first by slapping him lightly, then by shouting in his ear. When Kellen hardly moved, Jimmy gave up and went on to Hammy, who told him in no uncertain terms he was not going for a run, today or any day, unless it involved weed or a naked woman. When Jimmy continued to pull at him, Hammy threw a beer bottle at him.

When Jimmy went into Mark's room, he wasn't optimistic.

But Mark was sitting up in bed groggily, his guitar in hand. "Hey, listen to this," Mark started, but Jimmy grabbed him.

"Later. Come on, we're going for a run."

"What the hell—" But Jimmy had him out of bed, tossed the guitar aside and threw some clothes from his drawer at him.

"We can sing and write while we run. C'mon, it's beautiful outside."

At Jeff's knock on the door, Jimmy bounced out, still holding Mark. "Rock `n roll can't kill us," Jimmy sang out. "We're gonna live forever!"

The police officers guarding the door looked askance at them.

"C'mon," Jeff said nervously. "We're clear across the street."

He had somehow done it, too. The crowds of girls in the lobby, a standard feature in all their hotels, were suddenly not there anymore. "I told them Elvis was at a coffee shop down the street," Jeff said. "It seemed to work."

"I can't go running," Mark complained, all the way to the track. "I smoke a pack a day. Got no wind anymore."

"If you can sing, you can run," Jimmy said, as Jeff deposited them at the oval that Chicago high schoolers used to stay in shape. "First we stretch—" He bent and stretched his legs and quadriceps out thoroughly, as he'd been taught. It felt amazingly good. Mark just stood staring at him while he got ready.

Jimmy finished his stretches and pulled Mark with him onto the track. "I'll start slow. Let's go!"

Within two hundred yards, Mark was hopelessly behind Jimmy, who had truly tried to keep an easy pace with him. Jimmy eased up enough to let Mark, who was gasping for air, catch up with him. "Told you… I was out of shape," he puffed.

"You'll get it back in no time," Jimmy said encouragingly. "Come on."

He sped up again, just a little, and once again Mark fell behind. This time he stopped. "I'm no jock," he said. "Catch you on the next lap."

Jimmy sped up gratefully, running full out and enjoying the sensation of having his legs pumping hard beneath him. It had been a long time since he'd even run from fans, after they'd started using cars full of decoys. The screaming girls followed the decoys; then the real GooseBumps drove away in a dark sedan with blacked-out windows. It worked beautifully, protected the band and eased their fears.

Now that he didn't have to run to avoid the girls, now that he no longer *had* to run anywhere, he honestly missed it.

He ran the first lap almost at a sprint and still felt good as he passed Mark, who merely waved at him, a hand on his head. "Next one for sure," he said, and Jimmy kept running.

As Jimmy finished the second lap, rounding the short part of the oval, he saw Mark, a few hundred yards ahead, rubbing his hand over his forehead.

Something was wrong.

Jimmy stopped. He was beginning to gasp himself. "You okay?" he asked.

Mark said nothing, but suddenly, tears poured down his face, and he collapsed to the ground.

Jimmy ran to him, calling for Jeff, who appeared a moment later and gently eased Mark to the grassy part of the oval. "What's wrong, guy, what's wrong?" he asked.

"It hurts," Mark moaned. "It hurts so much."

Jimmy remembered how Mark had casually taken a pill in his house and mentioned that he got headaches. "Did you ever see a doctor about those headaches?" he asked.

"Doctors don't know anything. Jimmy, help me—do something—"

"Come on," Jeff said briefly. "We're going to a hospital."

Jimmy didn't mention that they had a show to play that night.

He just followed, holding Mark's hand, as Jeff carried the slim little figure carefully to the car, settled him on the back seat, and then drove like a bat out of hell.

* * *

Once in the emergency room, Mark turned stubborn. He didn't want tests. He didn't want anything except his pills. They would make him all right again.

The emergency-room doctor, who told him that he was a serious GooseBumps fan, tried to get him to have an x-ray, at least, but Mark refused. He was afraid of doctors, wanted nothing to do with their opinions. He had been fine when he woke up that morning. All he needed was rest. Jimmy argued strenuously that pain like that was a symptom that *something* was wrong, but Mark screamed at him that he didn't know what he was talking about, that if he couldn't do anything to help, he should shut the fuck up and leave him alone.

Reluctantly, and against medical advice, they finally discharged him, after putting an ice pack on his head and giving him the pain pill he always took. Within a few minutes, Mark truly was feeling better, and though the doctor insisted he sleep right up to show time, he went on that night and gave the same energetic performance he always gave onstage. After the show, he was the first to light up a joint.

Jimmy never asked him to run again, and Mark never went to a doctor for a thorough checkup. But he made sure, after that episode, never to run out of those little pills that eased his headaches, and he took them more often.

Within a month, Jimmy had kicked cigarettes. He used up dozens of boxes of lemon drops in the process, which did help keep his throat moist. While he could hear the improvement in his voice onstage, he never stopped writing songs with Mark. Their current tour would end in a month, and Jimmy was going home for a long rest. They were expected in the studio about four weeks after they came off the road, which gave them plenty of time to write the last songs they needed for the new album.

When they finally got a break, which Dary had promised would be a *real* break—no photo shoots, no interviews, no shows, no recording—Jimmy found himself thinking more and more about Laurey. He had no idea where she was. He could track down old high-school friends, but he and Laurey had gone to different high schools; she would have graduated by now, and he wondered what she was doing.

Finally, one night he couldn't stand it anymore: He got out her old phone number and after hesitating for some time, dialed it.

She answered.

"Laurey, I'm so *glad* you're still there!"

"Who is this?"

Jimmy was thoroughly disconcerted. He said, "It's Jimmy." When there was no answer, he said, more forcefully, "Jimmy Welton."

"Oh." She sounded cool and possibly indifferent.

"Laurey, it is you, isn't it?"

"Yes." She sounded a little more yielding now, cautious but not unfriendly.

"I've really missed you," he said, and in that moment, he realized he'd missed her since the day she was no longer around. Dary or no Dary, this was the girl he wanted.

"Well." There was another pause, and then she said, "I've missed you too."

After that, she opened up, and it got good again. She'd finished high school, was still working evenings at the park, but also had a full-time job at a senior-care home during the daytime. She was interested in getting a nursing degree; she liked taking care of people, and the old people she met and talked to were wonderful. She still lived at home and said matter-of-factly that she probably would live at home till she married.

Jimmy ascertained that there was no steady boyfriend, and that she still seemed interested in him. He started to tell her what the GooseBumps had been up to, but he didn't need to say much: she let him know she had all their albums and knew all the music. "`Wrapped in Gauze' is still my favorite," she said. "You've never written anything better than that." The conviction in her voice warmed his heart.

"Maybe you just like it because of the gauze," he said, joking with her. "Nurses wrap injured people in gauze—"

"Oh, you!" But she laughed.

He wondered if she remembered that she'd said she wanted the song played at her wedding, but right now he was so happy that he didn't need anything more. Throughout their short break, he wrote new songs with Mark and went out with Laurey, enjoying more of those kisses that had dazzled him so much when he first tasted them, though she refused to go further than that. She let him know she wasn't a groupie, and if they ever slept together, she'd be wearing a wedding ring.

That was fine with Jimmy. They were back together, and he was determined that this time it was for good.

Kellen had gone to Paris for more cooking classes, and Hammy was moving into his own house in Westchester, away from the family who overwhelmed him with their demands when he wasn't on the road. He'd maintained what Jimmy always thought of as his essential goodness—with fans as well as friends—but now he needed time on his own. Jimmy was glad he was getting it.

Jimmy didn't see either of them on their break, though Mark often called him, and he had to find excuses not to go to his house with its now-familiar music room. Unlike the others, Mark's family had never shown any pride in the band's achievements. They continued to nag Mark about his friends and treated him exactly as they had years before, when the GooseBumps were just another unknown group.

Jimmy once saw Mark run into his house after a tour and without thinking, reach over to give his mother a hug. She was talking on the phone and literally shrugged him away while continuing her conversation. She didn't indicate by so much as a twitch of her eyebrow that she'd even seen him.

Jimmy saw Mark's shoulders slump, as though this was a familiar reaction. He never saw Mark try to touch his mother again, and apart from his father's legal counsel to the group, for which he charged them thousands of dollars, there was no sign from him, either, that Mark had ever achieved anything. When he brought home the group's first gold record, it sat on the floor in the music room for weeks. No one bothered to hang it.

By the time their break was over, Jimmy was thoroughly besotted with Laurey and insisted she come with them on the next tour. He knew he was going to marry her, but thought he'd better wait till he was actually twenty-one before proposing.

Laurey surprised him by insisting on staying in New York. She could get into a nursing program there right after Christmas, and she had classes to take before that, to be ready for it. Jimmy knew he'd miss her fiercely, but if he'd managed to quit smoking, drinking and weed, he figured he should be immune from the temptations of groupies on the road.

The GooseBumps' next album—they couldn't get them out fast enough for their hard-core fans—was recorded right after the break, with Mark's and Jimmy's vocal harmonies as strong and unique as ever. They were moving into a new phase of their music, experimenting with new musical styles, using different instruments. Dary worried they wouldn't be able to replicate the songs onstage, but he was excited when the first new single from the album went gold in the first month.

The GooseBumps were a marketing juggernaut, as well. Every photo, article, TV appearance, or merchandise bearing their name was an instant hit, and Dary had re-negotiated their record deal after the first one to give them a much higher royalty percentage than they'd ever had before. They should have been thrilled with their upward climb.

Instead, things were starting to unravel.

The boys, now older and with more offered to them every day, began to pursue new interests. There was more to see and do, and they were starting to look in new directions.

The most exciting band in show-business history was about to come apart.

CHAPTER TEN

Autumn 1968

San Francisco

The questions had been coming for twenty minutes, the same questions as always. The boys, in front of individual microphones in their hotel's conference room, tried not to sigh; they'd been promised new questions this time, but they'd answered all of these a thousand times.

"Tell us how you came up with the name GooseBumps for the band."

This was always a question for Mark, who sat in a funky striped jacket and pants, black polka-dot shirt underneath, with a glass of water and an ashtray in front of him. He took a puff of his Marlboro. "Well, as you know, we're very tight as a band, always been great buddies. Jimmy and I—" He nodded at Jimmy, who smiled back— "We met on Halloween, when scary things are supposed to happen. So between meeting on a scary night and being such close pals—well, as you know, GooseBumps always break out in groups—you never see a single GooseBump, but you do see groups of two—and three—sometimes even four—"

He held out his arm, as he did now at every concert they played. Jimmy was getting heartily sick of it.

It was stale, but it still got a laugh, the reporters made their notes, and the questions kept coming.

"Did you ever think the GooseBumps would last this long?"

Mark answered once again; he usually did when they asked about the band's longevity. "We never really thought about that. We're just happy the fans like what we're doing."

Jimmy, seated next to him in a light-colored suit and white silk shirt, wedding ring glinting on his left hand, and trying not to sound as bored as he felt, added, "No one thought we'd last a year when we started out. When we had our first hit, they said we were already on the way down." As usual, he and Mark fielded the most questions; Kellen was fiddling with his new 'mod' glasses and probably inventing a recipe in his head, while Hammy had always been the quietest at their press conferences. Mark and Jimmy had long been the focal point for reporters, and this time was no different.

"Well, are you?" asked a woman reporter up front. The other reporters laughed.

Jeff, now their road manager, stepped in. His hair was thinning even more in front, but he leaned into the microphone in front of Hammy and said firmly, "The GooseBumps' popularity is not even a question. They're completely sold out here and at their three shows in L.A. next week, and even though our European tour this fall is a little shorter than usual, every single show is completely booked. As you can see, they're as popular as ever. No talk whatever of ending it."

Another woman waved her hand, and he nodded to her. "So where is Dary Dover?"

The boys looked at each other, perplexed. "What do you mean?" Jimmy finally asked back. "He's in New York. He doesn't tour with us anymore."

"I've been calling your New York office for days," one man spoke up. "No one has seen him."

"Maybe he took a few days off," Mark said, trying to sound calm. Dary's not being around was like the sun not coming up, and no one wanted to admit they didn't know where he was. "Life with the GooseBumps is stressful."

Another man cut in, "According to his secretary, he hasn't been in the office in the last week. He just went home one night and didn't come back."

Jimmy put a hand over his microphone and beckoned to Jeff, who came over quickly. Jimmy whispered to him, "What do you know about this?"

Jeff whispered back, "I didn't want to worry you. But we haven't gotten our paychecks for a few weeks. I've left messages too, but I haven't heard back."

"Will you let us know when he shows up?" someone asked.

Mark stood up, signaling an end to the questioning. "You'll be the *first* people we call."

And as usual, the GooseBumps press conference ended with a laugh.

* * *

"Where the hell is he?" Mark asked no one in particular, after he'd called Dary's secretary Sherry in the New York office and gotten the same answer as the reporters. Dary was simply missing, and no one had any idea where he'd gone.

Jeff paced back and forth in their suite. "He should have told someone if he planned to take off," he muttered.

"Maybe he didn't plan it," Jimmy suggested. "Maybe it just came up. I wonder if he's okay."

Mark shook his head. "We need to find him."

"It might be time to call the police," Jeff suggested. "File a missing-persons report."

Before they could think how to do that, the phone rang. Mark picked it up. "Yeah? Yeah, it's Mark, go ahead." He listened and began to grow pale. "No, of course not. Are you sure?" He listened again, longer this time, and when he answered, his voice was trembling.

"Well—we'll talk about it. You call us later, right, and we can all talk about it together? Yeah, that's great. Thanks. Yeah, stay there, for now. And run the numbers. Well, run 'em again. We need to know the whole story. We'll let you know."

Jeff turned from his pacing as Mark hung up. "Well?"

Mark looked frightened. "That was the accountant. He wanted to know if we'd authorized Dary to withdraw extra funds from the General Account. I told him no. Dary has power of attorney."

"Come on, man," Jimmy said impatiently. "Did Dary take more than usual from the account?"

Mark began to look acutely miserable. "He took somewhere around five million dollars. And then he vanished."

They all stared at each other.

"Oh, Jesus!" Jeff grabbed the phone and started dialing. "We need someone to look into this."

Before they talked to the accountant again, soberly and one at a time, Jeff had found out through a New York contact, a former police detective, that Dary had left his New York apartment six days before, driving his sleek black Cadillac. He told the concierge at the building to hold his mail, that he was taking a brief trip and would be back in three days. No one had seen him since.

Jeff called Dary's girlfriend and then his parents. They hadn't heard from him.

An hour later, the accountant confirmed that Dary had almost emptied the General Account, leaving only enough to pay the salaries of the New York staff for another month. The president of their bank hadn't thought to stop him when he asked for the money in cash, though it had taken several trips to store it in his car. In a way, he added, it had been quite funny, ferrying all that cash in boxes into his trunk.

"Oh, that's *hilarious,*" Mark said. "He's skipped town with all our money. *Our money*!"

"How bad is it?" Jimmy asked the accountant. "Are we wiped out?"

"No, Jimmy, it would take more than one crook to do that. You have royalty money coming in for the last two albums, plus the tour money, which is being paid, as you know, as you play each city. You'll bank about two million dollars from that alone. And there are publishing royalties too, which haven't come in yet. But Dary really did some damage."

"He must have been planning this for a long time," Mark said. His hands were so agitated, the fingers wouldn't stay still; they danced over the coffee table where the band was trying to eat breakfast. He'd pick up a spoon, try to scoop up some eggs and then give up. Hammy and Kellen had already given up the pretense of eating. Jimmy just stared at his untouched plate.

"But why would he do it?" Jeff asked. "Why? There was money coming in all the time, and he loved you guys; he thought you were the greatest. Did you have a fight?"

"C'mon, Jeff, we always fought," Mark said. "All that pressure on the road and in the studio. But even when we screamed at him, he knew we didn't mean it. We *needed* him, and we always made it up." He looked blankly at the road manager. "I thought we were fine."

Jimmy had an urgent question for the accountant. "What about my personal bank account? Did he—"

"No, I checked," the accountant said. "Your personal accounts are okay. And your savings. You can spend all you want from those accounts until we start to get things straightened out."

"Don't put anything more in the General Account," Mark instructed the accountant. "Deposit all the incoming money in our personal accounts. Split it four ways, and don't take out commission." He almost spat. "We won't be paying commission on *anything* anymore. But we *will* pay the office bills and salaries from those accounts."

"If I could have that in writing…"

"We'll wire it to you," Mark said. "But we have to have the tour money, and those royalties coming in." He put down the phone. Tears pooled in his eyes. "Why would Dary do this?"

* * *

It took a while to find out *why*, but a week later, they did find out *how*. Dary apparently had been signing for small sums of cash—a few thousand at a time—for more than two years, without incident. He'd apparently planned a big score recently and spent most of his time arranging how to walk out with the biggest money of all: the upfront tour guarantee money and the royalties, which were fortunately delayed by a bookkeeping snafu at the record company. If not, he'd have made off with more than a million in royalties, as well. The police speculated that he'd patterned his heist after the manager of a famous opera singer, who'd done the same thing a year before.

"Dary couldn't even do something different," Kellen said in disgust.

Mark shook his head. "He never was very original."

Unfortunately, the national press picked up the story as well. Some newspapers, spurred on by the illustrious GooseBumps name, sent reporters around the world, looking for Dary in remote corners. They found no trace of him, but learning that he had bilked the band out of seven million dollars over the past three years (that was the final figure) sent them scurrying for blood. The band had enjoyed unprecedented success and almost entirely good press relations throughout its career. Now they faced hostile reporters and angry, probing questions.

Mark and Jimmy, still shocked to their core, answered questions for the band; Kellen and Hammy did not even appear at the improvised press conference Jeff set up at the Plaza Hotel a few days later. The band had not yet left on their tour, because with Dary gone, they had to re-confirm all their dates and bookings. They were no longer sure what they were doing and had to double-check all their steps.

No, they told the reporters, they didn't know why Dary had done it; he'd left no word and no trace of his whereabouts. Well, Jeff would remain as their road manager and likely more; they'd have to figure out the hierarchy in their office. But they were going on as a band, no question.

Jimmy, sitting next to Mark as he fielded the questions, suddenly remembered the beautiful Patek Philippe watch Dary wore virtually all the time. It had been missing from his wrist, though, the day they signed their contract with him, and Jimmy had asked about it. Dary had told him he'd forgotten to put it on after his shower. Later, Jimmy realized it was likely pawned or given to someone as collateral for a gambling debt.

He also remembered another press conference years before, in a major American city (they all blurred together at this point, but he thought it was Miami); Dary had, as he often did in the early years, stood behind the boys as they answered questions from eager reporters. He never tried to answer for them but would step in if asked about contracts or tour dates.

Jimmy remembered a moment when Dary stared into the audience of reporters, looking frozen. Following his gaze, Jimmy saw a man in a hat and what looked like a fake mustache, glaring at Dary. Jimmy looked at Dary, who looked definitely frightened.

Following the press conference, Dary muttered that he had to see someone and ran out. When he returned, looking relaxed and in control again, the Patek Philippe was gone from his wrist. Jimmy didn't remember ever seeing it again, after that day.

When the press conference finally broke up, Mark called a meeting of the entire office to discuss the band's future. Everyone seemed relieved. They all needed direction.

Mark thanked everyone for staying with them and believing in them. He said for the foreseeable future, once they re-confirmed the tour dates and money, they would go out on the road again, though he didn't see them touring after that for a while, at least till they found Dary. The police were looking for him, and had alerted the FBI, Scotland Yard and Interpol. They also had private investigators, hired by the band, on his trail. He wouldn't be able to vanish and not account for what he'd done. The GooseBumps would stay close to home after the tour ended, to help as much as they could.

Also, Mark said, his father was coming out of retirement to handle their legal work and take on the duties of band manager, until they found a new one. Privately, he told Jimmy he'd never agree to another manager; this one had just about bankrupted them.

Jimmy, who didn't particularly like Mark's father, tried to persuade Mark to let another lawyer handle their legal affairs, at least, but Mark was adamant that his own flesh and blood wouldn't steal from him, and he wouldn't hear of bringing in anyone else. Jeff could still handle their road work, but he wasn't ready for the full responsibilities of manager. His dad would see they were taken care of legally; later on, if he wanted, he could probably be their manager.

Jimmy remembered the times Mark's father had snubbed him when he'd come over for songwriting sessions, and the coldness with which he treated Mark. He even remembered the night Mark got sloppy drunk in Chicago and began to sob in the late hours: "Why, Jimmy? Why does my own father hate me?" He didn't think he'd ever forget trying to calm Mark down, with Mark literally weeping on his shoulder.

The next day, Mark had acted as though he'd forgotten the entire episode.

Jimmy hadn't forgotten.

That night, after hours deep in talk about a future none of them could even picture, Jimmy asked Laurey to come into the city for dinner. Mark came without a date; Kellen and Hammy came, too. It was just the band, together again, like old times, before all the craziness and the big business and the things that were pulling them apart.

They agreed to table discussion of their problems for that evening and had a merry time in a private room, with Mark leading the jabs at Kellen for his obsession with cooking and Hammy for his newfound addiction to interior decorating.

The boys were laughing, but Jimmy could see the resentment in their eyes as Mark went on and on. He was drinking heavily and flared at Jimmy when he said Laurey had had enough.

"Come on, Laurey girl! Let's let this guy be the stiff! You're not the prude as he is, are you? I'll bet you're not. Here, try this. I haven't touched it."

He handed Laurey a full glass of brandy, which had just been set on the table.

Jimmy looked at Laurey as she picked up the glass and took a sip. Mark egged her on. "C'mon, Laurey, more, more! Finish it! Thatta girl!"

Laurey glanced at Jimmy, who shook his head slightly. He'd been more careful with her and with everything involving money, since the discovery of Dary's thievery, and she was beginning to resent it. She'd told him several times she would never steal from him, and he should trust her, but he was having a hard time trusting anyone, after Dary. Now she looked at him defiantly for a minute, then drank down the entire glass.

The others applauded. Laurey made a slight bow, the brandy already beginning to hit her.

Now that Laurey had drunk the brandy, Mark didn't seem interested in her anymore. He kidded with the others, who tried to respond, even as Laurey sat there, almost silent, her eyes getting larger and larger.

About ten minutes later, Mark said to her, "You know there's a rooftop on this restaurant, don't you? It used to be a rooftop garden, back in the 20's. Why don't we go up and look around? It's beautiful, Laurey, really."

Jimmy wondered if he would make a pass at her, even knowing she was Jimmy's wife. They had always been scrupulously careful not to go after each other's girls on the road. But Mark was pretty drunk himself, and since Dary's defection, he was angry all the time. Jimmy wouldn't put it past him, and he started to get up, to take care of Laurey.

Mark elbowed him rudely. "We don't want *you*, do we, Laurey? Let's just have a look on our own, okay?" He took Laurey's arm and led her out of the room.

Jimmy, Kellen and Hammy sat silently for a few minutes. "What's he up to?" Jimmy finally demanded.

"Dunno, buddy," Kellen said. He'd been drinking pretty steadily himself all evening, which had made him more than usually sullen. Jimmy noticed their intake even more since he'd stopped drinking himself. He was appalled at how much they were all casually pouring down, both on the road and at home.

"He didn't look too steady," Hammy volunteered. "Maybe you better check on them."

In the end, Hammy and Kellen went with him. Some instinct in Jimmy told him to run, and as he reached the last staircase to the roof, he was sprinting.

When they got out on the roof, what Jimmy saw made his blood run cold.

Mark and Laurey were laughing and singing one of the GooseBumps' latest songs, and while Mark sat unsteadily on an electrical box, Laurey was walking, in wavering, teetering steps, one after the other, on the brick parapet edging the roof. Mark was cheering her on.

She had about four inches of brick holding her up. The street was four floors below them.

Jimmy ran to the ledge, terrified out of his mind. "Laurey," he said, fighting to keep his voice calm, "give me your hand. I'll help you down."

"Don't wanna," Laurey said, in a defiant tone he'd never heard from her.

"Damn right, Laurey," Mark chimed in. "She's a happy girl, Jimmy. Happier than she's ever been with *you*. She's flying."

"What?"

"That brandy." Mark held up a finger. "It was laced with LSD, and she's tripping. She's having the time of her life."

Jimmy felt a rage so murderous he had to clamp down on himself to keep from breaking Mark's bones right there. "You mean you—?"

"She's loving it!" Mark insisted. "Look at her, how happy she is. If I'd asked first, you think she'd have said yes and tried a trip, right here? And she *needs* it, man. Living with you has to be an A-number-1 *drag*."

That was the end. He'd take care of Mark, all right. But first came Laurey.

He walked next to her, praying silently that she wouldn't move her foot the wrong way. "Come on, honey," he said. "Come down and let's go home. You've had enough for tonight."

She ignored him, kept walking.

How many steps could she take before she took the fatal one?

He knew she wouldn't listen to him. Mark had made sure of that.

He kept walking beside her, and as she stopped and hesitated, he saw his chance and grabbed her. She began to cry as he pulled her off the slippery parapet, and then to claw at him with her hands. Kellen finally grabbed her arms and forced them down, and she cried harder as Jimmy held her against his shoulder.

He didn't care. He had her safe. He would take her home at once and stay with her until she came down. He had never been so frightened in all his life.

But first… ?

He looked at Mark, laughing uncontrollably. "Had yourself a good time up here, didn't you, Laurey?" he said. "And you'd have had more fun if old fuddy-duddy Jimmy hadn't messed up the party, right? We could have had ourselves a good old time, if he'd just left us alone. You'd have liked that, wouldn't you? Wouldn't you?"

Jimmy pushed the still-crying Laurey at Kellen and Hammy and grabbed Mark, who was stoned out of his mind and thoroughly drunk as well. Mark put up no resistance at all. "You son of a bitch, you could have killed her!"

Jimmy had never started a fight in his life, but now he drew his fist back and smashed it into Mark's face.

Mark put his hand to his face and laughed. "You never could write songs, jerk," he said, laughter ringing out, despite the blood spurting from his broken nose. "You never could play. You brought this band down every time you strummed that stupid guitar!"

Jimmy hit him again, this time catching his shoulder. "I don't even know why I kept you around," Mark mocked him. "Except maybe for your pretty face. That was one sure way to get girls."

Jimmy punched him in the stomach and Mark doubled over, sagging to the ground.

Jimmy picked him up—he was limp as a rag doll—and hit him again.

When Mark got his breath back, he laughed softly. "You never wrote a good tune in your life, asshole. Everything you ever did was recycled, re-invented, re-tooled. Music for morons. It was all I could do not to die laughing every time you played me something you'd written." Even in this state, he sounded like a poet. "You're just lucky I was willing to drag you along for the ride. *Prince Charming*." The words burned into Jimmy's furious mind like the acid Mark had forced on Laurey.

He didn't say a word back, but just kept hitting Mark, punishing blows all over his body, until Kellen grabbed him.

"Enough," Kellen said. He and Hammy, still holding Laurey, were also trying to handle Mark, who was by now out cold. "Leave him and take her out of here. I'll call Jeff."

"Don't blame you a bit," Hammy added. "He was *asking* for this."

Jimmy gave Hammy one grateful glance for his understanding and then hurried Laurey home to Long Island and sat up with her all night, until the effects of the acid trip began to wear off. When it was over and he told her what she'd done on the rooftop, she was as furious with Mark as he was.

"It's over, honey," he kept saying. And in his mind, it was. He never wanted to speak to Mark again.

The newspapers reported that Mark Morgan, the superstar guitarist and singer from the GooseBumps, had taken a bad fall at his home and broken his nose, his jaw, his left arm and his right leg. They also said the police were interested in talking to Morgan about rumors that he was using illegal drugs.

Mark called Jimmy several times, trying to apologize. Jimmy refused to take his calls.

Meanwhile, they had new songs ready to record, but the news about Dary seemed to wipe them out. They wrote separately now, but after six years of backbreaking travel, touring, recording and playing, they were coming to the end of their explosive creativity.

In the end, the GooseBumps, torn apart by the rift between Mark and Jimmy on top of Dary's betrayal, agreed to a short final tour of London, Paris and Berlin, to pay looming bills left over from Dary's management. Jeff went on the road with them, Jimmy refused to speak to Mark offstage, but they still sang their hearts out in every show—to overflow crowds screaming so loudly they couldn't hear the music, which all the GooseBumps had resented for some time. Why bother to play if no one could hear?

Their last show was in London, and they played for two hours, singing all their hits and doing impromptu encores, reluctant to leave the stage this final time. When they finally came off, to fans, as usual, rushing toward them and wanting to embrace them all, Jimmy almost felt as though he wouldn't mind being trampled under their feet; he felt that bad about ending this vital part of his life. The crazy days of hot and cold running groupies, booze and drugs and traveling the world and playing and singing their hearts out, were over. He'd never known any other professional life; he had no idea what to do next. He was only twenty-four.

Back in New York, they got ready for their last recording session, a contractual obligation. Dary's betrayal was never far from their minds. They knew he'd be caught eventually, with so many people looking for him, but the band would never be the same. Dary had taken some vital piece of them with him.

When they added up the music they had to record, they were one song short. They needed twelve songs for a decent album; even stretching out every song, there were still only eleven cuts at best.

Mark argued that they couldn't be forced to write something else. They'd already written eleven new songs, some of which would be hits. He talked to their record producer, who now spoke to him and Jimmy separately; Jimmy refused to be in the same room with Mark except to record or perform.

Their producer said to Jimmy a few hours later, "Why not just re-record an older song with a new arrangement? Kind of a last hurrah?"

Jimmy thought about that. There was nothing left in the tank, and Mark was taking a long time to heal and babying himself absurdly, in Jimmy's mind; he appeared at the studio in full convalescent gear, with casts on his arm and leg, and bandages all over his face. Jimmy thought he was ridiculous. He should consider himself lucky that Jimmy didn't have him arrested for attempted murder.

"Well, maybe one," he said finally to the producer. "What'd you have in mind?"

In the end, Jimmy agreed to re-record "Wrapped in Gauze" with a new arrangement. "It's one of the best, Jimmy, it always was. Why not re-do it at a slower tempo?"

Their producer came up with a suitably beautiful arrangement that was almost a ballad, and Jimmy sang lead, as always, with Mark singing his lovely harmony behind him, which Jimmy considered ironic, given how little harmony they had left in their relationship.

When they finished the final take and overdubs of the song, just before midnight on their seventh day in the studio, the producer shook their hands in joy. "It's as beautiful as the first time I heard it. Wouldn't be surprised if this one jumps up the charts too."

"I hope so," Jimmy said wearily. "But for better or worse, it's done now."

It was all done. The record cover design had been approved, with even the cover photos of Mark and Jimmy separate. The final takes were finished, and mixing would begin the next day. The record would be released in a few weeks.

Jimmy and Mark shook hands separately with the engineers and others who had helped them in the studio, and thanked Jeff and his staff for their help. Once more, they patiently answered the questions of a few intrepid reporters who had managed to sneak into the session, with Hammy and Kellen finally, belatedly chiming in, trying to disguise the silence between their bandmates.

Then they walked out to their waiting cars, all of them separate, none of them speaking.

The GooseBumps, the most phenomenal success in twentieth-century popular music, were finished.

Chapter Eleven

April 1977

Stockton, California

Victoria Dunne always turned on the radio when she washed dishes; it made the unpleasant task go faster. She took the ribbon off her ponytail and re-tied it before she put on dishwashing gloves and called up to her sons.

"Come on, guys," she called. "You'll be late for school. You get up now, Dave!"

It was always her youngest who just made the final bus by a hair.

He didn't disappoint her. Michael was downstairs in time for a bowl of cornflakes; Dave ran out clutching an apple, his books in a jumbled mess as usual, hardly even listening as Victoria called, "Doctor's appointment after school. Come home quick!"

Victoria was still learning to manage the household on her own. Her husband, a plumbing supplies salesman, had had a midlife crisis, "or something", as she said self-deprecatingly when trying to explain it to others, and left her for a twenty-two-year-old blonde art student in Berkeley. Victoria was stuck with the bills, two boys and a mountain of unanswered questions about how this had happened.

She reminded herself to ask the doctor about Dave; he'd complained of stomach pains for a while now, and she hadn't done anything about it. Well, today was her day to deal with it.

Meanwhile, there was the sinkful of dishes she'd been too tired to wash after dinner last night.

Luckily, a new song was playing on the radio. "And here it is," the DJ announced cheerily, "the last known recording by the GooseBumps, the *re*-recording of one of their first hits, 'Wrapped in Gauze'."

She turned it up louder and began to sing while she filled the sink with water and soap suds.

"Sparklers flare in the dark of night—"

She just loved this song. She had grown up singing the original version, and dancing to it, too. It was upbeat and great. But this version, so melancholy, so bittersweet, recorded at the very end of the GooseBumps' career, was marvelous, too.

She sang along as she washed the dishes, not having to think about the words. For a split second she thought of the handsome young faces on the covers of her old albums. Did they ever miss the marvelous music they'd made? Did they ever play it or sing it now? Did they even *care,* after all these years?

Mark and Jimmy were still writing, recording and playing on tour, separately. They hadn't spoken since the band broke up. Kellen had become a chef and opened his own three-star restaurant in Chicago. Hammy, the quietest band member, though he had been the loudest as their drummer, had simply vanished into the ether of has-beens.

She finished the load, turned on the dishwasher and went upstairs to shower and dress. She *hated* washing dishes.

* * *

She watched as the doctor went over Dave, asking gentle questions, telling him to breathe for the stethoscope or open his mouth to check his tonsils. She reminded Dave to tell the doctor about his stomach pains.

The doctor listened and asked quiet questions, never raising his voice. Dave told him the pains had been coming for at least a year. Sorry for not mentioning it before. But Dave was a charming boy; the doctor smiled as he said he wished he'd known sooner. He asked other questions about the pains. Dave told him it hurt often after he ate. No, he didn't think it was spicy foods; he'd gotten pains after eating ice cream. The doctor asked Dave to lie down and pressed here and there on his stomach. Did that hurt? Did that? Had he been hurting when he walked into the exam? Dave told him no. He usually hurt only after eating.

When the exam was over, the doctor said to Victoria, "Why don't you and Dave come into my office when he's finished dressing?"

She had never been in his tiny inner office, and now she felt a frisson of unease as they walked in. These exams were all routine: stick your tongue out, breathe when he tells you to, and maybe a booster vaccination, then a smile, a lollipop and "See you next year". There was no need for a talk in the doctor's inner sanctum, was there?

Dave didn't seem worried. He pulled on his shirt and tucked it into his pants (for once, without her reminding him) and together they sat down in the little office. The doctor was already there, writing on a pad.

"I'm a little concerned about those stomach pains," the doctor said to Victoria. "I'd like Dave to have it checked out." He kept writing for a minute, and then his nurse walked in and handed him a slip of paper. "Ah, good." He handed it to Victoria. "This is a very good gastro guy I know in San Francisco. I can set up an appointment for you. He'll do the tests in the local hospital, have the results in a few days."

Victoria took the slip. This was out of her territory; she had never dealt with any serious health issues with the boys before. But she was the mother, and she was in charge. She smiled at the doctor and said, "Fine. As soon as possible, please."

* * *

The results were in before Victoria had prepared herself to hear them.

Cancer! How could a boy of twelve get cancer? How was this possible?

She didn't know what to do first. Call her ex? Tell Dave? Tell Michael? Call the school?

The doctor advised her to start treatment immediately, to let Dave and the school know and then handle everything else as needed. This was a lot to deal with, and Dave needed treatment as quickly as possible. Once they established that, they could do everything else in small bites.

Victoria asked the inevitable question. "How bad is this? I mean, it's not—he'd not going to die?"

The doctor answered gently, "This is bad, Victoria. I have to be honest with you."

"But you've had other patients who—" She couldn't bring herself to say it.

"No, actually," the doctor said as gently as possible. "I've never had a patient this young develop cancer."

"Well, but you've had other patients who did? How did they do?"

The doctor sighed. "Let's get Dave into treatment as soon as possible."

Victoria found her voice. "How bad is this? What are we looking at, here?"

The doctor looked her as kindly as possible. "We'll see how he responds to treatment. Some people do incredibly well with chemotherapy and radiation. They've beaten it. But it's going to be hard on his system, and we'll do our best."

"Surgery?" Victoria asked. She was thinking she needed to stop at the library as soon as she left the office and pick up every book they had on cancer.

"I'm afraid Dave's growth is too big for surgery," the doctor answered. "It's too deeply rooted. We couldn't get it all, even if we went in. But chemotherapy has done some really good things. You'll be surprised. He won't have an easy time of it, but we'll do our best."

Victoria stood up and shook hands with the doctor. She didn't know that the tears were pouring down her face; she felt nothing but an emptiness deep inside her. She had a million things to do and no idea where to start. But she would do whatever she had to do.

In the car on the way to the library, she snapped on the radio, hardly knowing what she was doing. "Here it is again," the bright-voiced DJ announced. "It's 'Wrapped in Gauze', the remake, by the legendary GooseBumps, and everyone's asking for it this week. Enjoy!"

She didn't know when the song began that she was singing along with it. She had no idea how she got from the doctor's office to the library. But she did know that when she pulled into the tree-shaded parking lot ten minutes later, her voice was hoarse, she was almost blind with tears, and somehow, she felt a million percent better.

* * *

Dave handled the news very well, though Victoria broke down, even as her friends tried to tell her it wasn't good for Dave to see her like this. She tried to apologize to him, choking on her tears, and Dave put his arms around her and said, "It's okay, Mom. Don't worry."

That made her cry harder.

Michael was speechless and almost as upset as she was. He hadn't hugged his brother since Dave learned to walk and started annoying him, but he wrapped Dave in his long bony arms and hugged him until Dave pulled away.

Long after Dave went to sleep, she sat with Michael in their little kitchen. The size of it no longer mattered. The fact that it never got the morning sun and was often gloomy no longer mattered. The old wallpaper she wanted to replace but couldn't afford to replace no longer mattered. Suddenly, every problem she'd ever had narrowed to one: Dave.

"He'll be all right, Mom," Michael said to her. He was patting her hand while she tried to drink a mug of hot coffee, but she kept spilling it out of the mug. She wanted to fix him a sandwich or something to eat, but he said he couldn't swallow anything. He looked pale and suddenly much older, though he was only three years older than Dave. She found herself praying that he would never get sick like this. It couldn't happen twice in one family, could it?

She hoped the stack of books she'd checked out of the library had answers. She hoped *someone* had answers.

She'd had a terrible conversation with her ex that afternoon, before Dave came home from school. At first, he was mad at her for calling his office, as usual; he never liked her to call the office, even when they were married. Then he was heartsick at the news. He asked her repeatedly if she shouldn't get a second opinion. She explained that the tests had already been done twice. He told her he wanted to bring in another specialist. Exhausted, finally, she told him to consult whomever he liked; she was starting treatment with Dave at once, and he'd better be sure the insurance was up to date.

"I don't care what it costs," she told him. "Don't bother me with that. I'll spend whatever I have to. Nothing matters except getting him well. So don't even think about cheaping out here, or you'll regret it for the rest of your life."

Dave, the ebullient twelve-year-old who rode his bike too fast, played basketball every day, in season or out, and had a crush on a girl in his history class, charmed all the nurses at the hospital. He wasn't too sick to joke with them, and they adored him, bringing extra portions of the soup that was the only food he could keep down, and making excuses to slip into his room to say hello when he was awake.

Victoria, the mother who had never thought she'd have to deal with this, dealt with it. She talked to oncologists, internists, x-ray technicians, financial specialists, hospital administrators. She brought Dave his favorite bread from the bakery at home and tried not to cry when he could only swallow a single bite. She held his head when he vomited from the chemotherapy treatments. She cleaned up after him when he didn't make it to the bathroom in time. She lost twenty pounds without realizing it, slept three hours a night, never left Dave's side on treatment days.

When the doctors cleared Dave to go home after the first set of treatments, though he'd have to come back in a month, she took him home and dealt with his tears when he realized his thick, shiny brown hair was falling out. She told him she'd never really liked all that hair, anyway, and this was easier than waiting in line for a haircut. She made him laugh when he had nothing to laugh about.

She kept turning on the radio to hear "Wrapped in Gauze", and after a while she bought a Walkman and got the tape of the band's last album, playing it constantly. Dave asked her what she was always listening to, and she played it for him. He had heard of the GooseBumps but hadn't known any of their songs; she bought their albums on tape, and he listened to them while he lay in bed, recovering from the brutal treatments. When he heard "Bawk Bawk" for the first time, he shouted with laughter, and when he was strong enough to stand up, Victoria taught him the dance she'd danced as a teenager, and he flapped his arms like a chicken, bobbed his head and did the high whistle at the end. Victoria laughed until she cried.

Dave's father came to see him, at first often, then sporadically, trying to joke, to talk about sports or business, bringing small gifts of food Dave couldn't eat and didn't want.

She didn't blame him for not knowing how to act, and for staying away. Who wanted to deal with this, if they didn't have to? It didn't occur to her that *she* could have walked away as well. He was her child. She would never walk away.

As the spring gave way to a hot damp summer, and a murderous madman who called himself Son of Sam stalked young girls in New York, the doctors still held out hope that Dave's 'little visitor', as he dubbed the tumor, would respond to the chemotherapy. Victoria made a point of discussing all the news of the day with both boys, telling herself that as long as Dave was still interested in what was going on in the world, as he always had been, there was still a chance, no matter what the doctors thought.

By autumn, they no longer had hope, and they suspended the chemotherapy treatments, which was a huge relief to both Dave and Victoria. The tumor was too big, and it wasn't going away.

Victoria took him home to recuperate, certain the doctor were wrong, and talked to his school about getting him back on a regular schedule. They said they'd provide a tutor to help him make up the work he'd missed in the spring.

But Dave did not thrive, even with the good food she provided, the organic fresh fruits and vegetables, the farm-grown eggs and the thick steaks (the doctors warned her against putting him on a vegetarian diet). He could not stand for long, walked only as far as the bathroom or the kitchen, and slept for long hours each day, and when the tutor came, he often could not concentrate, either. The tutor came faithfully twice a week for three months, but at the end of it, she told Victoria regretfully that Dave was not ready to return to his studies and she had other students in the district who needed her. When Dave was well, she said brightly, they could get him caught up then.

As autumn turned toward Thanksgiving, Dave stopped caring about the news of the world, and when he no longer responded to his father's jocular commentary about sports, his father stopped coming to see him.

Everyone knew it was just a matter of time.

One afternoon, while Michael was still at school, Victoria brought Dave a lunch tray and found him wearing her headphones and listening to a tape. She clicked it off. "Hi, guy, it's lunchtime, right? What do you think? Applesauce I made myself—and don't you dare complain about it—and some of that soup you liked in the hospital. I got the nurses to get me the recipe. Sneaky, huh?"

"Mom," Dave said, in an exhausted voice she had never heard before, "it's okay, really."

She put the tray on his bedside table and just looked at him.

He looked at her. "I'm not getting better."

"You need time, dude. That was no walk in the park, all that chemo."

"Mom—" He looked pleadingly at her and reached for her hand. "I need you to be okay with this."

Dave had never talked to her like this.

When that thought registered, she sat down in the chair by his bed. He wrapped his hand around hers, the fingers so white, so thin. She thought she could still see the marks of the needle they had stuck in his hand when they couldn't find a vein in his arm to take blood from. He repeated, "I need you to be okay with this. I'm okay with it. I've thought about it a lot."

"What are you saying, Dave?"

"I'm not gonna get better, Mom. I don't know why this happened, but I've—" he hesitated, but only for the right words, "I've *come to grips* with it. I don't mind anymore."

"Oh?" If she said anything else, the tears were going to start to pour, and she didn't dare let them.

"Some people live a long time, and they don't get anything out of living. Some people don't live long, like that Anne Frank we learned about in school last year. She was only fifteen when she died, and she had an amazing life." Dave stopped for breath. It had taken a lot for him to get out that much. When Victoria said nothing, Dave went on. "I've had you and Michael and Dad, even if he isn't around much, and I've played basketball and football, and we went on that great vacation to Disneyland when I was eight—remember--?"

She made a moan and put her head down. She *wasn't* going to keep it together, after all.

Dave held her for a long time, his wasted arms giving her so much comfort. She wrapped her arms over his, to make him hold her tighter.

Finally, when she began to come out of it and fumble for a Kleenex, he said, "I won't miss school. Do you think that's weird?"

She shook her head, dabbing at her face. Another makeup job ruined. "Nobody misses school. I remember hearing once that when you're facing the end of your life, no one ever says, 'I should have worked more'. You care about the people you love and the good things you did, and that's all."

"In that case, I've had a good life. I mean, I'll definitely miss Michael, and I didn't think I would." Dave leaned back on his pillows. "I'll try to eat a little now, and I'm glad you got that soup recipe. Can you make it a lot?"

"Sure."

"I just thought you ought to know, Mom."

They sat in silence for a while. Dave spooned up the applesauce and tried not to say, "Yuck", though Victoria thought she caught him forming the word once or twice.

"What were you listening to, Dave?"

Dave managed another spoonful of soup. "That 'Wrapped in Gauze' song. I really like it."

"Me too. I grew up with it."

Dave put down the spoon and wiped his mouth with a paper napkin. Victoria tried not to scold him for the little he'd eaten. "You know, we used to have all these talks in music class about what songs mean. Mr. Green talked about it all the time. He'd show us a song lyric and want to know what the writer was thinking about when he wrote it. I never liked those classes."

"Me either. Silly. You either know or you don't know. And if you don't know, the songwriter hasn't done his job."

Dave thought about this. "I think I know what this song is about, though. He writes about things in his childhood that are always there and always will be, and how he's wrapped in the gauze of love. Like how remembering them helps him to feel loved."

"That's a good analysis."

Dave was quiet for a moment. "Who wrote this? The GooseBumps?"

"That one was written by Jimmy Welton, who was one of their guitarists. He and Mark Morgan wrote all their songs, and they were always credited together even when they both didn't write everything. I remember Jimmy talked about it once in an interview. He said he remembered growing up and how great it was to know that things would always be that way, so secure. He said his father had just died, and he and his family had a tough time, until he became famous. So he wrote the song to feel better, and then he bought back the house they'd lived in, where he grew up. I think his mother still lives there."

"I'm glad it came out all right." He looked at his mother. "Which one were you in love with?"

Victoria blushed. "I don't know what you're talking about."

"Mom… "

"Okay. I thought Mark was cute and a great songwriter, but I really fell for Jimmy."

"Because he was sooo handsome."

"Because, well, he had those gorgeous crystal-blue eyes, and he was a great musician."

"Oh, right, Mom. Of course."

"You know I value talent over looks."

"You always did."

Dave snuggled down on the pillows, and Victoria started to pick up the tray, to take it back to the kitchen, but he put a hand on her wrist. "Stay with me a while, Mom, okay? And play the song again, will you?"

She put down the tray and turned on the Walkman, and without thinking, she got into the bed and cuddled next to him. The song started to play, and they both heard it, and Dave smiled. He looked beautiful to her. She wrapped her arms around his back, and he laid his head on her shoulder.

They curled closer together as the song wound down to its final chords.

"Doesn't matter where else I go

When I'm here, I'll always know

I'm wrapped in the gauze of love."

Then those final beautiful chords played, the ones she could never forget. And when she felt him leave her, she held him even closer and knew he was wrapped in the gauze of her love.

CHAPTER TWELVE

Spring 1986

Jimmy was used to interviews, but after all this time, most of them still asked about nothing but the GooseBumps. As though the last eighteen years didn't matter, and all he'd done since then hadn't actually happened. As though all the songs he'd written and sung since then might as well not exist.

The young reporter from the Cleveland weekly paper consulted her yellow pad and asked another question. "What do you remember most about being a GooseBump?"

Jimmy paused as though he were really thinking about it, though he'd answered this question often. "Arrangements," he said finally.

The reporter paused, waiting for him to elaborate, as she had no doubt been taught in journalism school.

"Arrangements for getting in and out of places. Arrangements for getting to different countries, and arrangements for living and sleeping inside the same places we worked."

"Did you really do everything together?"

"We *had* to do everything together. We couldn't go anywhere except the stage or recording studio; we were pretty much prisoners the rest of the time."

The girl shivered. "That doesn't sound like much fun."

Jimmy smiled at her. "It was great."

Then a curveball question. "How come you don't sing any GooseBump songs on your tours?"

Jimmy took a deep breath. He'd also answered *this* one a lot. "People get tired of the old songs. I like them, but the fans seem to want more of my newer songs."

"*I* don't think they're tired of them. There's a big '60's nostalgia craze going, you know. I think they'd like to hear them. Won't you even consider it?"

Jimmy smiled, automatically charming her as he'd done with other reporters for years, but there was a note of finality in his voice. "Those days are over."

She looked quickly at her notes. "You were—what?—twenty-four when the band broke up? You were so young. Your fans were young, too. Now that they've grown up, I think they'd love to hear those songs again. To remind them how it was. It was a great time."

"I agree. But you can't re-live your youth. You shouldn't even try."

She looked at him, at the vibrant blue eyes, the glossy dark hair he could still shake onstage, the still unlined, glowing skin. At forty-two, Jimmy Welton was *as* gorgeous, or *more* gorgeous, than he'd ever been.

"How do you stay in shape? I mean, most rock 'n rollers aren't as—"

"'Well preserved' as I am?" Jimmy laughed. "Is that what you meant?"

She blushed. "Well—"

He had made a career of being diplomatic and gentle with both fans and reporters; he wasn't going to change now. He smiled and answered her straight. "Well, I was drinking and smoking—and yeah, doing weed—for a while there, but I gave it all up cold turkey after a few years. I've felt a lot better since. And now I go everywhere with my family; they're the best company I know. I get enough sleep and eat good food and try to jog every day."

"And you work. A lot." It was a statement, not a question.

He acknowledged that was true; he'd always spent more time in the studio than the other GooseBumps, trying to get the sounds right, experimenting with new things. Sometimes he didn't leave a session until two or three in the morning, but the results on the albums were worth it.

"And now they're teaching your songs in universities."

"That's gratifying. It's wonderful that they think we have something to offer the next generation."

"Do you know there are already more than two hundred books about the GooseBumps? And three documentaries?"

He knew; the authors and filmmakers were always reaching out to him, asking for 'only' an hour or so of his time. It usually ended up being a lot more than that, but he gave it gladly. It was nice to be remembered.

"Do you think anything you do now or in the future will ever be as popular as the GooseBumps?" the reporter was asking, and now he was revising his original opinion that she was a sweet young thing. These were penetrating questions. He put on his game face and thought about how to answer.

"I don't think about how popular my stuff is going to be," he said finally. Carefully. "I always hope people like it. And I've gotten feedback that they do. I don't compare my time in the GooseBumps to anything else. It was fantastic, and I loved every minute. And if nothing I do now or in the future is as popular, it just means my work in the GooseBumps was really popular. And I'm okay with that."

She looked at him, waiting for him to go on. He'd long ago learned the first rule of interviews: Like a negotiation, once you've stopped answering a question, whoever speaks next loses.

When it was clear he had nothing to add, she went on. "How about a funny GooseBumps story that everyone else *hasn't* already run? Have you got one?"

Jimmy thought about it. He'd been pestered for funny GooseBumps stories for years and only recently remembered one he hadn't thought of. "Yeah, I think so. This one's about Kellen."

The girl got ready to write, poising her pen over the yellow pad.

Jimmy went on. "We were in… Berlin, I think—and Kellen was signing autographs for a group of fans. Dary brought them in and told him and Hammy to sign till he could round up Mark and me. Well, Kellen never liked signing autographs anyway; he liked to joke with the fans and pose for pictures, but he hated all that signing. Said he got writer's cramp.

"Anyway, a guy came up in a mustache and hat and sunglasses and asked Kellen to sign one to his mother. Kellen was polite. He said he was only signing his name, and he hoped everyone else was okay with that.

"But this guy persisted, said he really wanted it for his mom, and why wouldn't Kellen do him this big favor?

"He was obnoxious. But we'd always tried to accommodate the fans whenever possible. So Kellen wrote her name and started to sign his name. And then the guy wanted him to write Happy birthday to my good friend above his signature. And when Kellen wouldn't, he told Kellen he was a cruddy guitar player who knew nothing about rock 'n roll.

"Kellen hit the ceiling and told the guy to get lost.

"Then the guy took off his glasses and hat and pulled off his mustache."

"And it was someone Kellen knew?"

"It was me."

The reporter laughed heartily and wrote frantic notes on her pad. "You guys had fun together."

Jimmy took a deep breath and smiled; these were good memories. "Yeah, we did."

"So a GooseBumps reunion—"

Jimmy hesitated. "I don't see it happening."

"But you still talk to each other."

Jimmy said nothing. She went on, digging deep now. "So, what's with this feud between you and Mark? Did you ever make up that fight you had years ago?"

Before her eyes, Jimmy turned from a warm, easy interview into stone. He said nothing, and she could feel the ice behind the crystal-blue eyes.

He glared at her for a long moment, and then said, as though nothing had happened and he was still on the previous question, "I don't see a reunion in the near future."

"But it could still happen? You know the fans, the whole world, would go crazy for it, and any place you played would be sold out in an hour. You'd all make a fortune."

He didn't bother to respond that he already had a fortune, saying only, "Anything could happen." Meaningfully, he looked at his watch.

She took the hint and stood up, thanking him for the time. He said gallantly that he'd enjoyed it and hoped she'd mention the new album right up front. She promised she would.

He saw her out of his hotel room and turned back to the living room, where his seventeen-year-old daughter Sandra, a dead ringer for the young Laurey, said without turning around, "You took long enough."

"Part of the job, honey."

She pouted as she painted her toenails brilliant purple. He squinted at her. "Is that necessary?"

"It's cool. Dad, I swear, sometimes I can't believe you were ever in a rock band. You act like one of those squares from the fifties who never let their daughters out of the house alone."

"Not with purple nail polish. Even the hippest rock-star dads draw the line at that."

She smiled at him. "Different era, Dad. Okay? We're not living in the Dark Ages anymore."

Laurey came out of the bedroom, carrying a bundle of towels. "You done? Can we go out for lunch now?"

Sandra rolled her eyes. "*Other people* cook their own meals. *Other people* live in *real* houses that they stay in all the time, except when they're on vacation. *Other people* don't go running around the country trying to be a rock star when they're over the hill, and—"

"Sandra!" Laurey's voice was loud and chilling. Sandra quieted down sullenly. "We've had these conversations. Your dad is one of the best musicians and songwriters on earth, and this is his life, so it's our life, too. We're lucky that he loves us enough to want us with him, and that's what we want, too."

"It's what *you* want," Sandra muttered, but her mother was going on.

"This is the life he's chosen, and the life I've chosen. And if you really don't want to be here, well—"

Jimmy's other two daughters, ten-year-old Maggie and seven-year-old Glenna, rushed into the hallway from the living room. The family fight was more intriguing than the TV they were watching.

"Is Sandra in trouble again?" Maggie asked. She was the practical one, the one who saw things for what they were, and the one who knew that Sandra was often just one family fight away from chucking it all and going back to Long Island.

Jimmy took up the argument. "Okay, Maggie. Sandra's expressing an opinion, but it's an opinion we've all heard."

"Anyway," Sandra went on, "I don't see why you spend so much time on interviews. All that woman asked you about was the GooseBumps. Don't they want to know about your life *now*?"

Jimmy sighed. Laurey looked distressed.

Sandra, seeing an advantage, pressed the point. "They don't, do they? They still think you're about twenty, with that mop of hair and those funny songs—"

"*Great* songs," Laurey amended loyally. Jimmy kissed her lightly on the forehead.

"—And no one cares that you've had children and one of them is almost grown up—"

"I hope you're not talking about *yourself*," Maggie said primly. "*I'd* never call you almost grown up."

"—They just want to re-hash the old days and wallow in nostalgia, and honestly, Dad, with all the people who keep writing books and teaching courses at colleges and having GooseBumps conventions, you'd think *someone* would care about that. Is that why you keep making albums? Just to prove you've grown up, and you're not a GooseBump anymore?"

Jimmy put his arms around his oldest daughter and gave her a tender kiss on the top of her blonde head, with its expensive layered haircut. "I'll always be a GooseBump, Sandra. But I'm not old, and most people *don't* end the best parts of their lives before they're twenty-five."

Sandra was silent for a moment, digesting this. It was the first time her parents had ever tried to explain the paradox to her, which had made them wealthy beyond imagining but also yearning for a new kind of success. "Was it really the best part?"

It was Jimmy's turn to pause. "It was fantastic, honey, and I lived it with my three best friends. It was unforgettable." Then he added, "Having you three is unforgettable too. And expensive, including the purple nail polish. But I still love you."

Sandra hugged her father. "I don't care if you sing or play or write new songs, or the old GooseBumps songs, or any of that. I just think you're great."

Little Glenna, who'd kept quiet as always until she knew the direction of the argument, now piped up, "I think you're great too, Daddy, and I don't mind touring. I think it's fun, except when we have lessons."

"Glenna, you hate school. So that's a step in the right direction." Jimmy leaned down to kiss her too and then retreated to the hallway. Sometimes his kids were more than he could handle by himself.

Once that was sorted out, Laurey drew Jimmy gently into the bedroom. "This came in for you," she said, and handed him a message slip, marked with the caller's name ("Mark") and a phone number.

The handwriting was Laurey's.

"He called just as you started the interview," she said, looking a little guilty. "I said you'd call back."

"We've barely spoken in eighteen years, honey, are you crazy?" Jimmy was incensed all over again. He could still close his eyes and see Laurey balancing on a brick parapet high above New York. He didn't think he could ever forgive *that*, ever!

"You stayed close to Kellen and Hammy."

"Sure, because Kellen isn't interested in anything except turning out the most perfect French cooking on Lake Shore Drive, and Hammy, bless him, just signs whatever they ask him to sign when the record company puts out a new compilation album and shows up for documentaries and conventions. I'm not even sure that young girl he's always with isn't his cousin."

"Jimmy!" Laurey punched him on the arm, and he grabbed her and wrapped his arms around her. From the first time he'd seen her in that Cinderella dress, Jimmy had never seriously looked at any other girl. He had his share of groupies, but they were gone now, and he was free to be with his beautiful princess.

She let him kiss her, hard and passionately, but then she pulled away and said, "Will you call him?"

"Where was he, did he say?"

"No. Just call him. Don't be afraid."

He wasn't afraid, just disgusted at the way things had ended, but that wasn't his fault, was it? Dary had done one part of the damage; Mark had done the rest.

He took the slip into the bedroom, shut the door and reached for the phone. Strange; the area code was local, and in a minute a low, hoarse voice said, "Hello?"

Jimmy asked for Mark.

"This is Mark… hey, Jimmy, it's you!"

Jimmy didn't know what to say. The voice he'd heard sounded nothing like the Mark he had known, but he supposed that people changed in eighteen years. "What are you doing in Cleveland?" he asked. It seemed the simplest question to ask.

"Working with the cause, man. As always."

"And the cause is—"

"You don't know?" Mark began to sound more like himself to Jimmy. The roughness in his voice, he diagnosed, was from too many cigarettes over too many years.

"Save the whales. World peace. End the wildfires in California. Abolish income tax. Hell, I don't know."

"It's really my wife's doing," Mark said, and Jimmy thought back to the blurred photo he'd seen in some newspaper, of Mark holding a glass of champagne up to a tall Nordic-looking girl with a gorgeous smile and quiet eyes. "She's been a crusader longer than I have. She's been into it for years, and she dragged me into it, and now I wouldn't do anything different."

"Oh?" Jimmy smiled; he was remembering the first year he knew Mark, before the GooseBumps hit, when they'd just finished working on the arrangement to "Wrapped in Gauze", and Mark said to him ebulliently, clapping a hand across his guitar, "I never want to do anything else, Jimmy. Never in this life!"

He said nothing until Mark said, "You remember when we finished 'Wrapped in Gauze'? Remember what I said then?"

"That's just what I was remembering."

"Hm. You would. Well, since we're both in Cleveland, could we get together?"

"You still haven't told me what you're doing here."

"You playing a show tonight?"

"Yeah." Jimmy consulted his watch. "In about five hours. And I need to nap and eat before we warm up."

"Nap and eat—what the hell happened, you square? We used to be up all night with groupies, smoke weed, drop acid and still do a show the next night! You're giving rock `n roll a bad name."

"Let's face it, Mark, I've gone to the dogs," Jimmy said, but his heart was warming again at the sound of Mark's voice. He had missed him more than he realized, and he also realized that this man had been and still was the best friend he'd ever had. Whatever had come between them, nothing could erase what they'd always had. "But yeah, I'd be glad to see you. I'm available till, say, 3:00. Where should we meet?"

"Can I come to you? I hear your whole family travels with you. I'd love to meet your kids."

"They'd be glad to meet you," Jimmy said. "Can you be here in an hour?"

"I can be there in half that."

"Okay." Jimmy told him the hotel name and suite number and said goodbye. He told Laurey and the girls that Mark was coming by and went to change into something jazzier. He hoped Mark would think he was still hip enough to be a GooseBump.

When the knock sounded on the suite door, Jimmy felt unaccountably nervous. It had been so long.

He hesitated at the door, then pulled it open.

Mark stood on the threshold.

He looked like hell, though like Jimmy, he'd obviously tried to spruce up for this meeting.

He was gaunt, his hair long—longer than in the GooseBumps days--and uncombed. He wore straight-legged white slacks and an embroidered dark blue velvet jacket that was out of place for both the season and the era; it would have looked more appropriate in the '60's. He was a forty-three-year-old burnt-out rocker, and despite his continuing worldwide fame, he looked ten years older than Jimmy and far less happy.

He and Jimmy looked at each other for a long moment. Then Mark walked into the suite and gave him a hesitant hug.

Jimmy hugged him back, hard.

They looked at each other again.

"Long time," Mark said finally, and Jimmy nodded.

"Yeah. Too long," Jimmy said, and with that they erased eighteen years of silence.

Laurey came out of the bedroom to say hello, accept a big hug and introduce their daughters to Mark, who treated all of them with a joking roguishness that made a big hit with Sandra.

"How can you stand this square?" he asked her.

"I know, right?" she said, her voice warming to him as so many girls had, over the years.

"Stop talking about me like I'm not here!" Jimmy exclaimed.

Laurey wisely took the girls downstairs for ice cream (Sandra insisted on giving Mark a hug) and left Jimmy alone with Mark.

They sat in the living room, silent for a moment. Finally, Jimmy said, "I feel like we should be writing a song, or something."

Mark laughed. "Haven't done that in a while."

Jimmy said, "Maybe we should try again."

It was out, what he'd wanted from Mark since he'd seen the phone message. He'd known it from that first second, and he also knew he couldn't *not* try to make it happen. Songwriting without Mark had been a drudging exercise; with him, it had always been exhilarating and joyous. That was what his new songs were missing, that sense of joy.

But Mark just laughed again. "That's hard work, man! *Hard* work! Remember when we sometimes had to write an album's worth of songs in a week? And Dary thought a week was plenty of time?"

"So what're you doing now, Mark?" Jimmy asked. "I really want to hear about it."

Mark reached into his pocket and pulled out a pamphlet, which he handed to Jimmy: "A Word about God's Place in Our World."

"You're recruiting?" Jimmy said after a glance.

"Finding others to carry on the work. I won't be here forever."

Jimmy looked at him. Mark certainly looked older and a little tired; his ebullience at seeing Jimmy hadn't masked that entirely. "You okay, Mark?"

Mark just laughed. "What's okay, at our age, Jimmy? Rockers are supposed to be dead before forty! How come we're still alive and kicking? Must be something wrong with how we're living!"

"What's your doctor say?"

Mark shook his head. "Since when do I go to doctors? I'm just feeling a little older these days, that's all. Letty—my wife—thinks I still drink too much and smoke too much. I tell her I put down the whiskey and cigs long enough to marry her, and if those count as sins, I won't make it to heaven, no matter how hard she's praying for me. I go to church twice a week, read the Bible every morning, speak to church groups and anyone else who'll hear the Word from me, and I seem to be fine. God's a wonderful thing to have in your life."

Jimmy's mind was exploding. He told Mark about the reporter who'd asked—again—about a possible GooseBumps reunion. "Would you ever want to do it, Mark? We've been away for a long time, but—"

"You haven't been away for a minute, Prince Charming!" Mark exclaimed. "You've never stopped touring and writing songs, but for the rest of us, it would be quite a road back. Kellen and Hammy would do it in a heartbeat, if we agreed, but—"

"Then why *can't* we agree?" Jimmy asked, as excited as he'd been in years. "I'll do it if you will, Mark. We did end with a lot of bitterness, but the Dary business is straightened out now, and we should get together on this. That reporter was right; a GooseBumps reunion would be big!"

"Now hold on, Jimmy," Mark warned. "This kind of thing takes talking about. Even *if* Kellen and Hammy agreed, we'd still need rehearsals and a road manager and—"

"I still have Jeff," Jimmy interrupted. "He takes care of everything on the road for me, and you know he's great. Let's not think about it, Mark; let's just do it!" For the first time in their relationship, Jimmy was the one throwing caution to the winds.

Jimmy's enthusiasm carried the day, right through the meetings with Kellen and Hammy, both of whom agreed, with some reservations, to a new GooseBumps tour, if anyone was interested.

Jimmy had Jeff put out feelers through the press. He was knocked flat by the passionate response from old GooseBumps fans, new GooseBumps fans, fans who hadn't been born when the GooseBumps split up. Just on the strength of a *rumor* that they were getting together again, their old albums began to sell hundreds of thousands of copies and hit the charts. *Again*.

Jimmy took charge of the arrangements, because he'd kept the structure of a band throughout all the years. Jeff scheduled a full tour, starting in Seattle, working down the West Coast, then heading to the South and ending in the Northeast. It would be about two months of tour dates, several in each city, and demand was immediate and unprecedented: the new GooseBumps tour sold out all their dates in every city in the first forty-eight hours. Scalpers were charging thousands for tickets, and desperate fans were paying.

Mark and Jimmy, as always the band leaders, announced the tour at a joint press conference attended by hundreds of reporters. Kellen and Hammy were already getting back in shape, returning to the instruments they'd put down years before, and re-learning the songs they'd once known so well. The shows would be comprised of *only* the old GooseBumps songs, which the fans still loved.

As the beginning of the tour approached and Kellen and Hammy, now slimmed down but looking older than forty-four and forty-five, respectively, arrived in Seattle to meet Mark and

Jimmy, they were greeted by fans gathering in large groups around their hotel and the arena where they were playing. The arena held twenty-five hundred people, and it had sold out in eight hours on the first day tickets went on sale. The excitement was palpable.

Each GooseBump had a separate suite at Seattle's best hotel, which accommodated them and their families. Kellen produced a good-looking young woman he called his sous chef, along with two small children, while Hammy, now a partner in a major building franchise in New York, had brought a hearty-looking woman and four teenagers of his own. Jeff ordered round-the-clock guards for each band member. GooseBump frenzy was starting all over again, and he was going to be prepared for it.

Early on the morning of the first show, with rain slicking the streets of the city, the band and Jeff gathered at 7 am to look at the arena marquee, which read proudly: "GooseBumps Reunion Tour—The End of the Beginning", with all their names in huge lights.

The band, no longer boys, smiled self-consciously at each other. The days of sharing rooms and bathrooms were long over; they were men now, with adult responsibilities.

"We're back in the music business, boys," Mark declaimed, his arms raised toward the sign.

"Mark! Jimmy! Could we have your autograph?" Three girls had come around the corner and staked out a place at the head of the line.

"Oh, my God," Jeff said under his breath. "Again?"

"Absolutely," Mark said with a big grin, smiling as the girls produced slips of paper—a bus pass, a bank slip, an old envelope—and handed them a pen.

Jimmy signed under Mark's name and called over Kellen and Hammy to sign as well. "First in line deserves something special," he said with a grin.

"Oh, we almost came last night," one of the girls said. "We can't wait!"

Rehearsal was scheduled for noon in the arena, where sound and light checks were going on all day.

The band went over their entire play list, which they'd last used nineteen years before. It included "Souffle", "Bawk Bawk", "Bridge Across Tomorrow" and "Wrapped in Gauze", which they'd decided to do in the original arrangement.

Rehearsal went on longer than usual because Hammy and Kellen needed to re-establish their playing rhythm. Jimmy, who had never stopped playing and singing, began to feel a little impatient about how long they were taking.

Then he saw Mark drop his guitar and put his hand to his head.

Remembering the time he'd collapsed on the running track, Jimmy stopped rehearsal and ran over to him. "Mark, you okay?" he asked.

Mark's face crumpled, and his hand still on his head, he pitched forward and fell on his face.

Jimmy yelled for Jeff, who had been talking to the sound man. He came running.

"Do you need your pills, Mark?" he asked urgently. "Do you have them with you?"

Mark didn't answer. Gently, Jeff lifted him up, but when Mark felt the light in his eyes, he moaned and tried to drop his head.

"Put him down! Mark, where are your pills?" Jimmy asked again.

The technicians were moving toward the stage. "Call an ambulance," Jimmy told one of them, and the man ran off.

He sat on the stage next to his collapsed friend and picked up his hand. "It's okay, Mark," he said soothingly. "We're getting help for you."

Mark opened his mouth to say, "Letty—" and couldn't say more.

"Get his wife," Jimmy told Jeff, who ran off himself.

Kellen and Hammy sat down beside Mark on the other side. "Jesus, what's happening?" Kellen asked uneasily.

"It's happened before," Jimmy said, and now he wondered whether in all the ensuing years, Mark had ever bothered to find out what was wrong with him. He wouldn't put it past him to have left it alone all these years, just taking pills when his head hurt and never asking the right questions, because he was so afraid of doctors.

The ambulance arrived and two medics ran into the arena, led by the tech who had called them. Jeff was still trying to find Mark's wife.

"Who's going with him to the hospital?" the medic asked as they lifted Mark onto a stretcher. His face was drenched with sweat, and his fingers were opening and closing convulsively.

He opened his eyes for a split second, in the glare of the house lights, and said, "Jimmy."

The others stepped back as Jimmy jumped off the stage and went up the aisle, then sat on the floor of the ambulance with the medics who monitored Mark's blood pressure, temperature and heart rate.

Jimmy scarcely heard when the sirens went off, shrieking at the traffic ahead of them. He had Mark's hand in his—such a small hand for such a flighty, restless man—and held it tight. He didn't want to let go.

The medics murmured among themselves, while Jimmy focused totally on Mark. His eyes, which had been tightly closed against the light, looked more peaceful now. As they careened through the streets of the afternoon traffic, Mark opened his eyes briefly, found Jimmy, and satisfied, closed them again.

"Jimmy?"

"Yeah, Mark? I'm here."

"I'm glad. Missed—you." His hand tightened for a second on Jimmy's. Jimmy patted him reassuringly.

"Me too. More than I realized, till you came back."

"Sorry—about Laurey. Really sorry."

"I know. Forget it. It's over."

"I don't—think you're a square. You've—got the best—voice I ever heard."

"Hey, thanks. And it only took an ambulance to get that outta you." Jimmy smiled at him, and Mark, opening his eyes briefly again, smiled back.

"Head hurts. So bad. Worse than ever."

"Hang on, Mark. We'll be there soon. Everything will be fine." He hoped he was telling the truth.

"Sing me—a song, Jimmy."

"What song, Mark?"

"Sing—'Wrapped in Gauze'."

And as the ambulance siren screamed through the city and Mark's vital signs grew weaker, Jimmy began to sing, very softly, "Sparklers flare in the dark of night…"

As Jimmy paused where the final instrumentation usually played, Mark whispered, "I love that song. Always—my favorite."

"Mine, too." Jimmy realized as he said it that he meant it.

"It was our best song, man." An agonized breath. "We were—a great—band."

Those were his last words.

* * *

The sudden, shocking death of Mark Morgan, the legendary GooseBump, of a massive cerebral hemorrhage in an ambulance on his way to the hospital on the very day the GooseBumps reunion tour was supposed to begin, was headline news around the world. Every TV station, every wire service, every newspaper and magazine in the world ran it as an extra. Newscasters broke into television programs. Radio shows were interrupted and then suspended. Everyone who had ever known him or even spoken to him once was immediately contacted for comment. The headlines went on for weeks. The girls who received his last autograph became instant, minor celebrities.

The tour was cancelled, and the ticketing firm processed thousands of refunds. Many fans asked if their ticket costs could be rolled into creating a memorial to Mark, whose songs they still loved. The two solo albums he'd made after the GooseBumps broke up and released to tepid reviews and slow sales years before, suddenly hit the charts, to massive acclaim. His epitaph was that of a poet born into a difficult time, when sensitive people had to be rebels to survive. His final years as a crusader for Christ became part of the message of love he had spread as a GooseBump.

The GooseBumps were shattered. Only hours from re-creating their extraordinary success, they had lost the man who had founded and formed them and kept them playing and singing through great albums, long tours and the blistering heights they had scaled and then deliberately turned their backs on. Jimmy, who gave interview after interview, never told anyone but Laurey about his conversation with Mark in the ambulance, and she spent many days trying to comfort him. She knew Jimmy and Mark had had a complicated relationship, and that it would take a long time to process his grief.

But unlike Kellen and Hammy, who gave their interviews and then went back to their ongoing lives, Jimmy's life was playing and singing, and that was where all his grief lay. It was music that had brought him and Mark together, and long after Letty, in an ostentatious black veil, had had Mark cremated and scattered his ashes over the Atlantic Ocean—"where he could always hear the waves singing and the voice of God", she said to reporters—he sat night after night in his empty house, staring at his empty guitar, unable to write anything new, with no desire to play or perform. He spent his nights for the next year thinking of his time with Mark and waiting—hoping—for the music and his sense of purpose to come back to him.

CHAPTER THIRTEEN

New Year's Eve 1999

Tallahassee, Florida

The bridge was so beautiful at night, thought Carolyn Van Benne as she got out of her car, locked the door and pocketed the key. She always walked that bridge when she had serious thinking to do, and tonight, she had serious thinking to do.

She began up the first slope, looking up at the lights that would burn all night long, feeling her long legs in their warm leggings stretch out beneath her. Her soft boots were warm enough, too, and she had on a wool scarf and a hat as well. John always laughed at how she bundled up for winter, even in Florida. She just retorted that her Connecticut past made her cautious: She dressed for icy winds and blowing snow, though in the five years since they'd moved to Florida, she'd never experienced it.

The question was, she thought as she kept walking toward the cables that hung between the two high columns, why *should they adopt a baby?* John had been adamant that after five years of serious trying, it was time to look at alternatives. He wanted a child, and he wasn't picky about how that child came into their lives. It would be lovely, as he'd often told her, if she were the one to deliver it. But if not, there were babies out there who needed their love. They had enough money to adopt and enough room to welcome a new life.

But Carolyn couldn't get excited about this, much as she wanted a baby, too. She and her friends had discussed the proposition over lunches and at parties. She didn't see herself as the mother of an adopted child. Her own child, yes. She knew she could love her own child, a child of her own body, with no reservations.

But *someone else's* child? How to love someone who didn't really belong to you?

John, of course, insisted that any child they adopted *would* belong to them. He had already consulted an adoption attorney, who sent him home with all kinds of information about children around the world they could pick from. Carolyn hadn't known about the appointment or been asked along. She also wasn't thrilled when John spent countless weekends trying to show her that she could love someone who didn't come from her and yet would always be part of her. "The baby is part of you always, like a puppy," he'd said with his winning smile. "I had a puppy when I was a kid. Atlas. He wasn't born of us, but we loved him just like he had. You'll see, Caro. You'll see."

She *didn't* see, not at all, and it was beginning to truly piss her off that John was taking this attitude. He just *assumed* everything would be all right. What if it wasn't? What if making room for an *adopted* child (she couldn't think of it any other way, though she tried hard) was more than she could manage, in her heart? What if she never felt that flare of love for the child? What if she was stuck for life with someone she couldn't love? Would that be truly fair to the *child*, who had a right to expect love from its parents?

The path was getting steeper, and Carolyn could feel a wind cutting off the water as she strode up the walker's side. Usually it was never this cool, but tonight she stopped to tighten the scarf around her neck. *Any colder,* she promised herself, *and I'll pull out my warm mittens.* She always kept them in her coat pocket, but so far, she'd managed without them.

As she came around the curve leading to the apex of the bridge, she saw the woman.

She looked young—mid-thirties at most—and it seemed like she was stretching before a run, because one slim leg seemed braced against the bridge wall. She was wearing a thin jacket—nothing like Carolyn's winter gear—and looking over the side into the flowing waters below.

Carolyn didn't think twice as she came abreast of the woman. It was New Year's Eve, and obviously this woman was ringing in the New Year the same way she was. "Be careful, now!" she called. "Don't jump!"

She gave the woman a cheery smile and a wave and went on.

She kept going, without stopping, because the wind was getting colder and she wanted to get done and go home.

When she'd gone a few hundred yards, she heard a sound behind her. She couldn't have said what it was. She stopped and listened. Heard nothing more. Went on.

She crossed the bridge, then turned around and went back.

She didn't see the woman again.

Carolyn returned to her car without reaching a conclusion. It was an issue that was going to follow her, obviously, into the New Year.

She turned on the car heater to high and shivered all the way home to John.

* * *

Two days later, sitting over breakfast at their new dining table, she heard John say, "Oh, my God. Oh, my *God*. That's awful."

"What?" she asked, pouring cream into her second cup of coffee. She had extra time before the first deliveries at the floral shop, so she was taking a rare late breakfast with John. Between his hours as an architect and hers as a local florist, they didn't have that many hours together.

John Van Benne, a good-looking man in his early 40's, handed her the newspaper, turned to an inside page. The headline read: "Local Principal Jumps Off Bridge on New Year's Eve".

Carolyn read the story with growing horror. A local high-school principal had jumped from the Tallahassee Bridge on New Year's Eve. Her body had been recovered the next day. She was

33, unmarried and loved by everyone at her school. No one knew why she had done it.

She looked at the photo. The woman had shoulder-length brown hair and a nice face. No hint of what had driven her to this.

Carolyn began to feel very sick. She thought back to the woman she'd greeted so cheerily that night. Was it her? She'd only had a brief glimpse, and the woman's back had been to her.

"John," she said, "I walked the Tallahassee Bridge that night."

"Oh, was that where you went?" Then John realized what she was saying. "Caro—did you see this woman?"

"I—I don't know. I might have."

I might have driven her to it. She was looking over the water. She wasn't on the top ready to jump. It might have been what I said that was the last straw for her.

All of a sudden, she felt worse than she'd ever felt in her life. Every bad thing she'd ever done paled in comparison to this.

John was staring at her. "Caro—what did you do?"

"I don't know!" she cried. "I went past someone, that's all. I don't know if it was her. I don't *know*!"

But it didn't matter. In Carolyn's mind, *she* was the deciding factor. *She* had pushed this woman, with her thoughtless, off-hand remark, to throw herself into the dark waters below.

How could she have been so stupid?

* * *

Two hours later, she was knee-deep in flower arrangements for a wedding this weekend. She hadn't stopped thinking about the woman who jumped—she hadn't even caught her name in the article, just thought of her as the Jumper—and her mind kept whirling. What should she do? Call the police? Turn herself in?

Could you go to jail for precipitating a suicide, without realizing it?

As usual, she had the shop radio on while she worked. She liked listening to music—sometimes even dancing to it—while she arranged flowers. Now she made a determined, and successful, effort to push the Jumper out of her mind.

The morning DJ had a deep, soothing voice, something she needed today. "And now, folks, a great song from a great band… "Wrapped in Gauze" by the GooseBumps!"

She knew it, of course. She'd known it all her life. As the song started to play, she relaxed into it and began to sing along. There was nothing to be done, after all. She could wish for that moment back; she could regret that she hadn't helped. But that was all she could do.

Her own life, with its own issues, came back to her as she sang and mixed the flowers together in a tall white vase. Baby's breath. Ferns. Cut the thorns off the roses… that was better.

"Baseball games and lemonade

Lining the streets for the kids' parade."

The familiar words rolled off her tongue. She finished one vase, put it in the shop refrigerator and turned to the next. Though most people didn't look at table decorations for long, Carolyn liked to make them beautiful.

Could she *truly* love a child who didn't come from her own body? Could this child be a *real* addition to her life, or something she would always secretly regret? John or no John, Carolyn didn't want to take on the responsibility of a child she didn't think she could love. Always, before this, she had said she needed 'more time' to make a decision. She had the feeling now that that decision was imminent.

She finished the next vase as the song was winding down, and sang the final lines along with the radio:

"Doesn't matter where else I go
When I'm here I'll always know
I'm wrapped in the gauze of love."

The last chords died away, and the DJ's voice came back. "That was 'Wrapped in Gauze' by the GooseBumps, a great band that will live on and on. What a tragedy we lost Mark Morgan so young; I'd have been the first guy in line to buy tickets for a GooseBumps reunion. Hell, I *was* the first guy in line in our city… I camped out all night for tickets when they announced their reunion tour in 1986. Well, that was thirteen years ago, but it seems a lot longer. A lot of water under the bridge."

Carolyn winced and snapped off the radio. Why didn't they have shows for women who were considering adoption? She supposed she could look it up on the Internet; there were bound to be stories about women who'd adopted, and what they'd been through. Or maybe a group here in town that met regularly to talk about it…

All of a sudden, she forgot the wedding decorations. She ran to her office, where she kept thick stacks of telephone books, and dug into the yellow pages. That's what she needed: An adoption support group. She ran her finger down the list in the phone book… there. "Adoption for Moms".

She dialed eagerly.

A warm, sympathetic voice answered. "Adoption for Moms, Agnes speaking. How can I help you?"

Feeling better than she had all day, Carolyn leaned into that sympathetic voice, as she'd leaned into the song a few minutes before, and began describing her problem.

* * *

Agnes *did* help Carolyn, a lot. They had lunch that day, and for many days afterward, and when Carolyn finally opened up about her fears of adopting a child she couldn't love, Agnes helped ease those fears.

She was a tiny woman in her late 50's, who had adopted three children after the age of thirty and passionately loved them all. Though she only stood five feet tall, her conviction about women becoming adoptive mothers blazed bright, and she often spoke to Carolyn about something that bothered her before she got her second child, a little girl.

"I love *Good Housekeeping* Magazine," she said during one lunch at a local Mexican restaurant Carolyn liked. "And they used to have a feature called 'My Problem and How I Solved It', and in one issue the problem was that a woman who'd just given birth to her second child didn't love the second child as much as the first."

Carolyn listened so intently she forgot to eat as Agnes, her brown eyes snapping fire, went on. "And what the woman eventually realized was that she loved her first child more because she'd just *had* her longer, and that she needed time to establish a relationship like that with her second child. And that ended her crisis." Agnes sat back with a satisfied smile, certain that she'd given Carolyn the answer she was looking for.

Carolyn wasn't sure a magazine solution was enough.

What she knew was that it had something to do with what happened on the bridge on New Year's Eve. *Something* had happened there, and she still wasn't sure how guilty she was. But until she closed that chapter—and how could she?—she didn't know how to solve her problem. *Good Housekeeping* wouldn't do it for her. She felt so bad now that she didn't even want to go back to the bridge.

But after the umpteenth time John asked if she were ready to move forward and she'd snapped that she wasn't, to stop *pressuring* her, something began to give way inside her. He was on hold as much as she was. They needed to do something soon, or her relationship with him, so solid up to now, might start to unravel as well. At this point she felt certain that something would happen, and the answer would present itself.

So Carolyn began walking the bridge again, though now she never walked it at night. She changed her schedule to free up an hour in the early morning, and she made a point of walking with the other walkers, bikers and joggers getting in their exercise before work.

About a month after the new year had begun, Carolyn got up at seven, brushed her teeth, got into her walking clothes and walking shoes and drove to the base of the bridge again. It was an overcast day, cool and a little foggy, and there were fewer joggers; probably most had decided to stay in bed. Carolyn stretched her legs, rotated her arms until they felt loose and began to walk, humming "Wrapped in Gauze" under her breath. It had been playing every morning on her radio at work, and it was in her mind more often now than it had been in years.

As she came up the curve toward the apex of the bridge, she saw a woman on the side. She wasn't walking. She wasn't biking or running. She just stood there, watching the few walkers and bikers, as though waiting for them to pass. She looked over the rail to the water below.

In Carolyn's mind, an alarm bell rang. Something was very, very wrong.

Ordinarily she would never walk up to a total stranger, but after her latest experience, she didn't think for a minute of the consequences.

As soon as she got close to the woman, she said, "Hello. Are you all right?"

The woman said nothing and continued to watch the passersby.

Again, Carolyn repeated, "Are you all right?"

The woman still said nothing. She was a slight woman in a pink sweatshirt, nice beige slacks and expensive flats, not the best clothes to walk a bridge. That alone set Carolyn's teeth chattering.

When the woman refused to engage with her, Carolyn stopped walking. "I'm not going anywhere until you talk to me," she said. She didn't touch the woman, but the look in her eyes—tense and purposeful—made her meaning clear. She moved closer to the woman, not close enough to touch her, but close enough to grab her if she tried to go over the rail.

The walkers continued to walk, the joggers to jog, and the bikers to bike. Carolyn watched them, then turned to the woman. "I'm sorry to disturb you," she said, "But a few weeks ago a woman jumped off this bridge, and I think I was the last person to talk to her. And when I heard it had happened, it made me feel sick. And so ashamed."

The woman, whose hair was combed and whose face, though not made up, was clean, did not answer, but Carolyn needed some kind of absolution. "I don't know if I could have saved her if I'd said the right thing, but what I said that night was absolutely the *wrong* thing. And I'll always regret it."

The woman glanced back at the rail. Carolyn put a light, unthreatening hand on her arm. "No," she said. "I'm not leaving. If you won't talk to me, then we'll just stand here. But I'm not walking away this time."

So they stood. The air was still cool, and Carolyn shivered in her light windbreaker. She should have worn something warmer, but then, she didn't know she'd wind up standing on the apex of the bridge.

Fifteen endless minutes went by. Neither of them spoke. Carolyn never moved away from the woman's elbow. But she hated the silence. She never liked standing around with people saying nothing; even at home she turned on the radio or the TV, just to hear the noise.

Finally, unable to keep silent anymore, she started the conversation. "My name is Carolyn Van Benne. I'm a florist downtown. I have my own shop."

The woman merely looked at her. Carolyn went on hurriedly. "I was walking that night because I was trying to make a decision. Have you ever done that? Taken a walk just to think?"

She glanced at the woman, but this time, instead of just looking at her dumbly, the woman nodded. Carolyn felt a spark of relief. So she could understand what was being said to her. That was good.

Encouraged, Carolyn went on. "I came up here to walk and think. My husband and I have talked about adopting. But I've been worried that if—if I didn't have the baby myself, it wouldn't *feel* like it was really mine. You know what I mean?"

The woman's large dark eyes regarded her soberly for a minute. She nodded again.

"Well, anyway," Carolyn said, now warming to her confidences, "I just don't want to adopt a baby and then find out I can't love it or feel like it's mine. I'm pretty sure if it were mine, I would definitely love it, but you just don't know with someone else's child. And it would be horrible to go through everything to adopt and then… "

The woman continued to look at her. But Carolyn was beginning to wonder if the look in her quiet eyes was accusing.

She went on anyway. The words poured out compulsively. "So I came up here hoping I could decide, and I saw this woman. She looked like she was stretching before a run. And—" She had never meant to repeat the silly words she'd tossed off so lightly, but now she somehow felt she had to. So she took a deep breath and went on. "And I said—'Be careful now. Don't jump!'" And in a storm of regret and guilt, she began to sob.

The tears poured out of her: the fear that she'd caused it, the sure knowledge that she would never really know, the agony that it might have been the final thing that pushed the woman over the edge. She'd wanted to cry for weeks and couldn't. Now, standing next to this total stranger, she did.

She cried and cried, and then suddenly, she felt an arm across her shoulders, and the woman was speaking softly to her, so softly she wasn't even sure it was her voice, but whatever it was, the words were very clear. "Whatever you said, and whatever that meant to her, she's at peace now," the woman said, and the comfort of those words was like stepping into a warm bath for Carolyn. She said nothing, just cried a little less and listened, as the woman went on. "You spoke to her, and you meant to be friendly. You had no idea about her situation. And now she's resting in peace, and however she got there, can you try to feel good about that?"

Carolyn reached into her pocket and pulled out a tissue, something she always carried along with her keys. "And I was trying to make *you* feel better!" she said, and she laughed at the absurdity: first sobbing like she would never stop, and then suddenly laughing. She didn't know what was happening to her.

The woman saw that she had stopped crying, and she gave Carolyn a little squeeze across her shoulders. "Well, and you did," she said. "Are you gonna cry anymore?"

Carolyn shook her head. She was done crying. "No," she said. "I'm gonna—I'm gonna sing!" The wind was dropping, and the clouds were beginning to part. She was no longer feeling chilly, standing on the bridge. She actually felt like singing a happy song.

"What shall we sing?" the woman wondered.

Carolyn thought of the song she'd heard on the radio, even as she was gratified that the woman wanted to sing with her. "How about 'Wrapped in Gauze'?" she asked. "Do you know that?"

"Sure do," the woman said, and they launched into it, standing on that bridge. Carolyn put her arm around the woman and the woman squeezed her shoulders tighter.

Carolyn had never thought of herself as being a good singer, but they made a rousing duo, singing on that bridge in the morning light.

"Doesn't matter where else I go
When I'm here I'll always know
I'm wrapped in the gauze of love."

As they finished the last lines, smiling at each other, a police car drove toward them. Carolyn pulled away from the woman and flagged it down.

The driver lowered his passenger-side window and asked, "Can I help you?"

"Yes, I hope so. The woman over here—" Carolyn looked over, at the woman who'd just been singing with her. "I think she needs help, but she hasn't told me about it. I'm afraid she's thinking of jumping, so I stopped to talk to her."

The driver was already out of the car, walking easily over to the woman. "Hi, there," he said easily, moving quietly toward her. "I understand you may need some help."

The woman was back to being dumb and expressionless. She said nothing but went quietly with the officer when he explained they couldn't have people loitering on the bridge. He said he'd take her downtown and put her gently in the car.

Carolyn handed her business card to the officer. "Could you please—I'd really like to know that she's okay." She gave the woman a quick smile; the woman's lips twisted involuntarily into the semblance of a grin. "Hope your day goes better," she said softly to the woman. The woman nodded at her.

The police car drove off, and Carolyn resumed her walk. *That was great,* she thought, *singing with that woman.* And then, unbidden—*I'd like to sing that song to my child.*

She had no idea where it came from, but suddenly, she had her answer. She could hardly wait to talk to John.

* * *

The phone rang as Carolyn was preparing John's favorite pork-chop recipe for dinner. He was stuck at work but had called to tell her he would be home soon.

She put down the half-breaded chop, wiped off her hand and grabbed it. "Yes?"

"Ms. Van Benne," said an official-sounding voice.

"Yes?"

"This is Russell Marchand. I'm the officer who stopped for you on the bridge this morning?"

"Oh… yes?"

"We just dropped off the woman you were talking to. She's home now."

"Is—is she all right?"

"I think she will be." The voice relaxed for a moment. "She sat with us for a long time today. And we finally got her to talk."

"Oh?"

"She said she'd gone to that bridge today to jump, and having you there stopped her."

Carolyn felt a soaring sense of well-being she hadn't felt in a long time. *She* had helped! *She* had made a difference! She cleared her throat, which was becoming dangerously stuffy. "I'm so glad. Really."

"She told us her name was Annie, and she'd lost her baby daughter and felt she had nothing left to live for. Her husband left her a few months ago. She just lost her job, too. She was feeling hopeless." He paused again. "She said that singing that song you sang together, before we got there, made all the difference. Gave her hope."

"It gave me hope, too."

"She told us that, too." Carolyn wondered how Annie knew.

"She was wondering—she said if you want, you can have all her baby things. She'd like to know they're going somewhere useful." The officer paused.

"I'd love them!" Carolyn cried, but mostly because it meant she'd see Annie again. "Do you have her number? I'll call her."

Russell read it out and Carolyn repeated it back. "Right, that's it. And Ms. Van Benne, you did a really good thing today. Thank you."

By the time John arrived home, Carolyn had a tray of pork chops, salad and potatoes ready for him. She also had the welcome news that she was ready to become a mother, and Annie's soft assurance on the phone that she was welcome anytime.

CHAPTER FOURTEEN

Summer 2008

New York

Jimmy realized, as he started to kneel, that his knees hurt again. He tried to avoid too much physical exertion these days, because somewhere along the way, he'd picked up arthritis, at least in his left knee. But he still did his shows, full out, with the same energy as in his younger days. And that wasn't as easy anymore, at sixty-four.

The knee stopped hurting as he reached the ground, where he laid the sheaf of lilies he'd brought, as he'd brought them faithfully, every year since 2000. He prayed briefly that Laurey was happy and healthy, wherever she was, and that she still loved him.

Because he still loved her.

He said a silent "Amen" and a "See you soon", pressed a kiss to his fingers and pressed his fingers to her gravestone, there on the hill in the loveliest cemetery in Long Island. He hoped Laurey thought of him once in a while, even if she was sitting on the throne of heaven, since he still thought of her all the time.

Then he looked at the gravestone again, and his eyes filled.

"Come on, Dad," Sandra said, tugging at his arm. "Don't cry. She's happy. You need to be happy."

"I'm very happy," Jimmy said, letting her help him up. The tears were beginning to pour down his face. "Can't you see how happy I am?"

Maggie got on his other side and cupped his elbow, lifting him easily. She was the athlete, who pumped enough iron to start a factory but had a soft side as well. "Easy, Dad." She fished out a Kleenex. "Here." He took it, blew his nose and wiped his eyes.

Glenna, his baby who was now twenty-nine, put her arms around him tenderly. "I'm glad we came," she said. "I'll sit next to you in the car, Dad."

Jimmy smiled weakly at her. She was going to hit him up again for tuition for that art course in Europe, and he already knew he would say yes. What was the point of having money if you didn't spend it?

The driver drove them to the little bistro nearby, where they always ate after visiting Laurey. They'd been doing it since her funeral, and like lemmings, they just kept coming back, year after year. The owner, a passionate GooseBumps fan, was always thrilled to see Jimmy and always gave them the back room so they could have privacy.

Once they were seated, though, Jimmy was silent. He couldn't think of a thing to say to his three grown-up daughters who were there because they loved him.

"Dad? What're you thinking?" Glenna asked. She stroked his hand affectionately.

"Mm… I was thinking of when your mom and I met."

"Playing Cinderella and Prince Charming at that park," Maggie sing-songed. "The same place you met Mark."

Jimmy smiled at her. "Have I ever mentioned that before?"

"Only in every single interview since I was born," Sandra said, studying the menu. "Damn, they never change this menu, do they? It's exactly the same as when we first came here."

"I don't remember what I ate the first time we came here," Maggie said, glancing at her father. "I was so upset—"

"We all were," Glenna said. "I couldn't eat for days after… "

Maggie scowled at her. "You still don't eat. I don't know how you're walking around."

"Leave her alone," Jimmy said automatically. "Don't fight today."

"Dad, put on your glasses," Maggie said. "Or you won't see the words on the menu."

Jimmy reached into his pocket. "Stop bossing him around," Sandra said.

"She's entitled," Jimmy said. "She's my road manager now."

Sandra scowled. "I don't know why Jeff didn't want to stay."

Jimmy managed a smile. "He's getting older, honey, and he's not well."

Jimmy knew just how 'not well' Jeff was. He'd be attending another funeral soon. Jeff had left to spend his remaining time with his family, travel around the world (wherever Jimmy hadn't played in the last forty years) and take tons of pictures to be remembered by. Maggie was a more than adequate substitute; she was competent and detail-oriented, and even though Jimmy had never expected one of his girls to become a permanent part of his entourage, Maggie thrived in the hectic atmosphere on his tours. He had never regretted giving her the job.

A petite, hard-worked waitress came by and asked if they were ready. Sandra and Glenna ordered salads, Maggie a huge burger. Jimmy hesitated and finally asked for scrambled eggs. The waitress left after asking shyly if he'd pose for a photo; he said yes automatically. His daughters stared at him.

"Dad? Since when do you order scrambled eggs here?"

"I'm getting fat," Jimmy said defensively. "My stage pants are getting tight. I need to cut back."

"Oh, yeah," Maggie said. "And how many women just about faint seeing you onstage? And how many still cry when you sing? Do you think *they* think you're getting fat?"

"It's my job to look good up there," Jimmy said.

"Why do you even still tour, Dad?" Glenna asked. "I thought you'd had your fill of that. God knows I would have."

Jimmy drank some water and tried to think how to answer. Writing, singing and playing music was his life, and he never wanted to do anything else. He also never wanted to stop. His malaise after Mark's death had finally left him, and he went back to work with a vengeance; it was one of the most productive times of his life, writing and playing new music, which he wished Mark could hear, and he was loving it all when Laurey got sick.

He'd immediately quit touring, called off his recording commitments and told Jeff he was walking away. But when a few months later she was gone, and he sat home alone trying to deal with his grief, the only thing that helped was that piano, that guitar, and those magic chords which could be put together in so infinitely many ways.

He went through his grieving, as family and friends urged him to do. And then one day, he picked up his guitar again. He would never have the love of his life back, but at least he'd have his music.

"I like touring, Glenna," he said, forestalling her complaints. "And yes, I'll pay for that art school. Don't know why you need more schooling, but it's okay with me."

Glenna squealed and hugged him, but Sandra was frowning. "Dad, don't you think it's time to get out there again?"

"Out where?" Jimmy was buttering a roll. He would skip high-caloric meals, but by God, he still loved his bread.

"You know, Dad—out with some nice ladies. It's time, don't you think?"

"I was married to a nice lady, Sandra." Jimmy smiled as he looked at her, but Sandra knew better than to say anything else. The love he and her mom had had was for life.

"Dad?" Maggie dug into the breadbasket, slathering fresh butter on the homemade rolls. She was rail-slim, and he liked to see her eating heartily.

"Yes, honey?"

"How come—" she swallowed a bite of bread and washed it down with water—"how come you *still* don't sing GooseBumps songs in your set? Don't you think fans want to hear it?"

At this point, he really didn't know why he still refused to include those iconic numbers in his set, except that the last time he planned to, Mark died. Maybe it was simple superstition, or just sheer cussedness—but he wasn't ready to sing them again.

For one thing, Kellen was gone.

He'd died suddenly, in a one-car accident while on vacation, going over the side of a canyon while visiting Arizona in 2001. His obituary, the leading story on the news that night, mentioned his award-winning culinary career only *after* ten minutes of lauding his years with the GooseBumps.

What surprised everyone was how durable the GooseBumps and their music had turned out to be. The record company had issued a new greatest hits double album right after Kellen's death, which sold a million copies within a month and blasted the GooseBumps once more to the top of the music charts. After all these years apart, the GooseBumps catalogue was more popular than ever; Jimmy had seen sales figures that claimed as a group, they had sold upwards of a *billion* units, and they sold more every week. Every documentary, every book, even his concert footage were all still hot sellers.

All Jimmy knew was, his royalty checks got larger and larger, and Hammy, who still played with Jimmy for a gig or two every year, was still deluged for interviews with reporters and archivists who spent their lives chronicling the GooseBumps and their influence on popular music and culture.

They had thought they might last two or three years, five at most. No one had any idea they'd last generations, or that Jimmy, in his 60's, would still be recording new music and touring.

The waitress brought their food, and he took his time with the scrambled eggs. Maggie, he knew, would ask again if she didn't get an answer this time.

She was relishing her burger, when he ate his last bite of eggs and said seriously, "Maybe I should add a song or two to the set list."

"A GooseBumps song?" Maggie swallowed and stared at him. "You mean it?"

He thought about it. "Maybe they won't want it."

"They'll want it," Maggie said confidently.

* * *

He and Hammy had a happy reunion a few weeks later, when they met to discuss and rehearse a three-night gig Hammy had agreed to play with him in Florida, where he now lived on a distant Key with his second wife. They hugged each other, asked after each other's kids and grandkids, and settled in chairs on Jimmy's porch with a pitcher of iced tea.

Jimmy poured a glassful over ice and handed it to Hammy, who took a slug and grinned. "If Mark were here, he'd never believe we're drinking tea."

Jimmy laughed. "He'd never believe we were still *here*! He always said rock stars should be dead by thirty. We survived a lot longer than we should have, Hammy."

"True. I saw Mick Jagger a few months ago. He'll be taking up knitting any day now."

Jimmy drank his tea appreciatively. "I used to think those guys were so hip."

"They used to think *we* were hip. And now I talk to my doctor about another hip replacement."

Jimmy laughed again. It was pleasant sitting on the porch, talking to his old friend. Then he brought up a subject he knew Hammy would wax eloquent on. "So, Hammy, what about Dary? Where do you think he was… really?"

After almost thirty years without a trace, they'd learned Dary had finally gotten his, at last. Jimmy thought of the day in

1993 when he heard the remains of a body had washed ashore in the Caribbean, and Interpol, who'd chased him for years, thought the remains were what was left of the GooseBumps' notorious manager.

Jimmy and Hammy were doing one of their bi-annual gigs together when the DNA test results came in. They learned that Dary Dover, the manager who'd left them in the lurch and stolen seven million dollars from them, was the man who'd been chewed almost to the bone by sharks in the warm tropical waters.

"What a way to go!" Hammy groaned when he heard it. "Eaten by sharks! Talk about karma!"

They weren't sure how he'd fallen in the water, but an American cruise ship had made a stop near where the body was found, and the ship's passenger manifest listed a male passenger who never turned up to claim his luggage when they docked in Miami.

Forever after, they played the "Where had Dary Dover been?" game. Jimmy suggested he was a bigamist with a wife and ten children, though he'd had a girlfriend when he disappeared, who claimed she was desolate over his desertion. Hammy's favorite scenario was that he'd lost big in Vegas and was pursued by the Mafia, who finally cornered him on the cruise ship and tossed him overboard. On other days Jimmy put forward the story that he was an escaped convict who was a master of disguise and had disappeared from New York dressed as a woman. On those days, Hammy went with long-term amnesia. Kellen, who kept up with them both through phone calls and Christmas cards until he died, always insisted he'd escaped from a mental institution, then been found and re-hospitalized.

Knowing he had turned up at last and gotten what was coming to him (seven million dollars, for all they earned over the years, was not peanuts to either of them) made them both feel a little better. Knowing, they agreed, was better than not knowing. On some days Jimmy thought that he was glad Dary had had enough money to take an expensive cruise, even if it hadn't ended well. On other days he wished him all kinds of bad luck and thought that perhaps Dary jumped from the ship because he had a fatal disease and didn't want to suffer a long, slow death.

Hammy stirred his tea. "Ah, he's dead and gone, Jimmy. I'm not mad at him, and I hope he's resting in peace. I don't wanna play this game anymore." He drank some more. "We knew he was a gambler when we met him. Who else would want to manage a band of teenagers when he'd never managed anyone before?"

Jimmy shook his head. "I didn't realize he had a problem."

Hammy set down his glass. "You mean all those times on the road when he'd show up late for our shows because he was playing poker all night? Or selling the artwork he bought with our commissions, to pay off some thug who showed up at our hotel suite? Or coming in without the Patek Philippe watch he *said* he'd just forgotten to put on? C'mon, Jimmy, you know it was just going to some casino or other until he won it back!"

Jimmy felt deflated. He'd admired Dary, his show-business savvy and his good advice. (For all Dary's flashiness, he did make suggestions, like those first stage suits, that helped them as a band.) His persistence and hustle had made them stars. He knew Dary had tried to destroy them—or just been too pressured or greedy *not* to steal from them—but remembering back to the beginning, what he liked to think about was how much Dary had believed in them and hustled to get them gigs and record deals. He liked to remember the sold-out concerts where Dary would loll against the bandstand, listening blissfully with closed eyes as they entertained screaming crowds.

Dary's defection was really the beginning of the end for them. Jimmy had always wished things had played out differently, even if they *were* destined not to be together forever.

There was silence for a few minutes, while he and Hammy drank their iced tea and looked beyond the porch to the green lawn in front of Jimmy's house. Not realizing he'd made a decision, he finally said, "Hammy, I'm thinking of playing some of the old songs again, on my tours. What do you think?"

Before his eyes, Hammy became suddenly excited, transformed. "I think," he said emphatically, "that's a *great* idea. Why didn't you do it long ago?"

Jimmy shrugged. "I thought they'd like the new stuff just as much."

Hammy poured himself another glass of iced tea and sipped before he said, "As far as the world is concerned, *nothing* we've done since the GooseBumps has *ever* been better than what we did *as* the GooseBumps."

Jimmy wanted to argue with him, but with a sudden and painful clarity, he realized that his old friend was right. Even without Kellen, without Mark (whom he still missed fiercely), those songs he'd written as a teen and in his early twenties were the best work he'd ever done, and every year, as he struggled increasingly to write more, what he learned was that he could still write a song, but none of it would have impact of the songs they'd sung as kids and taught a generation to love as well. "Makes me feel like a performing monkey," he grumbled.

"Yeah, sure," Hammy said. "All those girls crying and screaming were a bad thing, right?"

"Never really minded 'em," Jimmy said grudgingly.

"Right, you didn't mind 'em. And you just hated all those awards and honors, too, right? And all the articles and books and college seminars too, huh, Prince Charming?"

Jimmy smiled, remembering how Mark used to taunt him with that. "You're just jealous, 'cause you were never the cute one."

"Damn straight." Hammy put a hand to his forehead, where his once heavy brown hair had receded and was now mostly gray. "Nobody misses *my* dreamy blue eyes. Not even me."

"I just wanted you to know what I was thinking," Jimmy said, sipping at his tea again. "If I were to—you know—put in some of the old stuff, what do you think I should do?"

Hammy gave him a look. "Gee, I don't know. Maybe things like 'Bawk Bawk' and 'Souffle' and 'Wrapped in Gauze'? You think any of those would get a good reaction?"

Jimmy didn't answer. It was already painfully obvious what Hammy wanted, and he could no longer think of a good reason not to do it himself.

* * *

He didn't fall asleep that night till after two.

He still didn't want to sing the old songs. They were *old,* damn it! They dated him, yes, and when he sang the newer stuff, which had been popular enough when it came out, it made him feel young and in control again. He was almost afraid that the old stuff would make him feel like retiring, and he wasn't ready for that. Not quite yet.

He didn't realize he'd fallen asleep, but suddenly he was in his old apartment in the Bronx, that old dirty window halfway open. It was, as it always was in those days, dark and cold, and though he knew it was summertime, in his dream, winter was coming on.

He sat on his old bed, legs crossed, his guitar over his knees, and suddenly, there was Mark, sitting across from him—not the Mark of his final days but the young, exciting, gifted boy who had enthralled Jimmy and brought him into the group by the power of his own charisma.

Jimmy was so happy to see him. Mark often appeared in his dreams, but this time felt different; it *felt* like Mark. In other dreams he kept trying to follow Mark, but Mark kept disappearing, around corners and into canyons; in those dreams he was a ghost Jimmy could never quite capture.

Now he sat opposite Jimmy, the old guitar in his hand. He strummed a few chords and said, "Hey, buddy. Why aren't you playing our songs? They're good songs."

Jimmy strummed a few chords; this conversation was worrying. "I have more songs in me, Mark."

Mark watched as Jimmy began to play, something he'd written only a few months before. But before he got halfway through, Mark leaned over and put his hand on the guitar. "Jimmy, sing *our* songs. *Sing our songs.*"

"But these other songs—"

"They don't have the heart of the old songs. That's why those songs still live, Jimmy. We *meant* them when we sang them. Sing *our* songs. Don't be afraid."

He got up, taking the guitar with him, and Jimmy knew that even though Mark was just standing at the doorway of his crummy little room, he wouldn't be able to follow. "Sing those songs, Jimmy, and see what happens."

Jimmy nodded, and he could feel the tears welling up in his eyes.

Mark repeated, "Don't be afraid. I'll be with you."

And then he was gone, and as usual, Jimmy didn't see him go.

And when Jimmy woke up, tears drenching his cheeks, he reached over to his night table for a pad and pencil and began writing a new set list, then and there.

* * *

Jimmy rehearsed the usual set with his backing band, which had been with him for years. He told no one except Hammy what he planned, because his two guitarists already knew the songs he intended to play; they'd *auditioned* for him playing those songs, note-perfect. They hadn't been happy when he told them he was done performing GooseBumps material, but they'd accepted it and were still making a great living touring and recording with him.

Hammy rehearsed fiendishly in secret with him, delighted to play the old songs again. He knew when Jimmy would go into his routine, and when Jimmy stepped to the microphone after the first hour of the concert, the Boston audience hushed.

"Thanks, everyone," Jimmy said. "We love being back in Boston. You're all wonderful to come out for us, and I'm thinking it would be great to do something a little extra here tonight."

The audience began to applaud, not knowing what was coming, but letting him know they were with him.

Jimmy said, "I'd like to do some older songs—"

The audience gasped and began to cheer.

"—Because, a long time ago, you may not know this, but I was in a little band—"

By now they were on their feet.

"—called the GooseBumps—" and now they were screaming. Screaming the way they used to, all those years ago. "So let's do some of those oldies, okay? Hit it, Hammy!"

Jimmy did the count-in and they started "Bawk Bawk", which he hadn't played in years. The guitarists, stunned at the sudden change in the program, hastily switched gears and played the backing chords with enthusiasm. Within a few seconds, the audience was dancing in the aisles, mimicking him doing the chicken moves, bobbing his head, dancing back and forth.

He hadn't had a response like that, to any song he'd sung, since 1968. It was the headiest feeling he could imagine. He hadn't remembered how much sheer *fun* it had been, to be a GooseBump.

He threw himself into the song, the moves, and the high whistle at the end.

The audience, which had been responsive and appreciative from the beginning, went out of their minds. They cheered so loudly he wasn't sure he could calm them enough to do another one.

Finally, he said, "You liked that, I guess?"

They screamed.

"Well, how about this, then?" he said, and began the opening chords to "Souffle".

They all knew it, and within a few bars, they were singing it with him. His guitarists, who had been disgruntled at not playing GooseBumps songs onstage, were suddenly all smiles as they sang along. The joy in their playing was palpable.

By the time he began "Wrapped in Gauze," the audience was ready for it, and they sang in a roar that he thought might literally lift the roof off the old building. He didn't worry about the harmony; his bass guitarist was right with him, just as Mark had always been, and the melody flowed out beautifully. As Jimmy sang, men held hands to their eyes. Women wept openly, even as they sang every word.

And in the very back of the auditorium, at the edge of an open door leading to the exits, Jimmy saw a shining golden light, the light that was Mark, and he knew from that moment on, everything would be all right.

CHAPTER FIFTEEN

2011

The night air whistled past Jack's car window. He breathed it in gratefully and looked at his watch; they were an hour from Las Vegas, on a highway that was all but empty.

He punched his friend Mike playfully. "Hey, by this time tomorrow, I'll be married, dude!"

Mike, who was driving, batted his arm away. "Today, you mean, dude. It's already past three."

"Think we'll get any sleep?"

"If we're there by five, I can guarantee us about three hours each."

Jack sighed. At twenty-eight, he wasn't used to being patient, and even waiting the few hours left before his wedding made him antsy. But they had everything planned, and it was going to be beautiful, and Carole was already there, at the hotel spa, tanning by the pool and otherwise dolling up for him. And after the wedding… ? They were flying to Hawaii in the morning. One glorious wedding night and then paradise for two weeks; he couldn't wait. He wondered if he should try parasailing; his friends said they'd loved it.

Jack leaned against the leather seats of Mike's sports car. He loved riding in it, even as a passenger. The headrest cradled his neck so beautifully. He wondered what the odds were of buying it from Mike, and decided they weren't good. It was a cinch he wasn't giving it to them as a wedding gift, even if he *had* managed to worm his way into being best man.

Next to him, Mike gave a huge yawn. Jack turned a lazy eye on him. "You want me to drive for a while, man? You okay?"

"I'm fine. All ready to hit the tables when we get there. You just relax."

"I'm okay to drive, Mike, really."

Mike yawned again. "So'm I. You get some zzz's, if you can. I'll wake you up at the hotel. We're almost there, buddy. Get ready for a taste of paradise."

Jack shut his eyes and leaned back against the luxurious leather headrest. He couldn't wait to climb into that big soft bed at the hotel, and then get up and get married…

* * *

Jack opened his eyes slowly and immediately felt a shoot of pain in his jaw. He wondered what had happened and tried to reach his hand up to touch it and find out what was wrong. Had he slept on his jaw?

He couldn't move his hand. Or his arm.

Or his head, which seemed to be stuck in place on top of his body.

Had they already gotten to the hotel? Was he still asleep?

He let his eyes travel upward. No, he was definitely awake and in some kind of room. But why couldn't he move his head? Or *touch* his head, for that matter?

He lay quietly, trying not to panic. Okay, he could hear something strange—a *whoosh!* sound to his left. He could breathe quietly, and every time he exhaled, he heard the *whoosh!* sound.

He told himself to stay calm and take stock: He couldn't move or change position, he was definitely awake but constrained and on oxygen. How and why? And by whom?

"Ah, you're awake," said a voice on his right. Jack tried hard to turn his head but could not, so he let his eyes travel upward as far as they could. He couldn't see the person who had spoken to him.

"Here, take a look," said the disembodied voice, and suddenly, Jack saw the outline of a friendly male face leaning down before him. The eyes were brown and merry, and the guy was wearing some kind of white coat. "Better?"

Jack wanted to nod but could not. He opened his mouth to speak and found he couldn't. Could he make sounds? He experimented, trying to bring forth a growl from the back of his throat. He could certainly make *that* sound. Nothing else was working.

"Never mind," said the voice comfortingly. "You can't talk yet, but you will. You're wearing an oxygen mask and there's all kinds of stuff around your mouth. You probably also have a sore throat." Now that he mentioned it, Jack realized he did. "You'll talk again in a few days. Meanwhile, we're feeding you through that tube in your arm." He tapped something on Jack's side that he couldn't see clearly.

Jack took this in in a daze. What had happened to him, that his mouth was taped, and he was being fed through a tube? What about the wedding? Was he married? He didn't remember being married. His head ached dully.

"I'm Dr. Fuss. And no, I don't make one most of the time." He looked like he was used to the joke. "You're at the Northwest Medical Center near Las Vegas."

Jack tried to smile at him but didn't think he'd get very far. Dr. Fuss went on. "I've been told you're terrific at giving speeches, so I'm glad to get in a few words here, before you start chattering again. Let me tell you what's happening."

Jack tried to remember the last thing he did before waking up in this room. He thought he remembered being in Mike's car and drifting off to sleep, but that was all.

Dr. Fuss stood by Jack's bed and looked him in the eye. "You were brought in two days ago. Your friend fell asleep at the wheel and the car drifted into the oncoming lane and hit a truck head-on. You with me so far?"

Jack looked at him and managed a blink. He wondered if Mike were okay but didn't know how to ask.

"Good. You blink once for yes, twice for no, okay? That'll work for now." The doctor patted his arm lightly. "Anyway, you were thrown from the car and pinned under another car that couldn't stop fast enough when you hit the truck. Your right leg was crushed. We had to amputate it. Your left leg is badly broken, and it's in a cast, which is why you can't move it." He tapped the left leg. "It's all there, though, and you can start collecting autographs on that cast pretty soon. *You're going to be all right.* Understand that?"

Jack tried to blink once, but he couldn't stop the tears from rolling down his face. Right leg amputated! Dr. Fuss said it like it was nothing! He blinked twice, and his anger rose. His life was shattered, and the doctor expected him to just *go on!*

Dr. Fuss grinned at him. "Good man. If I heard that from *my* doctor, I'd take a swing at him. Nevertheless, you *are* going to be all right. You need a lot of help and a lot of adjustments, but your life will get back on track. You'll see."

He started toward the door and then turned back. "Oh, your mother is on her way. She'll be here when you wake up. Get some rest. Doctor's orders."

Jack wanted to ask where Carole was, but blinking wouldn't communicate that question. He hoped he'd be able to speak soon.

* * *

Jack's mother was at his bedside when he woke. She looked like she'd been there for a long time. Her slim, straight back didn't touch the back of her chair, and her head, as always, was held high. She'd always been the strength of the family—when Tobey broke his back in that high-school football game, when Dad died—so it didn't surprise Jack that she looked quite capable of dealing with a simple car accident.

He wanted to thank her for coming, but that damn tape over his mouth made it impossible. He looked ahead and waited for her to realize he was awake.

She did, some minutes later. "Oh, Jack! I'm so glad!" She bent over him, and surprisingly, he could feel her tears on his face. Okay, he'd lost a leg and gotten pretty busted up, but she didn't need to make—he grinned to himself—such a fuss. Still, he was glad she was there.

When she finished crying over him, she brushed at the tears on her cheeks and said briskly, "Well, we have to know what we're up against here. Dr. Fuss said it would be a few days before we knew the extent of the paralysis."

Paralysis? What the hell??

Dr. Fuss hadn't mentioned paralysis, only the amputation and a broken leg. Paralysis was a whole other thing altogether. *Was he paralyzed?* How badly? Was it *permanent*?

Jack wanted to ask a thousand questions, and in his agitation, he tried to thrash around on the bed. His mother grabbed at him, holding him to her. "It's going to be all right, Jack. I promise you, we'll make it through this."

There was more sleep and more waking—days of it, in fact—before the doctor finally unwrapped Jack's mouth and allowed him to speak. He had a million questions and a lot to say; he was petrified that he was truly paralyzed, possibly quadriplegic; the thought of never using his legs *or* arms again was unbearable.

As soon as the tape was off and Dr. Fuss said, "You can try to speak now, Jack, even if you're a little hoarse," he was off.

"What the hell, doc? Am I paralyzed? What's going on?"

"We have to see," Dr. Fuss said calmly. "There's damage to your spine. As soon as we can run those tests, we'll know what we're dealing with."

"What happened to Mike? Is he here, in the hospital?"

Dr. Fuss exchanged a glance with Jack's mother. "No," he said finally.

"Is he okay? Where is he?"

"He was hurt worse than you, Jack," Dr. Fuss said. "You were relatively lucky. He didn't make it." He paused. "I'm really sorry."

Jack lay back in shock. Mike had been his best friend since the age of ten. Losing him was horrible.

He thought about this for some time. Then, "What else is wrong with me?"

Dr. Fuss shook his head. "Patience," he said again, and left the room.

Jack had only his mother to turn to, and he turned on her. "I might as well be dead!" he yelled. "My best friend is dead, and I'm trapped in this place, and I still don't know what's wrong with me!"

His mother tried to calm him, but it was hopeless. He screamed, and when he stopped screaming, he cried, for hours, in big gulps, almost choking himself. She had to call the nurse for an injection to calm him down.

By the next morning, he had cried himself out. He lay bleakly in the bed as his mother leaned close to him. "You're going to be all right," she whispered. "I promise, baby. You're going to be all right."

She hadn't talked to him like that since he was eight.

He looked at her from under wet-lashed eyes. "I want your help, Mom," he said in a purposeful whisper. "I want you to help me kill myself."

She merely looked at him over the top of her glasses. "Don't be ridiculous, Jack," she said, in the voice she'd used all his life when something was too silly even to talk about. To him, that had always been the end of the argument.

Now he wanted to push her. "Why not, Mom? I'll never be able to move on my own again. And if things are so rosy and great, where's Mike? Where's Carole?"

He'd heard nothing from his fiancée since before the accident. Why wasn't she there?

His mother adjusted her glasses, another gesture he'd seen from her all his life. "Carole may not be here," she said, "but that's neither here nor there. You *are* going to get better, Jack. Much better. I promise you."

"How do you know? Maybe right now is the best I'll ever be!"

She just looked at him strangely, in a way she'd never looked at him before. "The difficult takes time, boy," she said. "The impossible... just takes a little longer."

He never forgot those words.

Luckily, he had them to hang onto—when the doctors, after prodding and poking him with needles, told him his one remaining leg was paralyzed, and his arms might remain paralyzed as well. Only physical therapy and time would tell if he could get back feeling in them.

He held onto his mother's words when Carole, who refused to come to the hospital and even talk to him on the phone, sent a final letter explaining that she couldn't go through life with him as he was, that she had no training as a nurse and no inclination to become one. He held onto his mother's words when Mike's parents came to see him and wept unashamedly over their dead son.

He held onto her words the day he began his first physical therapy session, with a huge guy who introduced himself as "Hoover the Mover" and then picked him out of bed with one mammoth hand, as though he were a rag doll.

His mother remained at his bedside every day and went with him to physical therapy. When Hoover yelled at him not to be a wuss, to try moving his arms, she faced him down and told him to stop harassing her son. Thinking he needed cheering up, she brought in a portable music player and a stack of CD's and played them for him in the hours after his therapy sessions.

Her favorite was a double-album compilation of hits by the GooseBumps, which she told him she'd loved all her life. Even though she'd grown up after the GooseBumps had broken up, she knew all the lyrics and often sang them aloud, in her dry, sandpaper voice.

Jack tried not to listen. He hated her singing. He hated Hoover the Mover and he hated every day of physical therapy and Hoover's exhortations to try harder. He hated his mother's cheerfulness and understanding, and he resented the fact that he needed her to fight for him. He was twenty-eight, and he didn't need *her* to fight his battles!

He was angry at everything and everyone. He was angry about losing his leg, about being paralyzed, about losing Carole, though something in his head said quietly that it was better he found out now that she was so worthless. He went through his days listlessly, and sometimes it was all he could do not to scream at Dr. Fuss, who popped in regularly and told him he was on the road to getting well.

One afternoon, after a particularly grueling session, he finally screamed at his mother, as she was singing to the GooseBumps' last hit, a re-recording of "Wrapped in Gauze". "Shut up, Mom! I hate that song! I never want to hear it again! It sucks! Everything sucks!"

She went on singing, "Sparklers flare in the dark of night…"

"Didn't you hear me, Mom? Stop singing! I hate your voice! I hate how you always get the breathing wrong and how you sound when you try to hit the high note… "

His mother stopped singing. Tears pooled in her eyes. She pushed the "STOP" button on the CD player and ejected the CD, which she held out in front of him. "Okay, you hate it? Here. Throw it across the room. Smash it into pieces. Go ahead."

He wanted to snatch it from her and throw it right through the window on his left. He wanted to *so much*. He tried to reach out in front of him and grab it. He sent every signal he knew to his arms, to get them to pluck that miserable CD from her hand.

It weighed practically nothing; he knew he could throw it a mile. He struggled furiously to take that damned CD and destroy it, once and for all.

He couldn't.

He put his head down and cried.

His mother let him cry for a long time. She finally reached for a tissue to wipe the tears away. "It's all right, boy," she said softly. "Remember what I said. The difficult takes time. The impossible—"

"—just takes a little longer," Jack finished, his throat still clogged with tears. "When is a little longer, Mom? How long? When does it all come back?"

She was silent, mopping at his face with the tissue. Angry, he jerked his head away, the few inches that he could. "Some of it will never come back, Jack. We'll get back what we can and go from there."

"*We*? It's me, you mean! I'm the one who has to live with one leg and arms that don't work! It's me that has to 'go from here'! I should have died with Mike!"

He screamed these last words at her, lashing out as he had for weeks at the one person he knew was always on his side. He knew he was hurting her, and knew he could stop it, but he didn't want to; being able to scream at her was one of the few things he could still do without effort, and it made him feel, somehow, a little more normal.

Someday he'd apologize.

Someday, when he got it all back.

He had no idea when, or if, that might be.

His mother, tears dripping down her cheeks, sidled toward the door. He knew he'd hurt her horribly; it was just one more terrible thing he had to feel bad about now.

As he contemplated another way to kill himself, this time without his mother's help, he saw a young woman stride into his room. They had taken his neck out of its brace, finally, and he could turn his head carefully when he wanted to.

"Hi," said the young woman, surveying him with a smile. "I'm Claire. I came to introduce myself. I'm taking you to and from therapy from now on."

As much as Jack had hated every single minute of therapy, that was how much he suddenly blessed it now. Claire had beautiful silky red hair tied back in a ponytail, dancing green eyes, and a perky blue scarf tossed over her blue hospital uniform. He thought she was the most beautiful thing he'd ever seen.

"So," she said, looking at him with a smile, "what're you doing?"

"Screaming at my mother," Jack said, and wondered if he'd now lost his mind, along with his legs. In his previous life, he *never* would have started a conversation with a pretty girl that way!

Claire didn't seem to mind. She pulled up a chair to his bedside and went on, "Your mother looks nice. What were you screaming about?"

"A GooseBumps record," Jack said.

"Oh, I love the GooseBumps! I've got everything they've ever done, and I know it all by heart. I even went to a Jimmy Welton concert a couple of years ago. How could you scream at that nice woman about the GooseBumps? Or did that accident cause brain damage as well?"

Jack managed a snort, which was all he could do in the way of laughter these days. What did *he* have to laugh about, after all? He noticed his mother hesitating at the door, obviously wanting to leave them alone. "It's okay, Mom," he said. "I'll just visit with—Claire, here—until you get back."

"That's fine," his mother said, headed openly for the door now.

"Mom? I'm sorry." He felt he had to say that before she left.

"I know." And she was gone.

Claire looked after her thoughtfully. "She looks sweet."

Jack sighed. "She is. I'm a dick."

"Yes, you looked like a dick," Claire said, snuggling down in the chair. "So—how's therapy going?"

"Awful. I can't do anything Hoover wants me to do, and he just keeps yelling at me to try harder. Does he think I'm trying *not* to get better?"

"You couldn't blame him if he did. Some people *never* want to get better, can you believe it? They just want to feel sorry for themselves and have everyone else feel sorry for them. So they never get better, they just keep being crippled and pitiful." She stared at him.

"'Crippled and pitiful'. You're a real ray of sunshine, aren't you? What're you, the hospital entertainment?"

"Some people find me very encouraging." Claire didn't move and didn't take her eyes off Jack. "Of course, those people all *want* to get better and work hard to *get* better."

Jack looked at her. "Well, since Hoover's gonna keep bugging me and you're obviously gonna keep bugging me, I just gotta work harder, then, don't I? Otherwise, I'll just be crippled and pitiful."

"And we wouldn't want *that* now, would we?"

Claire became his guardian angel, relieving his mother from her long vigils in the hospital PT unit. She wore the same perky blue scarf every day, even when the temperature outside climbed into the 90's, and never stopped reminding him how much she loved the GooseBumps. Eventually he told her that he'd wanted to throw his mother's GooseBumps CD across the room, which at first horrified her, then fascinated her. She took to singing GooseBumps songs when she wheeled him down to therapy and kept singing them while he struggled to follow Hoover's baffling instructions to "Hold the stick" and "Push, now, push hard!"

He told her over and over that he hated the GooseBumps and especially hated the "Wrapped in Gauze" song his mother always sang. He said it sounded like the patients at the hospital.

That was Claire's cue to play and sing it every day, loudly and off key, on a portable CD player as she wheeled his chair down the hallway. He screamed at her to stop, and she just laughed and kept singing. She told him when he could throw the CD across the room, she'd give it to him to break.

Jack was moved from the regular hospital ward unit to a room near the PT unit, and he kept working. He was told he could make his arms work, but the links in his mind were not yet producing the kind of movement he wanted.

Claire stayed late to comfort him, eat dinner with him and annoy him with GooseBumps stories. He told her when he got his arms finally working, after he threw out his mother's CD, he would throw *her* through the hospital window. She told him before that happened, she would get him to sing "Wrapped in Gauze" with her, since his mouth obviously worked so well. He swore it would never happen.

Three long months went by, while Jack's face and broken leg healed from the trauma of the accident. The scars faded, but he remained helpless, trapped in a wheelchair he hated almost as much as he hated Claire's singing. His mother, who continued to arrive punctually every morning, had begun taking afternoons off while he worked in PT. She figured Claire got under his skin so well, she didn't need to be there. As long as he was angry, she knew he was improving.

One lovely summer morning, Claire arrived after breakfast to take him to therapy. The nurse who brought his tray had pulled open the curtains and unlatched the window. A soft, sweet breeze drifted into the room. "Hey, pal," she said, "today's gonna be a scorcher. Wanna sit in the garden at lunch, after therapy?"

Unaccountably, Jack felt wonderful this morning. The breeze carried such a sweet smell, it made him suddenly happy. "What I really want to do is walk into the garden," he said.

"Sure thing. Want me to help you up?"

Jack looked at her, stunned, as Claire looked back at him expectantly. "Well, friend, you're either going places or you're not," she said. "Today's as good a day as any to find out. Let's get you out of that chair and see what you can do."

He had been fitted a month before with a prosthetic leg, which he could not care for independently until he got the use of his arms back. But he liked wearing it, as though he were going to stand up and stride back into the world.

"Okay," he said, feeling just good enough to take the dare. "Let's take a stroll, shall we?"

Claire locked the wheels on his chair, stood between his legs and reached for his arms, which hung useless. "Let's go, dude," she said, and pulled.

A moment later, she had set him on his prosthetic leg.

He couldn't believe it. He was standing! He was so excited he actually yodeled, and a nurse ran into the room. "Jack!" she scolded, "who told you to stand on your leg? Who did this?"

He just looked at Claire. She looked back and said nothing.

"Well, since you're up anyway..." The nurse looked at him helplessly. "I think you could use a walker, huh?"

"Not till you can use your arms again," Claire sing-songed. "No stroll outside till you can lean on a walker and push yourself forward."

Jack felt suddenly deflated. The joy of being upright suddenly plummeted when he realized that without his arms, he couldn't sustain himself upright for any period without help.

"Come on, marching man," Claire said when the nurse left. "Let's get you to PT. Seems to me you've got some great incentive now!"

That afternoon, Claire gave Hoover the GooseBumps CD and instructed him to play it without stopping, until Jack achieved *some* movement with his arms, no matter how tiny. Whatever it was, it was a step toward throwing the CD against the wall, which Jack heartily longed to do, every single day.

Hoover tried. He tried to bend Jack's arms at the elbow. He tried to push Jack's arm backward. He tried to get Jack's hand to move across the table.

Jack watched him smugly. He hadn't seen the slightest improvement, and he was so pissed at Claire, he wasn't sure he even *wanted* to move his arms. She never stopped needling him or singing those stupid GooseBumps songs, and the only good thing, he considered, would be the chance to smash that CD, which he grimly promised himself would be the absolutely *first* thing he would do when he could move his arms again.

"Okay, final thing today," Hoover said finally, and he was panting a little, as though he too had worked a little too hard. He put a quarter on the table in front of Jack. "Push that two bits toward me and we're done for the day."

Jack concentrated. He always concentrated hard during these sessions, and he was always wiped out afterward. It was during those exhausted and frustrated periods that he often flew off the handle, at whoever was nearby. It always hurt his mother. Claire didn't seem to notice.

Jack focused on the quarter. He looked at it, gave his arm the command to move. He focused… focused…

His hand flashed out and pushed the quarter across the table in one mighty move, right off on the other side. The sound rang on the floor.

Hoover looked at him. "Holy God!" he said and let out a wild whoop. "Did you see that? *Did you see that, my man?* You are *amazing*!" He grabbed Jack out of his chair and whirled around with him, hugging him tight.

Claire, too, was transfixed.

When Hoover got finished skidding around the floor with Jack, he placed him back in the chair as though he were made of porcelain.

"Claire, did you see?" Jack shouted. "Did you see what I did? Hoover, put that quarter up here again!"

Claire still said nothing. She stared at the table.

"You don't have to, Jack," Hoover said, his joyful expression now quenched. "Really, I saw it and it was incredible, but you don't have to—"

"Put it up here again!" Jack said. *"Now!"*

Hoover retrieved the quarter and set it in front of Jack again. Jack looked at it. Concentrated. And his arm once again flashed out and knocked the quarter off the table.

Hoover looked at Claire, who by now was crying.

"Claire? Gimme that damn CD. I'm throwing it across this room and smashing it into pieces and—" He caught sight of her face. "Why are you crying?"

Claire tried to control herself. "The doctors—they all said you would never be able to do that," she said, and cried harder.

Jack was disconcerted. "What the *hell*? Why did they tell me I could, then?" He glared at Hoover. "And why did you push me every damn day to do it, huh? How come?" He shoved an arm at the table again. There was no coin on it to push off, but Jack felt better, and Hoover, his own eyes welling up, pounded on the table in triumph.

"Claire! Gimme that damn CD this second or—"

Claire took the CD out of her pocket, dabbing at her eyes with a Kleenex. "Here, Jack. All yours. Smash it to bits."

Jack took it in fingers which he was stunned were now working, obeying his commands. Nothing felt as good in his life as holding that wonderful piece of metal-coated plastic. He turned the CD in his hand, as Claire and Hoover watched, mesmerized. Yeah, he *could* throw it, but…

"I'm thinking—maybe I *don't* want to smash this thing to bits, right now," he told Claire as Hoover ran out of the room to alert the others in the PT unit of the miracle he'd just witnessed. "In fact, I think what I really want to do now is sing."

"Sing what?" Claire asked practically, still dabbing at her eyes.

Jack began to sing, "Sparklers flare in the dark of night… "

Claire began to sing with him, and for once, her voice was on key. Jack thought this might be more of a miracle than his being able to use his arms again.

They sang the entire song through—Jack had learned every stinking word of it in the days and weeks after his accident, when his mother sang it every day—and ended with the final promise:

"Doesn't matter where else I go
When I'm here I'll always know—
I'm wrapped in the gauze of love."

They looked at each other when they finished, and Jack reached out—oh, glory, he *could* reach out again!—and brought Claire into the circle of his arms. "They said this was impossible," she said to him, still tearful.

He smiled at her and whispered, "The difficult takes time. The impossible just takes a little longer." And when he kissed her and she kissed him back, they each knew, in their own way, just how far they had come.

Chapter Sixteen

New York

2015

Usually, Jimmy hated riding in a limo. Over the years he'd driven himself thousands of miles, flown around the world, taken trains and even once in a while, in the city, taken the subway. Always, he was recognized by fans, but they were nice now, not screaming crazy, the way they had been in the GooseBumps days. They stopped to tell him how much they loved his songs or asked for an autograph or a selfie. He always obliged when he could.

But today it was fitting he'd be in a chauffeured limousine, coming from Hammy's funeral.

Hammy, his dear friend and fellow GooseBump for more than fifty years, had died at seventy-four, from complications of pneumonia. He'd been sick since before Christmas, and as the new year turned from winter slush into spring sunshine, his hacking cough had gotten worse. Jimmy had visited several times, urging him to rest and do what the doctors said. Hammy always promised he would, but the next time Jimmy visited, the nagging cough was still there.

When Jimmy got the call from Hammy's wife, his first thought was: *I'm the last surviving GooseBump.*

Fans came out in flocks for Hammy's funeral, clutching old GooseBumps records and wearing old "I LOVE HAMMY" buttons, left over from the first heady, ecstatic days after the *Hollywood's Talent Palace* show, when the whole world seemed to embrace them. There were tears and prayers for this much-loved music icon and a touching eulogy from his partner in the building company he'd founded after leaving the group. He spoke of Hammy as the steady, unfailingly kind and generous person who kept people working in down periods and celebrated with them in high times. Jimmy, remembering Hammy's kindnesses when he first joined the group, nodded in agreement.

The press was out in full force, and they nabbed Jimmy before he could leave the graveside and asked for a brief live interview, to which Jimmy agreed. He was playing a concert that night, but he could spare ten minutes for his old friend.

"You're the last living GooseBump," said the young reporter with the microphone, instinctively straightening his tie around Jimmy, who at 71 still retained his elegance of face and figure. "How does that feel?"

Jimmy tried to think of a decent answer, but the best he could come up with was, "I never thought I'd be the last one. I loved Hammy, you know."

"I know you were all really close," the reporter went on. "What do you think of the continuing popularity of the GooseBumps? Why, after all these years, do people still remember them with such joy?"

"I hope because we tried to give them joy. That was always our goal, and it makes me so happy they still have a heart for the songs. They meant a lot to us."

"How did you get to know Hammy?"

Jimmy thought back to that night in 1961 when he met the long-legged drummer at the amusement park and tried to give a picture of that. The reporter jumped on it. "So you liked each other at once?"

"Hammy was always kind. He always encouraged you, and he was great to be with. It was impossible not to like him." Jimmy blinked against the tears rising into his throat. He was *not* going to cry on camera!

"So Hammy's legacy, you think—"

"He was a great drummer and a great friend. A great human being, which is the best any of us can hope for in this life. That's all. Thanks."

Jimmy bolted away from the reporter, who looked as though he'd keep asking questions as long as Jimmy stood there. He really needed to get away and get those tears under control.

Maggie caught his arm at the edge of the gravesite. "Let's go, Dad. Limo's waiting."

She sat next to him as they drove back to Long Island, where Jimmy had stubbornly kept the little house in Baldwin he'd bought back for his sister and mother all those years ago. He'd built an addition onto it thirty years ago, with extra bedrooms and a music room/recording studio, and it was plenty large enough now, with all his daughters on their own. These days, he often rattled around the house, aware that they needed their independence but lonely for their presence. His mother had died in 1990. His sister, now widowed, had moved out when she married in 1971. She now lived in Arizona for the weather, but she'd promised to be at his concert tonight, and he was excited to see her again. He loved Debby.

From years of touring where he only performed new songs, Jimmy had reverted, from that first concert in 2008 when he'd started playing GooseBumps material again, to set lists that featured almost an entire GooseBumps lineup. No one played them like he did, full out and with new, richer arrangements he'd done himself. And audiences around the world responded with roars and cheers, still under the spell of the 1960's band that climbed into the show-business stratosphere in just seven short years, before breaking up at the height of their success.

Since he'd begun—with Hammy—playing those old songs, GooseBumps' album sales had once again skyrocketed. They were now well into the billions in worldwide sales and digital downloads of their music, something Jimmy never would have dreamed possible when they began. But it had happened, and the sincere love of total strangers who still wrote him fan letters was touching. He was grateful for every one of them.

He was silent when they got home. Maggie went to the kitchen to fix a snack, and he went upstairs to his music room. He was getting ready to record a new album and wanted to go over the arrangements again, along with the set list for tonight's show.

When she came up with a tray, he was deep in his newest arrangement. "Dad, pick up the phone. A friend of yours is calling."

Jimmy saw a plate of shortbread biscuits and reached for them. "What's his name?"

"Luke something?"

Still thinking about Hammy, Jimmy picked up the phone. "Luke? Oh, Luke!" He put a hand over the phone and spoke rapidly to Maggie. "This guy introduced me to Mark!"

He talked quickly, sounding delighted. "How are you? Oh, that's great! You'll come tonight? I'll leave a pass for you. Hell, come backstage. I'm always there by five. Fantastic!"

He put down the phone and took a sip of iced tea. "Oh, I love Luke! We were friends at school, and I was working at the park when he came by with Mark—that's how I met Mark!"

Maggie looked less than enchanted. "I'll take care of the pass. But don't get all nostalgia-y with him, okay? I don't want you late onstage."

Jimmy was already nibbling on a biscuit. "Right. Promise."

"And I thought you were laying off the sweets to keep your girlish figure?"

Jimmy looked guilty but didn't put down the biscuit. "Just one. It's good for my voice."

"And I guess all those years ago, you thought cigarettes and weed were good for your voice too," Maggie grumbled, but she left the plate and headed for the stairs. "I'll be in the office if you need me. The car's coming at three."

Jimmy ate his snack and reluctantly put down the new arrangement. It would have to wait till tomorrow.

Once you were over 70, every performance took something out of you. So he always napped for an hour before a show. Then he could do two hours or more onstage, and the fans were thrilled that he gave them so much.

Today, he couldn't fall asleep. His mind went to Hammy, Hammy the sweet, generous guy who always had a kind word for everyone, who almost got pulled out of the car in that first riot at Marvin's, Hammy, who ate Kellen's first (ruined) souffle while Jimmy and Mark wrote a song about it. Jimmy turned on the little radio at his bedside, now playing a medley of GooseBumps songs, finishing with a tribute to Hammy and his wonderful drumming.

Damn, he wasn't getting any rest, anyway. He sat up and snapped on TV.

All he saw was the GooseBumps. Old songs playing over stills of Hammy's best photos, with footage of the screaming girls and some of their concerts—New York, L.A., Berlin, London. Footage of the GooseBumps—*God, we were young*—running from fans, running into hotel entrances, jumping into cars, onto trains, getting out of ambulances and running into the stage entrance of a concert hall. "Souffle" played over and over, as though written as a tribute to Hammy. Jimmy smiled; he knew why they'd written it, but Hammy would get a kick out of it if he knew. Jimmy hoped on some level he did.

He thought about it all again, as though he didn't have to re-live it for some reporter every other day. As a GooseBump, his life could not have been better. The walls in his music room were literally lined with gold and platinum records. He'd been honored at the Kennedy Center a few years ago, in a raucous and wonderful evening, for his lifetime achievements in music. In a few months, he would travel to D.C. to accept the Presidential Medal of Freedom, the highest civilian honor in America, for his body of work. He'd written songs for films, for other bands, for himself as a soloist and for the GooseBumps as a group, most of which had climbed the charts, though only his GooseBumps songs had become standards.

At least four hundred books had been written about the GooseBumps, including multiple biographies of himself; another author was working on a comprehensive one now, using him as a sort of co-author, instead of just the subject. He fielded calls from the writer at least every other day and gave him hours of taped interviews. There were a dozen serious documentaries on the groundbreaking band, and the Library of Congress had a special GooseBumps collection, including tape of all their recording sessions and musical discussions. There had even been a feature film about them, starring four young actors who were taught to play and sing just like them. It had been a huge hit, but Jimmy didn't like the album released with the film, which sounded like any generic four boys singing GooseBumps songs. He still preferred the original versions.

The GooseBumps' songs and legacy were taught in high schools and colleges across the country, and one ambitious music school had set up a special program where you could *major* in the GooseBumps, including classes on drumming like Hammy, playing electric guitar like Kellen, and songwriting like Mark and Jimmy. Jimmy had never visited the college but promised himself he'd get there sometime, if only for a commencement ceremony.

He had accepted at least a dozen honorary college degrees (he specified they had to be in a musical major) and spoken at many commencement ceremonies, to wild cheers and applause. He'd been at Marvin's when it was designated an historic site as 'the place where the GooseBumps began their historic, meteoric run', and at their downtown recording studio when it received a plaque as the 'home of the GooseBumps'. New York City had a special GooseBumps tour commemorating many of the places in the city where they'd played, as well as the miserable old building where Jimmy and his family had lived when he first met Mark and joined the band. He'd even agreed to will his house to the town of Baldwin, Long Island, when he died, so they could preserve it. The GooseBumps, after fifty-four years, were still big business to New York.

Ongoing tributes on YouTube. New album re-issues every few years. Documentaries, books, endless magazine special editions. The GooseBumps had literally achieved everything it was possible for a band to achieve. Their albums and song manuscripts had been buried in a 1960's time capsule, to be reopened in 100 years. Their songs—on tape—had woken up astronauts on the space shuttle. Jimmy had closed stadiums the GooseBumps had once played, where the last sound heard was his guitar, and opened new stadiums where the first sound heard was his guitar. He'd played at Royal Command Performances and at Super Bowl halftime shows, presented Grammys and picked up Oscars. He'd stood onstage with Kellen and Hammy the night they were inducted into the Rock `n roll Hall of Fame in Cleveland.

It's been a good life, he thought, *and I'm not ready to stop.* Maggie had suggested he think about retiring from touring, but he still loved it. He'd given up cigarettes, weed and (mostly) alcohol. He wasn't ready to give up his time onstage. Maybe at eighty; not now. Not yet.

He still missed Mark fiercely. He'd reconciled himself to losing Kellen, and he'd expected to lose Hammy for a while now; but Mark was the one who haunted him, who still came to him in dreams and encouraged him.

Three o'clock. Jimmy had showered and was ready when the car arrived. He tucked the set list into his guitar case as they headed toward Madison Square Garden. Maggie talked quietly on her cell phone, checking on the sound and light run-throughs at the Garden earlier in the day. No need to check on ticket sales; tonight was sold out.

There were hugs for Jimmy when the car stopped at the stage entrance of the Garden. He thanked the driver and darted inside.

He sat alone in front of his dressing room mirror, stage clothes hung neatly on a rack nearby. He'd already done three shows here; tonight was the last. Who knew when he'd play this venue again? He'd made a point of saying goodbyes as though they were his last goodbyes. Thinking of Hammy did that to him.

There was a knock, and Luke was there. Jimmy threw his arms around him. "Hey, Luke! It's been forever!"

It sure had been. Luke looked like a little old gray man, his hair thinning on both sides. He and Jimmy were the same age, but Jimmy had been coloring his hair for years, to look good onstage, and Luke had let nature take its course. He was a little bent over, as well, and walked more slowly than Jimmy, who still jogged every day and had never, thank goodness, suffered with back issues.

Luke hugged Jimmy back enthusiastically and took a seat next to him. "Have I ever really thanked you?" Jimmy asked him.

Luke smiled. "No, but every biographer says the same thing: 'Without you, there wouldn't be the GooseBumps'."

Jimmy could see Luke loved the attention; he probably dined out on it. "Luke, my life would never have been the same if you hadn't introduced me to Mark." *Okay, he needed to hear it; nothing wrong with stroking his ego a little.*

They were silent for a few moments. They had never been really close, but Luke helped Jimmy navigate a new school during those first bewildering months in the Bronx, and Jimmy remembered it with gratitude. "You really helped me at school, too. That wasn't an easy time."

Luke said suddenly, "Do you know, that first day I met you at school, I started thinking about introducing you to Mark? It was just a matter of time before I got you two together. I had a feeling."

Jimmy wondered if he gave interviews like this to biographers; God knows he himself read it often enough in accounts of his first meeting with Mark. Once Jimmy mentioned Luke's name casually in a newspaper interview in 1962, Luke became the go-to guy for all questions about the founding of the group. But then, *anyone* who had anything to do with the GooseBumps became instant celebrities. It was as much a curse for them as for the band.

Jimmy sensed that Luke had come for a reason, but the minutes went by and he said nothing, just chatted casually. Jimmy glanced at the clock; time to start making up. In a few minutes, the rest of the band would come in to say hello and start tuning up.

"Jimmy?" Luke was looking at him, and his look was pleading. *Here it came.*

Jimmy was used to this; as the wealthiest GooseBump (at this point, he thought it was hundreds of millions, but he wasn't sure), he got more requests every day than he could in good conscience turn down.

"Yes?"

Luke hesitated, his large head quivering. Then he began to tell Jimmy a long, involved story about his outdoor business going bust, a legal battle between him and his business partner, a judgment against him, an expensive operation for his wife, college fees he hadn't yet repaid.

Jimmy saw that this would last forever unless he stepped in. "Can I help, Luke?"

"Oh, Jimmy…" Luke didn't seem to know how to say it. "I always loved being part of your story, but… these last few years have really drained me, and I have to move forward."

"What can I do?"

"I—I told *Esquire* I could get you to do a photo shoot for them. That we were still good buddies, and all I had to do was ask—I know it was wrong, Jimmy, we've hardly seen each other in fifty years, but… what could I do?"

"*Esquire* paid you to get me to do a photo shoot? Is that it?"

Luke hesitated, then nodded. "Fifty thousand to get you in, but I don't get the money till the shoot is done, and—"

Jimmy silently cursed. These friendships were sometimes more trouble than they were worth. He genuinely liked Luke and didn't mind his re-telling the story of introducing him and Mark half a century before, but this was getting complicated. And yet, he himself wasn't about to hand out fifty thousand to Luke as a loan, either.

"Okay, Luke. Don't worry. I get that you need the money. Give me your number. Maggie's my road manager, and she handles my schedule. I'll tell her we'll do the *Esquire* shoot. She'll call you in a day or so."

"Oh, thank you!" Luke stood up, and Jimmy understood that he had accomplished his purpose. "Oh, Jimmy, I couldn't sleep nights. I was so worried about what you'd say."

"Forget it, Luke. Take care of your family. You'll stay for the show, won't you? I left a ticket."

"Love to." Luke swiftly leaned down to hug Jimmy, who was already opening pots of makeup. "Bless you, Jimmy. It's right that you're the last GooseBump. You always were the best one." As he left, Luke was calling, "I always told the truth about you and Mark!"

Jimmy shook his head as he began to make up. Poor guy. This was such a little favor, in light of the huge favor Luke had done him. It wasn't something Jimmy could ever forget.

Memories flooded his mind as he patted on base and powder, then stood up to change his clothes. Dary had insisted on their wearing identical suits onstage; now Jimmy wore simple black slacks, low-heeled shoes and colorful t-shirts, to be comfortable. It didn't seem to matter. The crowds never stopped coming and never stopped screaming. He smiled. How often had reporters asked earnestly, "When is it going to end?"

The answer was: Never. The GooseBumps had given the world something of enormous value with their songs, and the world had given them back unconditional love, for fifty-plus years.

Jimmy put on his stage pants and had to suck in a deep breath to zip them. Maggie was right. No more biscuits till these pants got looser. He'd never had a weight problem before, but the last few years, since Laurey wasn't supervising his diet anymore, had made a difference. He didn't want to die a fat old man who waddled everywhere.

With an hour to show time, Jimmy was dressed and made up. He sat with his guitar, noodling the strings, tuning it just so. The set list sat on the makeup table.

His band was outstanding, and he fully expected them to stay with him; they all had long-term contracts. Young guys, all talented, all GooseBumps fans who loved performing their songs. Good people to take onstage with him.

The band spilled in to hug him and ask if he was okay. They would; Hammy's death had gotten to them all, and most had attended the church service earlier in the day.

When they got the call to go onstage, they could already feel the excitement in the Garden. Thousands of fans, all thrilled to see the great Jimmy Welton, all pumped for a great evening. "Let's give it to them, guys," Jimmy said. "And let's do this show for Hammy."

"For Hammy!" They raised fists in the air, and Jimmy was gratified at the tears in their eyes.

"Let's go!" He still made it a point to run onstage, pumping up the energy level and getting them excited for the show ahead. Tonight he ran a shade more slowly, and a couple of the players looked at each other. Was the legendary Jimmy Welton starting to slow down?

They always started the show from the wings, where the first chords of "Driving Toward the Light" began. His drummer was already onstage, and the rest waited with him as the announcer said, in a lilting voice, "Ladies and gentlemen—Jimmy Welton!"

He ran on, and the others took their places as they began to sing.

The audience rose in a roar to welcome him. These were hardcore fans; some came to a dozen shows a year. All of them knew his songs and sang them right along with him. They weren't there to hear him sing; they were there to celebrate with him. He'd been with them all their lives; this was their night to enjoy it.

They sang "Driving Toward the Light", and the response was electric. Jimmy stepped forward, as he always did after the first song. "Good evening, everyone! Welcome to our little show!"

A Jimmy Welton production was never a 'little' show. The lighting, sound and video were perfect, the result of hours of rehearsal and adjustment. The show was never short; Jimmy had done short shows as the GooseBumps' career became more popular—and dangerous—but now he wanted to stay onstage as long as he could. Audiences loved it.

When they'd finished laughing and applauding, Jimmy spoke into the microphone again. He couldn't see beyond the footlights, even knowing it was a full house. Luke was out there, and Maggie; he'd introduce them later. But right now, he had something he wanted to say.

"As most of you know," he began, "today we said goodbye to—" He suddenly couldn't finish, and tears were pouring down his face. The audience, responsive as always, rose and yelled, "Hammy! We love you, Hammy!"

Jimmy pulled himself together abruptly. He *never* cried onstage, *never*. The discipline of fifty years onstage kicked in, and he brushed away the tears. "That's right. We lost Hammy, and since we all love him and know he's in a better place—"

More cheers and screams from the crowd.

"—let's dedicate tonight's show to Hammy, okay?"

They were out of their seats.

Once the cheers had died down, Jimmy stole a glance downward, the only way he could see even the first few rows of the audience. Most were in tears. He saw Luke dabbing at his face with a handkerchief.

"Yes, tonight is about great memories," he went on, "and so I'd like to introduce you to a friend of mine who really started the GooseBumps off." There was already a cheer from the sides; they knew what was coming. "—I had just moved to the Bronx, and he was one of my first friends at school. And on Halloween night in

1961, he said to me, 'Jimmy, I'd like you to meet my friend Mark Morgan.'"

The cheer that went up for that almost deafened him. These fans knew their GooseBumps history, all right.

"So let me introduce *you* to the guy who started it all for me by putting me together with Mark. Ladies and gentlemen, Luke Arlington! Stand up, Luke."

A spotlight hit Luke, as Jimmy had instructed earlier, and Luke hesitantly rose to his feet, gave a half-hearted wave and sat down. A roar of applause followed him. Jimmy introduced his sister Debby as well, who rose and smiled. She still looked trim and alert, even in her sixties. The fans gave her a huge ovation, also.

Unlike his earlier solo years, he was quite prepared to give most of his shows now to his legendary band. As he began the set list, he asked, holding up his arm as he had for years in those days, mimicking Mark's old gesture, "Anybody here have GooseBumps?" and the crowd responded by holding up their elbows as well, and—yes—*screaming*.

Jimmy continued the set with "Bridge Across Tomorrow," paying tribute to Mark, to Kellen and to Hammy, which the audience loved. He told the true story of how "Souffle" was written, including the fact that Mark's exuberant clap across the guitar strings caused Kellen's masterpiece to fall entirely. "Don't try this at home, folks," he warned to affectionate applause, and then sang it full out, to screams from the audience.

He talked about their initial success with "Bawk Bawk" and broke into a rollicking version that had the audience dancing, bobbing and whistling with him.

As he spoke, on the huge screen over his head, photos flashed of the young GooseBumps, playing, singing, laughing. He'd given the video people instructions to shoot the audience; this was going to eventually be a music documentary he would edit himself, after the tour ended.

"Bawk Bawk" was such a success they had to do an encore.

When that was over, there was a hush in the Garden. Everyone knew what was coming. Jimmy stepped to the mike. He didn't have to introduce the song, but when he said, "You know this next one, feel free to sing along," everyone in the audience did.

Halfway up the aisle, Victoria and her second husband Philip clutched hands. He hadn't been there when Dave died, but he knew this song would set her off. It always did.

Victoria allowed herself to feel again those last moments with her son, as Jimmy began to sing the long, slow version, "Sparklers flare in the dark of night…"

"Admit it," Philip said. "You're still in love with him."

"If he ever looks twice at me, brother, you're in big trouble," Victoria answered, her eyes swimming. She didn't reach for a Kleenex; Philip's hand on hers was comfort enough.

Closer to the stage, in the tenth row, Carolyn and her daughter Elizabeth held hands, too, and their eyes were moist. This was a special song for them, and for Carolyn's friend Annie, who had died last year. They both missed her terribly, and this song reminded them of her.

"Baseball games and lemonade—
Lining the streets for the kids' parade."

"He's so good," Elizabeth whispered.

"He's the best," Carolyn said. "So are you."

And she hugged the girl who had turned out to be the love of her life.

Down by the stage, Jack sat in his wheelchair, his hands eloquently moving in the air, along with the music. Claire sat on one side of him. She didn't realize the video people were catching the play of emotions and the tears pouring down her face, nor did she realize that Jack was singing directly to her as Jimmy wound up the final chorus:

"Doesn't matter where else I go,
When I'm here I'll always know—
I'm wrapped in the gauze of love."

Jack reached for Claire's hand. "I could never have done it without you," he whispered.

She clutched his hand. "You're never going to, buster."

Jimmy held the final note for eight counts, while the audience, many others moved to tears, sang along, dabbed at their eyes or just cheered.

Jimmy then did what he always did—took off his guitar, set it down, and reached out for his bandmates. They came quickly, took his hands, and bowed.

Bow to the audience, Dary had always counseled them. *Thank them for loving you.*

There was no way to thank anyone here for the love they'd been given, no adequate way to give it back, except to sing it out, as often as they wanted to hear it. Forever.

Jimmy looked up, as he always did, toward the doorway at the top of the box seats. Jimmy had seen him at every show since the first one, where he'd first sung the GooseBumps hits again.

As always, he was there, for the briefest of moments, in a wash of golden light, and as always, Mark was smiling. Tonight, though, Kellen and Hammy were with him, and they made typical, impatient-male gestures: *Go on, idiot. Milk it!*

He took his band's hands again, and they made another, final bow.

And for that briefest of moments, Jimmy knew that he had finally come home, and that he was, once more, wrapped in the gauze of love.

Enjoy this preview of

FORWARD TO CAMELOT: THE FINAL EDITION

By Susan Sloate & Kevin Finn

Then came the moment they had all waited for. Hundreds of heads leaned forward in anticipation.

Air Force One touched down lightly and taxied to the reception area. Airport personnel rolled portable steps to the passenger doors, set high in the side of the plane, and the door swung open. Aides and Secret Servicemen deplaned swiftly.

There was a pause. Nothing happened.

Then there was a stir at the door, and a flash of pink, and a roar went up from the waiting crowd.

The First Lady, in her lovely pink suit, short white gloves and pink pillbox hat, stood at the open door, and smiled automatically toward the fence, where the crowd had exploded into cheers and waves. Behind her, the President, in his elegant dark suit, striped shirt and figured blue tie, smiled and waved. The glare and heat of the Dallas sunlight was overpowering, but they looked cool, poised and genuinely pleased to be there.

Talk about star power.

They moved graciously through the official reception line—where Mrs. Kennedy smilingly accepted an armful of blood-red roses—then made their way, as I knew they would, toward the waiting crowds behind the fence.

It was eerie to be living through this moment now, just as it was happening, the dashing young President and his beautiful wife in her unblemished suit, with the matching pillbox hat set lightly back on her dark hair just a few feet away. The crowd roared and waved, cameras clicking endlessly. A tall, lean Secret Service agent shadowed the President.

Working his way through the crowd, Lee followed the President's movements, pulling me along behind him. "Stay close!" he insisted.

The President's driver eased the convertible toward the fence, to be ready when the President finally decided to leave his admirers. Kennedy was coming to the end of the fence. There wouldn't be another chance. Lee was leaning toward Mrs. Kennedy, who was moving slowly along the fence.

I reached out for the Secret Serviceman next to the President. "Secret Service!" I yelled.

Involuntarily, the man's eyes flicked to me. He could see I had nothing suspicious in my hands. "Don't let him get in the car!" I shouted, trying desperately to be heard above the roar of the crowd. "Don't let him—"

The Secret Serviceman, unable to hear me and uninterested, was moving away, his eyes trained on the President once again. I reached out and grabbed frantically at his sleeve and managed to yank him back.

I had to tell him. He could stop it, but only if he knew.

He hadn't expected anyone to grab him. I had pulled him off-balance, my strength increased by my terror.

He fell back a step from the President, then two, then three, as the President, not noticing, moved toward his wife and the admirers at the other end of the fence.

Meanwhile, I was transfixed by what was happening down there; I didn't say anything more to the Secret Service agent because I couldn't stop staring in that direction.

Lee had a fixed smile on his face and was calling out to Mrs. Kennedy, pushing through the crowd to the top of the fence. For a moment, he hung precariously there, then leaped lightly down, to land right in front of the First Lady.

With a little laugh of surprise, she jerked back instinctively.

Lee removed his cap with one hand. I thought it was a gesture of exaggerated courtesy. So did Mrs. Kennedy: she started to smile and reach out a hand to him.

When his hand came down from his head, it was holding a revolver. He pointed it straight at her head.

The President saw it, and his eyes widened in horror.

The Secret Serviceman behind him couldn't see it; his view was blocked by the President, and I had unwittingly distracted him by trying to get his attention.

The President, only a few feet from his wife, was at her side before anyone else could move.

"Put down the gun, Lee," he said calmly. Even in this moment of maximum pressure, he recognized Lee and remembered his name.

"Get in the car," Lee retorted. "Now, Mr. President—or your wife gets it."

A TAP OF THE DRUMSTICK

Scenes from a Song began as a humble entry for the 2018 Nanowrimo (National Novel Writing Month), that glorious November marathon for writers everywhere, where the goal was to produce 50,000 words of an original novel *in 30 days*. Though I didn't complete the entire first draft in November, I did finish it before the end of that year (okay, about *six hours* before the end of that year, but still...) Though Nano no longer exists, I'm grateful for the Nanowrimo organization, which provided a special place for 25 years that allowed writers to create and flourish. Thank you so much.

Thank you to Danny Raye, one of the great beta readers ever. Thank you for caring so much and for paying attention to the details!

Thank you to 100 Covers for the beautiful cover design (my third with them, so far), and for handling the formatting and typesetting, as well. I don't want to imagine what this book would look like without you. Phyllis Ngo, my project manager, handled all inquiries with unfailing good cheer and always helps me across the finish line.

Most of all, my thanks to the readers who follow and enjoy my work. At the end of the day, you're the ones who keep *me* wrapped in gauze.

About the Author

SUSAN SLOATE is the author or co-author of more than 25 published books. This includes 3 editions of *Forward to Camelot,* a time-travel thriller about the JFK assassination that became a #6 Amazon bestseller, was honored in 3 literary competitions and was optioned by a Hollywood company for film production. She also wrote the autobiographical Broadway novel *Stealing Fire,* which became a #2 Amazon bestseller and Hot New Release, and *Realizing You* (with Ron Doades), for which she invented a new genre: the self-help *novel.*

Susan has also written young-adult fiction and non-fiction, including the children's biography *Ray Charles: Find Another Way,* which won the silver medal in the 2007 Children's Moonbeam Awards. *Mysteries Unwrapped: The Secrets of Alcatraz* led to her 2009 appearance on the TV series *MysteryQuest* for The History Channel. She has also been a sportswriter and a screenwriter, edited the popular *Kyle & Corey* young-adult book series, managed two political campaigns and founded an author's festival to promote student literacy in her hometown outside Charleston, SC. She has appeared in multiple volumes of *WHO'S WHO IN AMERICA, WHO'S WHO IN ENTERTAINMENT* and *WHO'S WHO AMONG AMERICAN WOMEN.*

Visit her online at https://susansloate.com.

Other Titles by Susan Sloate:

Forward to Camelot: The Final Edition (with Kevin Finn) Covfefe Press, 2024

Stealing Fire Covfefe Press, 2018

Realizing You (with Ron Doades) CreateSpace, 2013

Amelia Earhart: Challenging the Skies (*Great Lives* series) Fawcett, 2011

Abraham Lincoln: The Freedom President (*Great Lives* series) Fawcett, 2010

Ray Charles: Young Musician (*Childhood of Famous Americans* series) Simon & Schuster, 2008

Ray Charles: Find Another Way! Bearport Press, 2006

Edited by Susan Sloate:

Kyle & Corey and the Game-Store Mystery Covfefe Press, 2021

Made in USA - Kendallville, IN
38106_9798998989407
08.15.2025 0019